I Love You, LUKE PIEWALKER

ELIZA GORDON

To Jayne Dandys everywhere ...

In your quest for the perfect love,
I wish you the luck of the double moons.

JOIN THE RAFT!

You know those adorable videos of sea otters floating together, holding hands? In the wild, they do this so they don't get separated in the tides—these are called "rafts." Fun trivia: Rafts are almost always of the same gender. You can tell when it's sea otter mating season because the females will often have vicious-looking damage to their noses. Seems sea otter boys like things rough.

Though you and I are not sea otters, we can still float together and keep in touch about books and related topics. And we don't even have to bite one another's noses to make it happen.

Join the Raft! Sign up for my newsletter for project updates and chitchat. Welcome aboard!

ALSO BY ELIZA GORDON

Dear Dwayne, With Love

The Revelation Cove series:

Must Love Otters (Book 1)

Hollie Porter Builds a Raft (Book 2)

Love Just Clicks (Book 3, standalone)

1

"SEX SMELLS FUNNY."

Dr. McCoy chokes on her coffee. "I'd say 'come again,' but I'm afraid to." She dabs at sputtered drops before they soak into her blouse. "How would you know, Jayne?"

"I'm not a complete newb. And my roommate—I know when she's had a carnal sleepover. She lights scented candles. To mask the smell."

"Ever thought that maybe your intimacy issues are heightening your sense of smell?"

"I can smell garlic from the next block. Just like when I was a kid and could walk by a house and tell you if the TV was on inside."

"Maybe you were a bat in your last life."

"That would explain a lot. Wait—do you believe in past lives?" I stare cockeyed at my therapist, attempting a read on her face. Sometimes it's hard to tell when she's kidding.

She shakes her head and fumbles with the diamond ring hanging from the thick chain around her neck. I've tried to ask her about it; she defers, says that's fodder for her own therapy visits.

"Are you jealous when your roommate has 'carnal sleepovers'?"

"No."

"Are you confused? Sexually, I mean?"

"I'm not a lesbian, if that's what you're asking."

"Do you have unusual fantasies?"

"What, like, sex with clowns or in front of an audience?"

"Would those be situations you'd like to find yourself in?"

I laugh. "No. No audience."

"Jayne, what I'm trying to help you find is what it is you *do* want. Once you're able to address that, we can dig deeper for what's keeping you from finding it."

We've been digging for almost seven months. We've ruled out a good portion of the psychiatric diagnostic compendium—while I'm not great with bodily fluids, I'm not OCD. I don't have to bathe in bleach after changing a tampon. I've seen semen a time or two, including when my poor prom date danced too close for just a moment too long and soiled his rented tux. Awkward.

And that one other time. *Shudder.*

Dr. McCoy has it narrowed down to psychological traumas of childhood: a tag team of cheap-perfumed church ladies who sat a group of eight- to twelve-year-olds in the sweating basement of an old stone building while our parents prayed away the week's sins upstairs. My folks only joined the congregation because the family court judge felt we lacked a spiritual cohesion; once Mr. and Mrs. Dandy decided not to divorce (again), we stopped going to church. Sorry, God. The Dandys apparently don't need you anymore.

But the damage had already been done: the Satan Squad—what the older kids called these spinster sisters—told us God would be watching, and would be *very unhappy*, if we were to touch ourselves "down there" or if we considered any sort of unclean thoughts, especially those with members of the opposite sex. They called it petting and told us how sinful touching tongues was in the eyes of the Big Man.

From eight years old, I was pretty much convinced God would strike me down if I touched a boy. And please don't say *masturbation.*

I will not admit anything here. Not even to Dr. McCoy. God could be listening. That is, if he's not busy with famines and plagues and the stock market.

Whatever. This isn't about religion or my lack thereof. This is about me paying $150 an hour to figure out why I can't get laid.

"Have you considered the online dating sites we talked about?"

"Not yet. I don't want to find some perfect guy and then scare him away when he wants to see my boobs."

"Hey, progress! You're imagining a man seeing you naked. This is very good, Jayne."

Awesome. I can now say "boobs" out loud without begging forgiveness from a bearded, robed man living in a posh, pillowy cloud house. Money well spent.

"Are you still writing stories?"

"Absolutely. Mucking about with people's lives on distant planets keeps me steady." She hasn't read any of my fiction but is supportive nonetheless—a refreshing contrast.

"Have you diverged from your regular fare to incorporate what we talked about? The role-play situation?" This exercise she gave me when we first started therapy: think about my ideal man and imagine everything from initial meeting to inviting him into my bed. If I can't do this for myself, play make-believe. Write about other people doing these things as a means to finding myself in such a situation.

My cheeks sizzle. No eye contact.

"Ahhh, so you did write something down."

"Maybe."

"May I see it?"

"No!" I sip from my water. "I burned it."

She stares at me. "When you're ready, you'll share."

I didn't really burn it.

I write and self-publish science fiction and fantasy stories for fun. Under a pen name. No one knows, not even Gretchen, my roommate and best friend since grade school. I make a few bucks here and there for the rainy-day fund. And I live in Portland, so we have a lot of rainy days.

But writing erotica? I only did it because Dr. McCoy, my *therapist*, recommended it. I did it in the name of medicine. My progress in this field could make me eligible for a Nobel someday.

One finished journal sits locked in my closet, in a fireproof safe to which only I know the combination. The latest journal, containing the unfinished sequel to the first novel, I carry with me everywhere. In case someone breaks into my apartment to smother himself in my underwear and steal my *Star Wars* collectibles. I repurposed the cover from one of my many copies of *Pride and Prejudice* and wrapped it around the journal so no one will pay attention if my bag spills. Also, if I leave paper out, our psychotic one-eyed alley-rescue cat, aptly named Quack, will eat it. She eats everything.

I mean, GOD, *what if someone found it?* What if I died in my sleep from a hemorrhagic fever picked up by touching the doorknob at the coffee shop, and once the hazmat team extracted my soupy corpse from my apartment, Sheila Dandy, face obscured by a thick biohazard mask, went through my stuff and FOUND that her daughter had written something naughty?

That her underachieving daughter had written *sex?*

I'm still not sure I wasn't the product of an immaculate conception. My parents haven't shared a bedroom, or even a friendly smile, since *Love Boat* was in reruns. What the hell is *Love Boat?* Google it. Yeah. That long ago.

Don't misunderstand: neither of my parents (this is really weird talking about my parents' sex lives) seems frigid. My issues do not appear to be an inherited condition but rather the result of an unfortunate series of circumstances. My parents simply don't like each other. And if they're not gloating about their own lives or those of my golden siblings, words are few. Like the last four sheets of toilet paper in a treeless world.

"I don't want to be a virgin forever."

"Technically, you're not a virgin."

"Doesn't your 'gentle blossom' stitch itself closed after so many years of inactivity?"

"Some people term it a born-again virgin, but that is a label only you can give yourself." Dr. McCoy leans forward, pats my hand. She must buy the expensive hand cream. Her skin looks younger than mine. "This is fixable. I promise. We're going to get through this. Together."

Unless Dr. McCoy sprouts a penis, I'm on my own here.

Time's up.

EIDER: CHAPTER 1

by Jaina Jacen (September)

Planet Eider, steeped in archaic protocol, had long forgotten the lessons of the Dead Planet.

For Illyria—a Class I highborn facing a future where her preselected husband would assume her father's esteemed place in government—the delights that suited her fellow citizens did nothing to inspire.

But when an old friend tiptoes back into her life, he reminds her heart what it feels like to beat again.

～

"Illyria!" *A pound on my chamber door.* "Time to rise. The collectors are here."

Of course they are.

Today is my Twelvemonth. The collectors seek yet another blood sample to store in the archives. Same day, every year, for every citizen of Eider, the procedure duplicates. The collector's needle stabs are softer, though, given my station. My father would not tolerate anything less than a deep bow, utterance of thanks for allowing them to breathe the same air as me, followed by a gentle withdrawal of my blood.

Taisa, my handmaiden, tidies my hair and feeds me a thick, nutrient-rich drink to ensure a satisfactory harvest of my red cells. "Mind yourself, Illyria."

"What ever do you mean? I'm not allowed to pinch this one?"

She snorts and ushers in the collector.

Upon his first step into the chamber, my senses are lost.

A hint of a distant past whispers in my ear—I know this face. Don't I?

I scan his uniform, as drab and common as all other members of his station, a high collar hiding evidence of stubble his shaver missed. The black coat offers only one clue: II, with a red circle next to it that indicates his job. Class II Collector from the Wellness Bureau. His hair, slicked against his head, dark under the low chamber light, but an errant curl has shimmied itself loose and bounces against his forehead. Funny—I understand that curl's desire for autonomy.

The collector's eyes, downcast, remain a mystery—until he rises from his bow and we make first contact.

I've seen those eyes before, a thousand times, in my slumber.

Before his bow is finished, I am undone.

2

"DANDY JAYNE, here for her morning kick-start."

"Mr. Walker." I throw a fiver on the counter. Every morning, same thing. Coffee, black. Lots of sugar. Warm apple turnover with light whipped cream. Precisely why Gretchen won't stop hounding me about joining her gym.

Seriously, you have to try Luke's apple turnovers.

His Goth-y twin hunches in the corner on the phone, eyes hooded and tired as per usual, fingers worrying the ring protruding from her lip. She's scary.

"Leia! Customers!" Luke squawks. She ignores him, turns her back. Someone behind me makes a rude comment about how the line is too long. But people wait, rain or shine, line or no line, because there is no food truck on the avenue like Luke Piewalker's. You wait because it's *that* good.

Well, and because Luke. Untamed dirty-blond hair and eyes, the color of éclair chocolate, that sort of never stop glistening. Quick sense of humor, generous with extra helpings of whipped cream and his winning smile. The days where my tasty treat has been collected and I sit alongside the food truck, I watch for Luke's adoring fans amidst the diners. Shorter skirts, tighter shirts, extra perfume, girls who stop by after salon visits to flip their locks and say, *Oh hey Luke how are you isn't my new hair cute are you free Friday?*

What? I'm not jealous. I do not need a man. Men mean sex. Remember?

The business boost also comes from the reality that Portland is filled with *Star Wars* geeks who want to see if there really is a set of twins named Luke and Leia Walker. Leia's only here because it's part of her work-release deal.

"Jayne, don't leave yet. I gotta show you something after ..." He nods at the snake of antsy patrons.

"Five minutes." I could wait for ten or maybe even fifteen, but then I'd risk the wrath of Surly Brian. Our building's security guard. My boss doesn't give a rat's ass when I show up—as if writing obituaries and garage sale ads and the occasional article is going to stop the eighty-year-old paper from publication. But thanks to one deranged chef with a knack for pipe bombs—it's amazing how nuts a man can become when your paper writes the review that allegedly sinks his restaurant—Surly Brian is now a necessity. Best be in by the time Brian goes for his morning shit, though. Once the doors are locked, you're waiting until lunch. Unless you have an extra fifth of fine Russian vodka in your trunk for bribe currency, or you're skilled with climbing rusted-out fire escape ladders.

I'm edging dangerously close to the point of no return—I have neither vodka nor the energy to climb rusted metal today.

With mere minutes to spare, Luke gets his sister's attention long enough to sneak out the back door. In his hands, he holds a mighty prize.

"Where'd you get this?" I say, fingering the figurine's robes.

"Private collector. Guy on eBay."

"Limited edition?"

"Mace Windu, ¼-scale vinyl model kit."

"Do I want to know how much you paid for this?"

"Let's just say I'd better sell a hell of a lot more apple turnovers this month." He smiles. The corners of his eyes crinkle. Impossibly long eyelashes. What is it with guys and long eyelashes? I spend six minutes per eyeball every morning just to get my nine eyelashes to look like double that number.

"This one's a beaut, Luke. Why is he behind the counter? You're going to spill cherry topping on his gorgeous bald head."

"I had to show you. I knew you'd appreciate it." He slides the action figure—not a doll—back into its blister pack. "You coming around for lunch?"

"Maybe. I brown-bagged it, though. The famine before payday."

"Today is bacon chowder. I'll save you a bowl, on the Empire."

"Don't let Vader hear you say that."

"Hey, you got your ticket yet?" The Portland Comic Con. Luke goes every year and reports back.

"Nah. You know me. Crowds, *et cetera.*"

"This year, the pie truck is an invited guest. We're on site for three days, and *that* means," he pulls an envelope out of his back pocket, "comp tickets. One with your name on it. I told them you're staff."

"Luke ... I can't."

"You have to. VIP access, baby. Peter Mayhew's gonna be there. Billy Dee Williams. Rumor has it Sir George himself might make an appearance."

"That's the rumor every year."

"This could be OUR year! Come on ... you have to go."

"I'm not great with these things. Plus, nothing to wear."

"Lame excuse. Leia has a shit ton of costumes."

"Leia's also a waif. She doesn't eat your turnovers every morning."

"LUKE!" His sister wails.

"You've got a few months to think about it. You're not a real geek until you've shaken Chewbacca's beautifully furred hand." He waves the envelope at me. "See you at lunch."

Easy for him to say. The helices of his DNA read *G-E-E-K*, a fact his twin struggles against with great flair. Their parents, as I've been told, met at a *Star Wars* convention in the '80s and it was love at first lightsaber. The Comic Con for Luke is like a family reunion.

I shovel in the whipped cream from atop the turnover. Luke's face shines as he serves his customers, a joke here, a free cookie there. I like watching him work, and I realize that makes me a little creepy. If I were to find myself romantically interested in a member of the opposite sex, I think Luke could, maybe—

Stop. He's a friend. I don't want to screw this up. And what's to say he'd even be interested in me? Just because we share a love of all things geek, I cannot do romance unless it's on paper. Luke and me, we're good as friends. No pressure, no weirdness.

But his comfortable demeanor and facility with wit are charming qualities, a stark contrast to his growly sister throwing napkins at people. He tried to convince her that wearing the Leia bun hairpiece would increase tips; she instead pierced another part of her face. I wonder what her probation officer thought of that.

Luke waves just as my cell phone alarm warns that I have three minutes to get down the block before Surly Brian locks me out.

I notice a text. "Frankie made partner! Dinner at Portland City Grill. Friday, 6 p.m. No jeans. Bring a date."

God, I hate my mother.

3

"YOU SPELLED the decedent's name wrong."

"I spelled it based on the email from his daughter." I open the folder and extract the correspondence from the dead guy's family. "See?"

"Shit." Mr. Clark runs his newsprint-stained fingers down his sloppy tie. Part owner of the building, he interprets that to mean he can ignore the rule against indoor smoking. The open window is supported by a long-forgotten copy of *Robinson Crusoe*—"That book ruined my childhood," Clark says—and the little purifier on his desk gave up the ghost long ago.

"Okay. Offer to run the obit for another week. Ask the daughter for a bigger picture of her father. Oh, and give them a coupon for a free garage sale or Missed Encounter ad. Send her one of our fancy pens," Clark says. He's talking about the kind with the nylon rope strung through the lid. As if any self-respecting person would be caught dead walking around with a *Rose City Register* pen hanging from his or her neck.

"Did you get a chance to read that article I left for you?" I ask.

"The one about the ducks?"

"Yes." An article about the best places around the Portland metropolitan area to watch wood ducks, Mallards, American wigeons, and double-crested cormorants—check out Oaks Bottom, Crystal Springs Rhododendron Garden, and Sauvie Island—and how to tell the difference between a Canada goose and a cackling goose.

"Not really sure our readers would be interested in that."

"Well, it's part of the magic of living in Portland—maybe I could interview someone at the Oregon Zoo or the Audubon Society of Portland?" He's shaking his head. Must talk faster. Throw out another salvageable idea. "Or maybe I can write book reviews?"

"Book reviews about ducks?"

I sigh. "No. Book reviews about books. Any books. You can pick." He eyes the copy of *Crusoe* in the window.

"Let me think about it." He lights up another cigarette, which means he's done talking to me. "And the new food guy started today —make him feel at home. I think the other kids are afraid to talk to him." Folks are afraid to get too close to the food writers—not only are they usually pompous overachievers only stopping here until a "real" publication finds them but they get the most threats of bodily harm. Standing too close to a food writer might cost you your kneecaps.

Hand on the door, Clark stops me again. "Dandy, I promise you'll get out of obits before year's end."

Mr. Clark first said this three years ago. He hired me because his wife was my ninth grade English teacher and she loved me. The one person in my life who said, "You're going to be a great writer some day." Kids love hearing that. When a dream is validated by an external entity, it can be life changing.

So far, the *Rose City Register* hasn't life-changed anything except how often I go into overdraft.

And Mr. Clark knows I want to be a staff writer, but he still relies on me to keep the chickens corralled. Reminds me at every annual review how important I am to keeping everything running smoothly —and I do handle much more than just obits and ads written by searching hearts who missed that pretty girl on the MAX. Seems our light-rail transit system boasts her share of empty hearts.

En route back to my desk, I freeze.

No, no, no.

Gretchen's lithe body, slipped into an impossibly thin pencil skirt and boots my calves can only dream about, has a book in her hands.

Pride and Prejudice.

The look on her face tells me the words she's reading don't belong to Jane Austen. Gretchen is my roommate and best friend from forever, but some things I just don't tell her.

For very good reasons.

"What the hell are you doing?" I yell. Heads turn like meerkats scanning for hyenas. I slap the book out of Gretchen's manicured hands.

"Jaaaaaaayne, did you *write* this?"

"I hate you." My stomach knots up. Dizzy. Shit. Sit down. *Don't freak out, Jayne. Five four three two—*

"Jayne baby, that was effing *hot*," Gretchen whispers at me.

"I hate you. I hate you. I hate you."

"No, you don't." She wheels her chair from her adjoining desk and grabs my clammy, clenched hands. "I'm sorry I read your book. It was sticking out of your bag and you're always nagging me about not having read Austen, and I was waiting for you to get done with Clark—"

"That was private, Gretchen."

"Jayne, open your eyes. Are you going to throw up?" She reaches under my desk for the rubber-duck-printed garbage can. The apple turnover dances in my throat. "Sweetie, I am so sorry. If I'd known ..."

"You're too nosy."

"Please don't tell me this is going to be a repeat of third grade." My eighth birthday. Gretchen read my diary while I was in the bathroom with diarrhea from some dodgy hot dogs. She didn't get diarrhea because she doesn't eat meat. She still reminds me of this. I still remind her that she read my diary while I was peeing out my ass.

"Why did you read it?"

"I told you—I thought it was your Mr. Darcy. But then—whoa—that is definitely not Ms. Austen's cup of chamomile."

"Please be quiet ..."

"Can I read more?"

I open my eyes and stare at her like she's just asked me to donate my still-beating heart.

"I'm not kidding—that shit is good."

"How much did you read?"

"Up to the part where he has his—"

"Stop." I flatten my sticky hand against her mouth. I feel her grin. "Oh God, I'm going to pass out."

Gretchen scoots my chair back and shoves my head between my knees. God, these are the ugliest shoes. I really need new shoes.

I slap her arm away and sit upright.

"Better?"

"I still hate you."

"You do not. And I'm taking you to Piewalker's for lunch so I can hear *all about this*—this—whatever *this* is."

"I was just there for breakfast. He's going to think I'm a stalker."

"He's going to think you like pie. Besides, he said he'd make me those vegan brownies."

A new face peeks over Gretchen's shoulder. "Vegan brownies? Sounds like something I should try."

I stand and straighten my pants, nudging the garbage can under the desk. Gretchen pops a hip out, as per Gretchen. As soon as her hips grew in, she learned how to pop them. They will likely require replacement before she hits forty.

Gretchen extends a limp wrist, as if waiting for Hipster Food Critic to kiss her hand. He shakes it and pushes his black frames up his nose.

"I'm Holden."

"Do you perm?" she says.

I elbow Gretchen's ribs. "And you are?" he deflects.

"Gretchen. This is Jayne."

He offers his hand to me. I shake it for real. One of the few things Sheila Dandy managed to teach me amongst all the bizarre rules she installed in my developing brain: shake a person's hand like you mean it.

His palm is clammy. Gross.

I try not to be obvious about wiping my hand on my pants.

Gretchen moves to block him out of our conversation.

"Gretchen, Mr. Clark says we have to be nice to Hipster Food Critic. Turn around," I say.

"Is that what Mr. Clark said?" Gretchen asks.

"Yes. And he's the boss." We speak as if this third individual were invisible. The loose, floppy curls are actually sorta cute. In that *I'm a food critic there could be bombs nearby* way.

"Fine." Gretchen swivels. "So, Food Critic, despite my personal disdain for people who perm their hair, I shall pretend to be a nice person. What brings you to our little paper?" Gretchen says.

"Name's Holden, it's a hundred percent natural curl, and uh, well, I needed a job. Student loans don't pay themselves."

"I wouldn't know," Gretchen says. She's bluffing. Sort of. Her parents made her sweat under the weight of student loans for a few years "to learn fiscal responsibility" before her addiction to shoes and Prada bags made said loans unmanageable. They paid them off. "Jayne, tell Hipster Food Critic here what we do at the *Rose City Register*."

"I write about dead people and dead people's crap for sale. Gretchen writes about fashion and culture."

"Impressive. Do dead people sell their stuff?" Holden asks.

"Yes. Portland is known for its zombie garage sales," I say.

He chuckles. "Ever come across any good finds?"

"I just write the ads."

"Afraid of zombies?"

"Afraid they'll overeat," I say.

17

"Oh, because your brain is ..." He twirls a finger around the crown of his curly head.

"Yes. Jayne's brain is huge," Gretchen says, raising a hand for a silent high-five. Of course, this begs the question about why I work here if my brain is so huge. Another day, perhaps.

"One of my college buddies found an original Picasso at a guy's yard sale in LA once."

"Doubt it," Gretchen says behind her hand. "Okay, great, well, don't you have food to critique?"

"Mr. Clark warned me about you." He wags a finger at Gretchen and leans his brown-corduroyed body against an adjacent desk. Jumps when a ruler invades his butt space.

"Mr. Clark knows many things. You should heed his warnings." Gretchen pinches my cheek. "I'm off. Student show at the Art Institute. You—lunch—be ready at noon. Bring Mr. Darcy."

Even my ears ignite.

"*Pride and Prejudice* fan?" Holden asks. I ignore him.

"So, um, are you settling in okay?"

"If by okay, you mean that everyone has been sort of rude and someone taped all the drawers shut to my desk, stole the cartridges for my pens, left me crayons instead of pencils, and no one told me about Surly Brian, then, yes. Absolutely fine."

"Do you remember third grade, Food Critic?"

"It's Holden. And yes. I remember third grade."

"Act like you're back there."

"Noted." He smiles. His middle two teeth are longer than their neighbors, though straight. Quite white. Not a smoker, then. Definitely looks like orthodontia was involved. "So, I guess I'm off to critique food."

"Good luck with that. Oh, and sweep your desk. Every day. Maybe consider getting a dog that can smell explosives. I hear beagles are friendly."

"Wait—what?"

I pick up my ringing phone and wink.

EIDER: CHAPTER 2

by Jaina Jacen (September)

"My Sovereign, are you ill?" Taisa's face has paled. If anything happens to me, she will pay the price.

"No. No, I'm fine. Thank you." This is a lie.

Young suitors have courted and carried on, seeking my father's favor above mine. But for my stubbornness, I am yet without betrothal. I will not be able to hold off my father's demands for marriage and grandchildren much longer. Like the old stories from the Dead Planet, I find myself seeking love beyond duty.

Foolish girl, my father chides. He married a woman he did not love —out of duty. For all our futurism, this life is archaic.

"Miss Illyria." The collector begins a sentence my handmaiden won't let him finish.

"Do not address her directly."

His head lowers and then upright, it shines again. "Her sleeve. Please lift her sleeve."

"Taisa, leave us. I don't need your nervous fretting to make me more skittish than I already am."

The handmaiden pauses but then exits.

We, the collector and I, are alone.

"I know you," I say.

"My Sovereign."

"You don't know me?"

"Only by way of allegiance."

"You said my name." It sounded like a waltz dancing from his lips.

"Everyone knows your name." He readies his supplies. "Your blood. May I take your sample?"

That familiar lonely twinge in my chest—it again makes itself known.

You do not know me, but I indeed know you.

And you are mine.

4

"HOW WAS THE FASHION SHOW?"

"Lame. Nothing new and fresh. Did you bring Mr. Darcy?" Gretchen asks.

"I am not going to pull it out here."

"It's a book, Jayne. I'm not asking to see your penis."

"Jayne is going to show you her penis?" Luke asks, placing food before us. We're at one of the food truck's three metal outdoor tables, the one with the perpetual *RESERVED FOR EMPIRE ROYALTY* sign on it.

Oh my God. "Shut up, Gretchen."

"She won't, Luke, but I'll show you mine," Gretchen coos, pulling on the white string of his apron.

"But then you'd tire of me and put me out in the back pasture with Daddy's thoroughbreds, and I would wilt from lack of riding," Luke says, his index finger bowing suggestively. He plops extra sugar packets on the table.

"Go away, peasant." Gretchen shoos him off. "You. Book. Give. Now."

"You've read enough."

"I didn't get to finish the scene."

"There's nothing left to finish."

"Uhhhh, yeah, there is. Let me see if they finish right!" She throws her head back and lets out a yowl.

"God, you're such a child."

"I'm going to reenact Meg Ryan's diner scene if you don't give me the book." She scoots her chair back, fluffs her enviable blond hair, and braces both hands on the table. Shit. She's gonna do it. Wouldn't be the first time. And the lineup at the food truck would really enjoy this show.

"Troll." I hand her the journal and dig into the bacon chowder, my eyes down so I can't see her reaction as she gets through the … deed.

Within a few pages, she fans herself. "This is really good."

"Quiet, you."

"No, Jayne, I mean it. You should come to my writers' group."

"No."

"Why not? Why do you always say no?"

"Because. I don't want your writers' group to read this stuff. I didn't even want *you* to read it."

"Yes, you did, or else you wouldn't have left it in your bag for me to find."

"Uhhh, maybe if you'd stay OUT of my bag, like a normal person."

"I needed a tampon."

"Liar." I scrape the bowl for the last chunk of bacon.

"That shit is so bad for you."

"Mmmmm, I know." *Slurp.*

"Why won't you come to my writers' group? What if I said you don't have to share anything?"

"Do they serve bacon?"

"I'm serious, Jayne."

"So am I." I dab at my mouth with the napkin. "Your people wouldn't appreciate me just sitting there. I'd have to contribute."

"Not at the first meeting. Please? Try it?"

"I can't." Gretchen stares at me, steals a chunk of my bread. "Be careful. Those carbs might make your heart explode."

"*Why* can't you? What, because Mommie Dearest might find out? Seriously, Jayne, you're a grown-up. You need to stop listening to the bullshit your parents poured into your ears."

"You don't know anything about it."

"Are you kidding me? I've been to your house a million times. 'Writers are sad sacks. Do you know Hemingway died drunk and alone?'"

"We all die alone. Drunk if we're lucky," I say. "And he killed himself. So, yeah."

"Or here's my favorite—'All that money on a journalism degree, and you write obituaries? Your father and I thought you'd be a real reporter.'" Gretchen changes her voice to match that of my nasally sister. "'Yes, Jayne, dear, why don't you go to Afghanistan or Iran like that Amanpour woman? Or, 'You know, you'll forever be waiting for the band to get back together. You could be homeless before then.' What does she even mean by that?"

Sigh. "She means that I should stop waiting for something miraculous to happen. Writers are always waiting for their big break. Like, how a band, once parted, hopes it will get back together so they can relive their glory days."

"Ohhhhhh. That makes sense. She may have a point." If Gretchen hadn't been my best friend since before we sprouted boobies, I'd leave. "Come on, Jayne—your sister picks people's zits for a living. HOW is that more glamorous?"

"Her new Jaguar tells you how glamorous it is."

"I wouldn't do her job for ten new Jaguars."

"Yes, you would. And speaking of the band, I have a name for you," I say. Neither Gretchen nor I have an ounce of musical talent, despite the fact that our parents subjected us both to piano lessons. But we often talk of our fictional band.

"Hit me, sister."

"Tauntaun Parade."

"Really?"

"What—you don't like it?"

"What the hell is a Tauntaun?"

"A reptomammal from the planet Toth."

"None of those words were English."

"They were all English."

"Jayne, it's a little ... geeky."

"What's wrong with geeks?"

Gretchen snorts.

"Ladies? Anything else?" Luke is back, a small white bag in hand. I grab my journal away from Gretchen and shove it in my purse. With my luck, she'd read an excerpt to him. To the entire lunch crowd.

"You trying to get rid of us?" I tease.

"You? Never. This one, though ..." He bobs his head toward Gretchen.

"You want me. All the boys do." Gretchen looks past Luke and nods. "Your sister seems to be giving the customers extra-special treatment these days." Leia is leaned over the food truck counter, lip-locked with a guy sporting a very stiff blue Mohawk.

"How does he get it to be so sticky-uppy?" Gretchen asks. Luke slaps his damp towel at the guy's backside. Mohawk Man jumps and unhooks his tongue from Leia's.

"Luke! Seriously!" Leia whines.

He turns back to us and plops the small package on the table. "For coffee break later. Vegan brownies, as promised." And then he's gone, chasing Mohawk Man away and yelling at his lazy sister to clean something.

Gretchen opens the paper sack and shoves her patrician nose inside to suck in the chocolaty fumes. "Oh God, these are going to be good."

"Don't get boogers on the brownies."

"Booger brownies are my favorite," she says.

24

"Up, child. I have garage sales to advertise," I say.

I have to drag Gretchen down the street, away from the windows with the new fall pretties beckoning her credit card. "Down, girl. Bad Gretchen. No shopping." The trees are pulling on their autumn wardrobe, one branch at a time, the Portland air hinting that this year's Indian summer will be brief so that fall may assume the stage. Mother Nature is still a little undecided about what she wants out of life—do I give the humans enough sun to inspire short sleeves, or do I make the little bastards cart around a sweater? I keep a down coat and extra socks at the office, just in case Momma Nature has a meltdown. Never know when Father Time is going to skip town again and leave her with all the stormy offspring.

While our office is within the purview of what we'd call "downtown," we're sort of in that seedier, outskirts part, the redeveloped buildings stopping before their shiny infection reached us. Like someone drew a chalk line on the sidewalk and said, "No more clean lines or pleasing façades past here."

We have mere minutes before Surly Brian locks us out.

"Oh! I have something for you!" she says, stopping at the corner. A large man smelling of onions and foul armpits stands too close. He sways and bumps Gretchen. "ExCUSE me!" He belches loudly in her direction.

From her bag she extracts a yellow rubber duck, the orange bill painted with big red lips.

"She's cute," I say.

"She's talented." Gretchen takes the duck from my hands and pushes a little button on its underside. It vibrates against her palm. Gretchen beams. "Personal massager."

"Is that—is that a *vibrator?*" I whisper.

"Do you love it?"

"Oh my *God*, Gretchen, no! What the—"

"I'll take it," Belching Belchman says.

"What?" we say in unison. His lunch is in his beard.

"I like rubber ducks. And vibrators. I'll take it."

The crosswalk chirps, signaling our go-ahead. Gretchen pulls me across the street, the duck still buzzing.

Yes. I like ducks. When I was three, I got lost in a petting zoo. My father found me in a little shed with a family of baby ducks snoozing in my lap. Which is where my love for real feathered babies started. Now that I'm a grown-up, I spend weekends volunteering at an animal sanctuary in Tigard. Dogs and cats and horses and two pot-bellied pigs and a goat named Fang—and ducks. My ducks. Domestic rescues from Westmoreland Park—people think it's cute to adopt baby ducks, but then the babies grow up and they poop a lot and get into everything so the owners drop them off at the massive casting pond in Westmoreland. Unfortunately, the park already has an established duck and goose population, and the domestics don't fare well against their wild cousins. I helped with these rescues, so they're "my" ducks.

But the rubber duck collection, that was sort of an accidental thing. At nine, a cute boy from London moved into our neighborhood. Naturally, we fell in love. For my tenth birthday, he gave me a yellow rubber duck with a Union Jack painted on its wings. I still have it. And the ducks are something my family only sort of makes fun of. I wasn't allowed to collect *Star Wars* stuff because "throwing money at toys intended for nerdy boys who eat paste and never get dates is wasteful." Address your hate mail to my mother.

However, I do not need a duck that vibrates. In fact, it sort of ruins the entire *thing* if I consider putting a darling, sweet rubber duck anywhere on my body.

"Too weird, Gretchen."

"Okay, forget she vibrates. Look at her little painted-on necklace —and her name is Valerie Vibrato! See? She's so cute and Italian!"

"Mm-hmm."

"She'll be our little secret. Put her on the shelf above your monitor so you can smile when you have Whiny McWhinersons on the phone." Which reminds me. I have to call the grieving daughter back about her father's screwed-up obituary. Offer her a free pen.

26

"Speaking of vibrating, what do you think of Hipster Food Critic?" Gretchen asks.

"Apparently his name his Holden."

"Oh, so angsty. His parents couldn't have been more obvious? Wait!" Gretchen stops mid-sidewalk. "Holden Caulfield is in love with a girl named Jane, isn't he? Oh, this is so perfect."

"Shut it," I snarl.

"I, for one, would never name my children after book characters. Too much pressure to live up to."

"No, your children will have proper snob names like Todd and Blair."

"And yours will be named after *Star Wars* characters. Your son, Han Solo, and your daughter—God, I'm not nerdy enough to know any girl *Star Wars* characters."

I could tell her there are many: Padmé, Jaina, Deliah Blue, Mara Jade. "I'm never having children."

"Right. That would require S-E-X!" She shouts the spelled-out word, turning the heads of the office drones in front of us making their own way back to their respective holes in the ground. "You know, if you keep writing scenes like those in your magic journal, you could be on to something, Jayne darling. Maybe it'll break down some of that voodoo standing in the way of a little SVF: sexy vagina funtime."

"Gretchen! Shut *up!*"

"Wait! That could be our band name! Sexy Vagina Funtime."

"Seriously ... please."

"Is therapy doing you no good? Why are you so uncomfortable with the word *vagina?*" Again, she says it loudly enough that the two dudes in front of us look again and smile widely. She'll have their phone numbers before Surly Brian has the key out of the door.

I ignore her the entire way up the stairs, glaring instead at the red soles of her very expensive shoes. Elevator's broken. Again. Sometimes it works, but you take your life into your own hands in that ramshackle steel box. I don't even want to know how a few frayed cables actually hold it up. Plus, the camera in the corner? It invites Gretchen to be her embarrassing self. Once she did a strip tease in the time it took us to go three floors. Always looking for her viral video breakthrough.

In the interim two hours, I ignore her Facebook and text messages and the rubber bands she shoots across the aisle. And when I don't eat the vegan brownie she plops on my desk at three o'clock, she knows I'm pissed.

"C'mon, Jaynie, you know I was kidding. I'm sorry for saying the V Word and embarrassing you."

"Again."

She wiggles Valerie Vibrato in front of me. I slap it away.

"Why do you do that?" I say.

"Why does she do what?" a male voice interrupts.

"Food Critic, did you sweep your desk for bombs yet?" Gretchen spits.

"Leave him alone, Gretchen. Remember, he's new. We have to be nice to him."

Gretchen snorts. "Hey, when I was new, no one asked me to lunch or invited me to join their secret club."

"That's a lie. I invited you to lunch and we've been in the same secret club since grade school."

"Oh. Right. Well, girls only." Gretchen stretches her arms in front of Holden. He looks down at her boobs and smiles. "*Those* girls? Dream on."

"Well, I have to go to a new Italian-Asian fusion eatery over on Hawthorne tonight. The table will be for two. Any takers?"

"You're just shooting wide here, hoping that one of us will say yes?" Gretchen says.

"Tough crowd."

"And you have no other friends in your real life who you can ask?"

"Trying to lay the foundation for strong ties within the office environment. Looking for future alliances."

"You get that from your Tony Robbins' eight-disc set?"

"I was going to ask to borrow yours, actually," Holden says. I giggle.

"Whatever your game is, Food Critic, I don't eat carbs. So I'm out."

"Don't brownies have carbs?" Holden asks.

"These are magic brownies."

Holden looks at me. "Jayne? Free dinner? I'd say good company, but that's for you to decide."

Gretchen sticks her finger down her throat.

"Thanks. I, uh ..."

"She can't. She has a meeting tonight."

"Oh. What kind of meeting?" Holden asks. I stare at Gretchen, not sure what meeting I have.

"A writers' group. She's one of our rising stars."

"Really? What do you write?"

"Wait," Gretchen says, her hand against his plaid tie, "we do not want to hear about your crushing stack of rejections from your epic dragon-meets-vampire-overlord trilogy."

"You should read that trilogy. It's really something else." Holden laughs. "Okay, well, maybe another time, then. Ladies." He bows. The chain holding his wallet swings as he walks away.

"I'm not going to your writers' group tonight."

"Yes, you are. Or else I'm going on all the social media sites and telling people you're writing erotica."

"You wouldn't."

She pulls her phone out of the slender front pocket of her skirt. "Wouldn't I?"

As I stuff the brownie in my face and watch Gretchen's teeny ass sashay away from my desk, the realization hits again: I need new friends.

5

"PLEASE, Gretchen, *please* don't bring up the journal."

She looks at me, finger hovering over the doorbell. Laughter and conversation float through a cracked window. Moths flit crazily around the porch light, hairy little addicts seeking their fix.

Maybe because Gretch can see the fear in my eyes or the lack of color in my cheeks, she relents. "Fine. But if they ask you what you write, and they will, don't tell them you write obituaries. Tell them you're experimenting with women's fiction right now until you find your voice."

"I write other stuff." She doesn't know about Jaina Jacen—my pen name. *Star Wars* geeks will know those names—the twin children of Hans Solo and Princess Leia. Fortunately, Gretchen wouldn't figure this out if I punched her with a *Star Wars* encyclopedia. I almost feel guilty that she doesn't know this about me, but the teasing ... it would never end.

"You write *boring* stuff—about ducks," she says. I give her a dirty look.

"Ducks aren't boring."

"Little boring," she says under her breath.

"What do *you* write, other than your fashion crap?"

"Nothing. I run my columns by these guys and they help with spelling. Not my strong suit, as you know. They keep inviting me because I bring them free shit from the fashion shows."

Makes sense. Gretchen has so many freebies from fashion-related events, we almost had to rent a three-bedroom apartment so she could have a separate space for her wardrobe. And she only keeps the job at the *Register* because her parents said she had to work or her allowance would be cut off. Their version of tough love.

Bell rung, the door swings wide to welcome us in. Overbearing fragrance from one of those plug-in air fresheners about knocks me over.

Seeing the stack of discarded shoes in the foyer, I'm relieved I put on socks without holes. Gretchen ignores the shoe-free policy. From a psychological perspective, I'm sure it's because she loves the edge four extra, stiletto'd inches gives her. This way, she looks down on everyone.

A few air kisses are traded, some polite handshakes. "Writerly people, this is Jayne. Jayne, everyone. Where's wine?" Gretchen follows a portly, red-cheeked older woman I think is named Beth into the kitchen. I sit on the edge of a foldout chair, waiting for whatever comes next. My pulse tickles my eardrum.

"So, how do you know Gretchen?" a blond in an expensive pantsuit asks, impatiently tapping her silver pen against a notepad. She could be Gretchen's cousin—she has that *I'm a rich kid but I'm playing grown-up* look about her.

"We've known each other since we were little. Now we work together at the *Register*."

"Do you write for the paper?"

Gretchen floats back in, two filled wine glasses in hand, and answers for me. "Jayne's more on the management side of things."

"Ohhhh," the blond says.

"So, what *do* you write, Jayne?" another woman asks, this one housewife-ish with disheveled hair and a stain on her pilled brown sweater. She looks like she hasn't slept in a year.

"I write nonfiction stuff. Articles."

"Like about world events and politics?" Sweater Lady asks.

"Not exactly. But, I, uh, I'm experimenting with women's fiction, until I find my voice." I steal a look at Gretchen. "What about you?"

"Right now, mostly stories about hot men and anything remotely different from real life." She sighs.

"Suzette has very young triplets," Gretchen adds. "She needs as much escape as she can get."

Beth calls us to order. They start with sharing publishing-related news—one woman has had a poem about loss accepted at a small lit magazine; someone else has had her story short-listed for *Glimmer Train*; another person brags about her signed copy of Chuck Palahniuk's *Invisible Monsters*, a first-edition beauty. It's all very sedate and proper. These might be my people, after all, and Gretchen seems calm enough to not embarrass me in front of strangers.

Until the reading starts.

These are dirty birds. Of the five people who read their stories, four are erotica. The mother of triplets? She reads a scene about one woman being taken by twin studs at a horse ranch. Involving whips and prods and toys I've never even *heard* of.

I excuse myself when she gets to the part about "his milky elixir of life winds its way through her luscious locks." This is apparently sexy.

More wine will be required to make it through this.

In the kitchen, I empty the opened bottles into my glass and swallow the inch left in another bottle before anyone comes in for their own refill.

When I reenter the living room, my warm, wine-filled stomach repositions itself in my feet.

On Gretchen's lap sits *Pride and Prejudice*.

"So, you guys, I've been working on something extra, outside of the usual fashion stuff. I want to see what you think."

How? How did she get it?

I am going to kill her. Dead. Turn her into a ghost.

Tonight. I might not even wait for her to fall asleep. I don't have a gun. I do have a hatchet. That's going to make a huge mess. I wish I had a syringe—I should've stolen one out of Mr. Clark's diabetic supplies. I could inject her with a gigantic air bubble and she would just choke out on her new embolism. Those are tough to find on autopsy, right? Then I could leave her body for Quack. She'd eat Gretchen. Gnaw through skin and muscle until she licked the bones clean. Then they'd pin everything on the cat.

"Did you find the wine okay, Jayne?" Beth asks.

"What? Oh. Yes." Both bottles. "Thank you."

"Come sit, Jaynie. Hear what I've been working on." Gretchen winks at me. I have to sit. If I leave now, it will look weird. Plus I'm buzzed. I can't walk home alone or I'll get mugged by bagpipe-playing hipsters on unicycles.

The room quiets, and she proceeds to read.

The hardest part isn't hearing my words unrolled for the willing listeners or watching their expressions change as the pages flip forward. Surprisingly, I find myself wanting to rip the book out of Gretchen's hand and read it the right way. She's not placing emphasis where it needs to go. She's reading it like a fourth grader would read *Superfudge*. No intonation, no inflection, no slowing down or speeding up at the sexy parts.

In essence, though, it sounds pretty good.

With the last word spilled, the room erupts in giggles and applause. Gretchen smiles proudly, as if she's done something wonderful, that the accolades falling at her feet are truly hers. A twinge of resentment bites at the edge of my brain. But the curl of Gretchen's lip, the flutter of her brow, meant for me, says so much more. She's just trying to help. She believes in me. She believed in me in the class-president elections in middle school when I didn't have a snowball's chance in hell against that Rachel girl (I lost); she held my hand the night I stood up to my parents and told them I wasn't going to law or medical school; she sat next to me in the lunchroom the days and weeks after the make-out party scandal when everyone else stopped talking to me, newly named Jaynie Prudie, because I refused to touch tongues with that kid Robert. Honestly, though—he was notorious for leaving his lunch in his braces.

I have to be grateful for Gretchen's interference, as annoying as it is, especially given my life's ratio of people who care versus people who think I'm a dud.

Gretchen will live to see another night.

"YOU WERE *BRILLIANT,* Jaynie! Don't you see that? They LOVED it!" She pulls into traffic, barely missing a passing bus. The driver honks. She flips him off.

"They love smut, Gretchen."

"Duh! Have you been in a bookstore lately? These are modern women, taking control of their sexuality, babe."

"I have to say, though, I was shocked when the triplet mom read her story."

"Dude, that was straight-up porn," she says.

"She should maybe not be having sex. She does know that's where kids come from, right?"

"Oh, she's not having sex. That's why she's writing it. She has books and books *filled* with those stories. Her husband is terrified to touch her now. He had a vasectomy the day after the triplets were born, and he goes in every month to make sure his sperm count is zero."

"Shit."

"Yeah. She keeps catching him masturbating in the bathroom."

"Gretchen, please, that *word.*"

"Maaaaaastuuuuuurbaaaaaaaatiiiiiiiiing." And we're back to Gretchen being a child. "Isn't therapy helping you at all?"

I wiggle my journal in Gretchen's peripheral vision. "Uh, *yeah,* this is part of the therapy."

"Well, damn, you tell that Dr. McCoy to keep on keepin' on. This is some good stuff." Gretchen swerves across the neighboring lane and makes an abrupt left turn into a parking lot. The Copper Horse?

"What are you doing?"

"I'm not ready for bed yet. That was such a rush! We're going to celebrate."

"It's almost ten, Gretch. Work tomorrow?"

"Yes, obituaries are exhausting." She slams the car into park and freshens the lips that look plumped with collagen. Except they're real. Her hands clench my cheeks and she twists my face in her direction, painting my lips with her gloss. "Blow me a kiss. Rub in the lipstick."

As we're walking toward the pub door, I see a familiar beat-up truck. The magnetic *Piewalker's* sign hangs lopsided from the driver's side door. The pickup rear gate is smothered in *Star Wars*-themed stickers, a coalescing growth of Vaders and Stormtroopers that eclipse any sign of remaining paint on the truck's ass end.

Gretchen claps excitedly. "Oh, yay! Your nerdy brownie boy is here!" She wraps her arm around my shoulders and whispers close to my head. "You should read him a bedtime story, Jaynie. I know the perfect one."

The wine, and the residual rush from the writers' group, has softened my usual murderous sentiments. While I won't be reading anything to Luke tonight, if he's even here—it may be Leia with the truck—it will be nice to hang out. He's funny. And I don't feel weird around him because I'm pretty sure I'm not his type.

To be honest, I don't know whose type I am.

Maybe I'm typeless.

"Stop." Gretchen straightens my top, adjusts the shoulders of my cardigan, fluffs first my hair and then my boobs. "Oh. Have these grown?" Her hands cup my chest and she bounces them. Two guys walking out of the pub stop to ogle the girl-on-girl show.

"You hot muffins busy tonight?" one says.

"Dream on, cowboy." She hooks her arm into mine and in we go. My heart sinks a little when I see a woman resembling Leia on the small corner stage strumming a guitar—but then a familiar voice greets us from behind the bar.

"It's my favorite girl and her vegan puppy!" Luke says. Since I'm neither vegan nor puppy, I must be his favorite girl. Gretchen pinches my ass.

"Go get 'em, tiger," she growls quietly.

We slide on to barstools, still warm from their prior tenants. "What can I get you lovely ladies tonight?"

"When did you start working here?" I say.

"Just helping out my buddy. He and his wife have a new baby, so he needs a few nights off now and again to catch up on sleep."

This evening has a growing theme: stay away from babies. You will never sleep again.

"Hunh. Well, lucky for us we picked *this* bar," I say. Gretchen shrugs. This was not coincidental. But when did he tell her, and why not me? I scan her face for a sign that she's in to Luke. That would be too weird. But why else would we be here unless she wanted to see him?

"Two crantinis, if you please, boy," Gretchen says, whisking her hand at Luke. He snorts and moves to make the drinks.

"How did you know he was going to be here?" I whisper.

"I'm nosy. I heard him talking on his phone while we were waiting for lunch."

"Oh." I pick all the salt off a pretzel to give my nervous hands something to do. "Are you ... interested in him?"

Gretchen laughs loudly. "Him?" She throws a thumb in Luke's direction. "God. No. But, you know, maybe you are ..."

"Yeah, of course. As a friend, though."

"Maybe more than a friend? He would be so safe for you, Jaynie. You guys have been friends forever. He's not scary. You could be perfectly nerdish together."

"I don't need you to play matchmaker."

"Oh, but I do. I'm like that old crony lady in *Mulan*."

"No, you're Yente."

"I've never seen any of your *Star Wars* movies, so I don't know Yente."

"She's from *Fiddler on the Roof*."

"Does the guy really play the fiddle on the roof, though? That's what I want to know. Like, wouldn't that piss off the neighbors if he was out there playing a ditty? What if he sucked? Do the neighbors throw tomatoes at him? How does he not slip off?"

"These are your deepest thoughts?" I ask.

"I'm just sayin' ..."

When I see Luke in action, the same thought crosses my mind that has been there for the three years we've known each other: yes. He's perfect. For me. We have so many of the same interests. He's funny. Handsome. Humble. Witty. Creative. Ambitious. Kind. And the way his Chewbacca T-shirt fits is not lost on me. Mmm, mmm, Chewy.

But if I say this out loud, even to my darling Gretchen, all will be lost. The moment I admit that I have any sort of male-directed affection, the thoughts tumble into a ginormous, fire-breathing fearball that looks like it came out of Quack's stomach—*What if he likes me back? Oh God, what if he doesn't like me back and really he's just being nice because that's what civilized people do? Worse, what if he wants to kiss me? What if he wants to see me naked?*

Forgive me, George Lucas, for this departure, but the anxiety of romantic involvement is my Kryptonite. I'm weakened, on my knees, bleeding unnaturally, gasping for air in that inhospitable territory called Men.

Which means I will be single forever.

Maybe therapy really isn't working.

At this moment, however, I can sit near Luke and soak him up. And then later when my housemates, the tall blond one and the scary furry one, have been properly medicated for sleeping time, I'll wring out my writerly sponge and give sweet Illyria her man. Oh, Mooney ...

Luke slides the pretty red drinks atop the bar, the lime wedges hanging on for dear life. "So, what brings you out so late on a weeknight?"

"We had our writers' group meeting. We're celebrating Jayne's future foray into—" I slam my elbow into her side, "into meaningful, proper fiction that ladies read over tea," she finishes.

I gulp the first sip. It burns going down. Too much vodka, not enough cranberry.

"Really? I didn't know you were writing anything, Jayne. You're holding out on me?" Luke wipes down the counter.

"No. It's nothing really. Just some ... experimenting."

"Anything I can read?"

"No!" I clear my throat. "No. Not yet. I'll let you know."

"Jayne's shy about her work. She shouldn't be—it's very good—but maybe someday ...," Gretchen coos.

"I like to write," Luke announces. What? No way.

Gretchen's smile widens, eyes glowing with the energy of her evil plotting. "Do tell, Luke."

"Mostly sci-fi." Oh my God. "And some fan fiction—you know, when you write stories about a world another writer has created."

"Fascinating! Isn't it, Jayne?" She pats her hand over her mouth in a fake yawn. So rude.

"Actually, yes, it is." How did I not know this about him? "Do you have anything published?"

"Some stuff online. Blogs. A few sci-fi forums. It's just for fun." I know many of these forums. Now I will hunt.

"I'd love to read your work sometime." What I want to say, but cannot, is *I love sci-fi we should talk more I'll show you mine if you show me yours.*

"Done." Luke offers a fist for a bump. The odor of bleach wafts from the bar towel.

My phone vibrates against the bar top. My sister Margaret. Oh, sorry. Dr. Margaret. I read the message and sigh dramatically. Because, well, Dr. Margaret.

"One of your adoring fans?" Luke asks.

"My sister."

"What does she want? Did she get a new car? No—wait. She got a new machine to suck shit out of people's faces," Gretchen sneers. "Actually, do they have those?"

"She's texting for Sheila to find out if I got the other text about Friday night."

"What's Friday? I didn't know we had plans." Gretchen empties her glass.

"*We* don't. My brother made partner with his law firm, so we're doing family dinner and I'm supposed to wear something other than denim."

"Oh! I can dress you up!"

"Nothing in your closet will fit me. I eat carbs, remember?"

"And bacon," she says.

"Hell, yeah. Bacon. Speaking of bacon, Luke, that chowder today, man ... Make that every week, would you?" This crantini is going straight to my head. "I'm supposed to bring a date. I ignored my mother's prior message, so now she's got Maggot bugging me."

Maggot. The name my toddler mouth bestowed upon my sister when it couldn't say *Margaret*. Who knew how fitting it would become.

"So, take Luke."

Luke stops wiping the inside of a glass and looks between Gretchen and me.

"I'm sure Luke has better things to do with his Friday night than to put on a tie and be bored to blood tears by my self-righteous family."

"Actually ... I don't." He smiles. The light from the overhead spots bounces off the very clean bar top and reflects in his eyes.

Shit. No more crantinis. Ever.

"Um, nah, don't worry about it. I never bring a date. They're used to it."

"But Jaynie, Portland City Grill is a nice place. In a high rise. And you won't have me there to protect you from Dr. Maggot and Farting Frankie."

"Farting Frankie?" Luke asks.

"My brother has colon issues," I say.

"He's gorgeous, but man, don't sit next to him." Gretchen fans her face.

Frankie managed to overcome most of those early humiliating days when the gastrointestinal specialists found drugs to curb the flatulence, much to the relief of his long-suffering classmates, but the name *Farting Frankie* is just too much for Gretchen to let go.

"I don't need protecting."

"Since when?" Gretchen says. Ouch.

"Jayne, honestly, this sounds like fun," Luke interjects. "From what you've told me about your folks, I'd love to come be the bleeding-heart thorn in their sides. Think of the pair we'd make sitting in the Grill with our unmatched socks and silly ideas about democracy."

I laugh. Luke always makes me do that. "Really? Because my father might try to pull you into a conversation about why the '80s was the best decade ever, despite the terrible music. Or how the Lehman Brothers were framed."

"I studied interdisciplinary politics in college. I can handle whatever they throw at me."

"God, you really are a bleeding-heart liberal, aren't you," Gretchen says, her tone a tiny bit too acidic.

"Another crantini, girls?" Luke deflects.

"Nah, this is enough for tonight. I'm going to be sucking back the Advil as is," I say, reaching into my wallet for drink money.

"On the house," Luke says, placing a hand over mine. I shiver. He's touching me. A boy is touching me.

It's nice.

His hand is so soft and warm and big.

"Then a tip at least," I say, voice cracking.

"Tip me in the morning when you try the new turnovers I've got planned."

Tip me in the morning. An image pops into my head of me leaving twenty bucks on his pillow. It's not a bad image.

"So, Friday. Do I pick you up, or ...?" I ask.

"Leia's got the truck, plus your parents might have a heart attack if we pull up in that. So, yeah, maybe you drive? Is that cool?" Luke says.

"Perfect. Okay, she'll pick you up at seven. See you then," Gretchen butts in and pulls me off the stool. "Ta-ta!"

I wave and feel his smile surround me like a favorite sweater, even as Gretchen drags me out of the pub and into the chilly night.

"You're so rude," I say. Her BMW chirps as she unlocks it.

"He doesn't have a proper car, Jayne. This is not a good sign."

"You're a snob."

She twists and points back at the well-loved pickup. "THAT is his ride."

"Weren't you just telling me how perfect we'd be together?"

"That was before I realized he has to share a vehicle with his sister. He's a *grown-up*, Jayne. Don't give your heart to this guy or you will end up living in the back of his food truck."

Hey, as long as it's filled with turnovers and bacon chowder ...

"Don't be so judge-y, Gretchen. It's a truck. For all you know, he could have a Ferrari parked in his garage at home."

"His éclairs aren't *that* good."

Yes, they are. Everything about Luke is that good.

Oh, dear.

EIDER: CHAPTER 3

by Jaina Jacen (September)

"Best wishes for Twelvemonth, Illyria," my mother says over her break-fast. I will expect nothing more from her for the day. Even her presence beyond her chamber walls is remarkable enough. I, alongside everyone else, tolerate her, despite her foul temper and harsh bearing. My father's schedule is organized so that he can avoid impromptu encounters; they have not shared a bedchamber since the birth, and subsequent death, of my younger brother. Genetic engineering is a dangerous business; while it works most of the time, cases such as my little brother's are a side effect of a field where nature doesn't always play fair.

When the first settlers stepped foot on Eider five centuries ago, this cannot be how they imagined their fresh start: loveless unions, a bloodline hierarchy that assigns station to one group over another, granting sweeter genetics and thus longer life to those deemed best to rule. This is why they abandoned the Dead Planet. That is why we're here.

But the frailty of humanity dictates that purity shall be stained by greed, power, and lust. And efforts to avoid all such spoils exacerbate the original problem.

Because of their shortsightedness, the room my heart holds vacant cannot be occupied by the soul who truly belongs there. One who knows my name only because it is printed on our currency.

My mother disappears without another word. Taisa slides a plate before me, though my interest is not on food. "The collector—what is his name?" I ask.

Taisa does not answer. Instead, she pours wine.

"Taisa—his name?"

Again, I'm met with quiet.

"He is Class II, yes?"

"The collectors are all from Class II."

We are not so far apart. One class only.

"Do you know his family?"

Taisa looks into my face, a rare and brave act when others are around. "I do."

"I want to know everything about him—"

"My Sovereign, inquiry is dangerous."

"For whom, Taisa? For you?" I smile. Taisa, though a Class III, is the closest thing I have to a friend. As I am not allowed out of the compound without armed escort, she sneaks in sweets and treasures and tales of adventure from starcrafts long traveled to distant settlements. She knows I will protect her.

Before she can open her mouth again, my father thunders into the room and assumes his seat at the table's head. Servants spring to action.

"Happy Twelvemonth, Illyria," he says. My father doesn't smile often, so receiving one this morning is a pleasant treat.

"Father," I say, bowing my head as per etiquette's dictate.

I squeeze Taisa's wrist where she stands next to me. "We're not done here," I whisper.

She clears her throat quietly and steps away. No need risk my father's ire if he were to see us touching. Such a preposterous fear.

This Twelvemonth marks an important milestone for me, beyond sweetcakes and dancing with tiresome suitors and wishes of good tidings from strange mouths. I am of age, and thus my voice will no longer hide behind my father's cloak.

I am the future of Eider. If change is to happen, it must begin with me.

6

WHILE I STAND in a light rain outside Piewalker's, the breeze carries the promise of sugary goodness. A real-life kaleidoscope, umbrellas bounce down the block, scurrying to hit crosswalks or grab the bus sloshing toward the stop. Luke's crowd, though thinner this morning, will fatten up for lunch. Friday midday is always busy as folks head into the city center for shopping adventures. And the food truck made Portland's *Best Of* list again—the mention in the *Huffington Post's* recent article on the nation's top 101 food trucks has been good too. All well deserved.

If he could just get Leia to stop making out with her random, spiky-haired boyfriends so publicly. I wonder what Christmas is like at *their* house.

Oh God. It's Friday.

Dinner with *my* family tonight. With Luke.

Something squeaks in my ear. I jump a foot. Spin around.

"Good morning," Holden says. In his hand is a green rubber duck, stamped with light blue raindrops, wearing a yellow rain hat. He extends his arm toward me. "You like ducks, right? Your desk—there are a few sitting around."

"Yeah. I like ducks."

"Now you have one more for your collection." He hands it to me.

"Thanks." The customer before me steps away, order fulfilled.

"Nice duck," Luke says. "Who's your friend?"

"Uh, this is Holden. The paper's new food critic," I say quietly.

"Oh no! A food critic!" Luke feigns fear, exaggerated biting of nails. He laughs and thrusts his hand over the counter. Holden shakes it.

"I've heard only rave reviews about your truck. Plus I'm off duty. Still trying to recover from last night's ordeal," Holden says.

"Bad meal?" I ask.

"Brilliant meal. Ate too much. I will suffer at the gym later." Right. Of course Hipster Food Critic has to go to the gym. Otherwise he'd never fit into his cords and thrift-store sport coats.

"There's a cure for that," Luke says, plating a still-warm turnover.

"Yeah?" Holden says.

"Never go to the gym." Luke smiles and smothers the turnover in whipped cream, passing it over to me. I start to pay but Holden touches my wrist.

"This one's on me."

Luke wiggles his eyebrows. This is very awkward. Why is Holden buying my breakfast?

"See you at lunch?" Luke asks. I nod.

Holden holds his unfolded umbrella over us as we move down the street. Where is Gretchen?

"So, is his lunch menu good?" Holden asks.

"Depends on if you like the best bacon chowder ever made in the history of the world."

"Ringing endorsement. Maybe I'll tag along for lunch and give it a try."

"He doesn't have it every day of the week. Pretty sure Fridays are a vegetable thing. He tries to alternate to keep the crowd happy."

"Right. Makes sense." He switches umbrella hands. "So, I hope it wasn't too forward, giving you the duck. I saw it at a touristy shop next to the MAX station and thought of you."

"No. Thanks. It's cool. People bring me ducks all the time." Which is sort of not true. Valerie Vibrato is the first one I've received in a while. "So, where'd you go to school? You mentioned student loans," I say.

"I started at U of O to get a degree in architecture, but I don't have the head for it. Much to my father's chagrin."

"Your dad's an architect?"

"No. He drives a garbage truck. But my parents were hoping I'd be their little success story. I finished at Portland State, but barely. With an English degree, a minor in folklore."

"I had no idea a person could major in folklore."

"Surprised me too."

"Then how'd you end up a food critic?" I ask.

"I'm good with eating and putting sentences together?"

My cell phone alarm twinkles from my pocket. "We have to hurry. Three-minute warning."

We scuttle down the sidewalk under oppressive cloud cover, careful not to slip on the leafy reminders of the changing season. Funny thing about the Pacific Northwest—some days, it feels like the sun never comes up—or, like, maybe she called in sick. "Hey, Mother Nature? Yeah, it's me, Sun. I was up really late last night and I've got some serious hot flashes and unreal solar flares going on this morning. I'm gonna pop some Midol and crawl back under the sheets for the day. We cool?"

While the humans know it's daytime because our alarm clocks and bosses remind us that we should be out of bed and behaving in a productive manner, days like today, where the mist is sneaky and dampens all the layers, even under my allegedly water-resistant trench coat ... Makes me long for flannel jammies and a movie marathon and a coma-inducing intake of sugar.

On approach to the office, we're greeted by the jingling of keys— Surly Brian's announcement to anyone in the vicinity that closure is imminent. I scan the block for Gretchen's car, in case she parked out front today. She left early this morning—something about taking her mother's Pekingese to the vet.

A black Town Car idles curbside. License plate: BRANT1.

Shit. Brant Cole. The paper's owner. Mr. Clark's second cousin, twice removed, on his mother's angry German side. Or something.

"Does he do that every morning?" Holden asks between breaths. "The key thing?" Right. Food Critic wouldn't know that he should not worry about keys but rather should have a scary feeling when the Brant Mobile appears.

Holden starts toward the elevator.

"Stairs. That elevator will be your end."

We're among the last to arrive, so I sneak into the tiny staff kitchen and shovel a few bites of turnover into my face. Man, so good. Luke is magical. As if I needed a turnover to tell me that.

Heart, stop thinking in place of Brain. You're impulsive and naïve.

I scratch "Death and pox to ye who purloins" across the box lid. I'm very protective of my refrigerated foodstuffs.

Raised voices careen through the open-concept office. Open concept only because our mismatched half-height cubicles were bought at an office rummage sale. Nothing but the best around here.

I'm not going to my desk yet. I sit too close to ground zero. I don't want to be nearby when Lord Vader blasts open the office door. More pathetic is watching Mr. Clark pander after his second cousin, twice removed, begging reprieve from whatever damage has been done this time. Brant Cole isn't much older than I am but he has enough bad manners and sour grimaces for an army of Sith lords. When he shows up, damage follows.

"Stay in your desk. Pretend you're working," I whisper to Holden as I slink by. I am going to the restroom to hide. Gretchen and I usually do this when Brant Cole surfaces in search of his next meal, but Gretchen's not here so I will have only the toilet to keep me company. I should be worried—no note or text this morning. I hope she still has that case of Stolichnaya in her trunk.

Our floor has two bathrooms. One is unusable after the pipe bomb took out a toilet and part of the wall. When the lath and plaster blew off, it exposed lead pipes. No bueno. In light of this weighty discovery, they're supposed to be renovating one floor at a time—water dispensers have been added to each office—but apparently, there is an issue with a lapsed insurance policy. Likely what Mr. Clark and his Imperial cousin are arguing about.

The second loo now serves the entire floor. Men and women. You take your chances coming in here most of the time. Because this is an old building, the stalls are made of wood. The floor tiles are old, and everything creaks. One misplaced fart bounces off the toilet bowl and echoes around the high ceiling for minutes.

Stretched along the face of the mirrors whose peeling silver edge broadcasts its age is a message: I AM BLUE AND SO ARE YOU.

I step closer. Is that ... paint? Someone has painted the message on the mirror. What the hell does it mean?

Hand on the stall door, I push. It snags. Old, tired wood. I bump it with my hip.

BANG!

I slam backward into the framework, eyes stinging. A foul taste coats my lips.

Room spins. Ears ring.

"Am I dead? Was it another bomb?" I yell to no one. "Help!"

Goddamn, my eyes sting! I wipe furiously to clear my vision. I must see if the wetness on my hands is blood or water from the exploded toilet. No smoke. Just a faint blue mist in the air.

No blood. Toilet porcelain is still intact. Water is not gushing on to the floor. No alarms have been triggered. No one knows that I am in this bathroom alone, having survived another assault from the demented restaurateur. Because that *has* to be what this is.

"Help!" I scream again. The stinging won't abate. And the taste ... so gross. I grope my way toward the two tiny sinks, twisting with both hands to get the water on.

On my third rinse, the stinging lessens. A thorough swish with water replaces the inky taste with the metallic tinge from our health-hazard pipes.

The main door opens. "Oh my God! Jayne? Your face!" Gretchen! I'm saved! "What—what the hell happened?"

I straighten abruptly and squeegee my eyes. Stare into the mirror. Scream. Loudly.

"I'm *blue*! I AM BLUE!"

"Okay, calm down. Shit, it's everywhere." Gretchen runs out and triggers the fire alarm. The whooping flares down the hallway. Footsteps and sliding chairs filter down from the floor above.

"Don't move. You might need medical help. Can you breathe okay?" Gretch asks.

"Why am I blue?" I yell again. A small crowd gathers outside the open bathroom door.

"Whoa, is that Jayne?" Holden asks.

The commentary buzzes like a game of Operator at a slumber party. *Yeah, it's Jayne! Why is she blue? Holy shit, she's blue? What happened? Oh sweet Jesus, is there another bomb? Let's get the hell out of here! We should never have hired a food critic in the first place.*

"Oh God ..." Gretchen mutters.

"What? What!? Am I bleeding? Is there another bomb? Am I going to die?"

I'm going to hyperventilate. I'm fucking *blue*.

"It's Friday, isn't it ..."

"Gretchen—you are not helping. Inspect me for damage."

She does. Sort of. Without touching me or even getting very close at all.

"We're going to have to scrub really hard to get this off," she says. "Should I call your mother? You cannot go to the Grill looking like this."

"Stop making me feel worse—I need help!"

"There's no blood, Jayne. Can you see? And hear? Does anything feel broken?"

I shake my head. My ear hums from the bang. But nothing feels broken. Except my pride.

"Can you look around by the toilet and see if there are more contraptions?" she says.

"NO. I'm blue ENOUGH."

"Okay, well, I don't mean to be a dick but I'm not going to touch you until the paramedics arrive. In case you're ... radioactive. Or something. It's best we contain this."

"If I were radioactive, I would be—glowing. Not BLUE!" I start toward the door but her raised hands preempt forward movement.

"Stop. Stay. Jayne, we need to make sure you're okay before you walk out of here."

"She's right," Holden says.

"Shut up, Food Critic. This is your fault. You people—you make restaurant owners crazy and then they do shit like *this* and I just came in to pee and now *I'm blue!*"

Holden turns to Gretchen. "She sort of looks like the girl from *Willy Wonka*—the original one, not the Johnny Depp remake—who turns into a blueberry." They giggle.

"That Johnny Depp one was weird. But he's very versatile, you gotta admit," Gretchen says.

"I AM NOT A GODDAMNED BLUEBERRY!"

"Okay, okay, sorry," Gretchen says, hiding her smiling mouth behind her perfectly flesh-colored hand.

"Where have you been, anyway?"

"My mom's dog. Her anal glands abscessed."

"God, gross. Stop. I don't even want to know what that means." I spit into the sink again. My saliva is the color of a summer sky. "Can you get me a glass of lead-free water, please? And shut the door. The fire alarm is aggravating the explosion headache."

Holden and Gretchen stay with me until the paramedics and police arrive. To hear the story told later, Gretchen makes sure to share how brave she was to stay with me as there could have been another bomb—a real one, not one filled with what the police estimate are bank-robbery dye packs.

Whoever did this rigged all three stalls. I just happened to be the first one in the bathroom today. Once the paramedic takes vitals and checks my appendages for damage, he tells me I should buy a lottery ticket. Yes, because becoming a human canvas for some sick jerk's inky prank means I'm ridiculously lucky.

He hands me a huge pack of alcohol prep pads and some sample-size ibuprofen for the headache. Tells me to watch for further signs of eye irritation. Says if I scrub hard with the prep pads, I should be able to get some of the ink off. Some. Not all.

"Moisturize a ton when you're finished, though," his female partner offers. "I hear lemon rinds and olive oil are good for removing ink too."

Great. I'm going to smell like a nursing-home dinner special.

Dinner. Tonight. There is no way I can go to dinner, with Luke, with my ass-y family, looking like Violet Beauregarde.

We're not allowed back inside until the police do a thorough search of the whole building. Four floors of office workers, at least those who stay, migrate around back to the parking lot. I see Mr. Clark hunched nervously under a wide black umbrella, standing next to Brant Cole, phone stuck to his ear.

Clark summons me over.

"Sorry about this, kiddo."

I nod, pulling the silver emergency blanket tighter around my shoulders. My clothes are damp from the efforts to wash off the ink. It would be helpful to hear Mr. Clark say the following words: "Take the rest of the day off. Go home. Have a stiff drink and a hot bath. You've been through a trauma."

Instead, Brant Cole ends his call, turns to Mr. Clark, and says, "Are you going to tell her, or shall I?"

Mr. Clark opens his mouth, but no sound comes out. Just a desperation-tinged squeak.

"Fine. Ms. Dandy, right?"

"Yes."

"I regret to inform you that we are reshaping the *Rose City Register* and as a result, we will be downsizing. We can offer you part-time hours if you are willing to retrain and move into the accounting and payroll department."

"What?"

"Do you have skill with accounting and payroll?"

"I've just been the victim of a terrorist attack, and you're firing me?"

"Technically, this," he gestures at me, head to toe, "is not a terrorist attack. Second, if you have accounting and payroll experience, we can reassign you to that department."

"But no writing."

"Writing obituaries and garage sale ads is hardly a writing position. Your current job will be amalgamated into another senior employee's duties."

"I don't have any accounting experience." I failed the last two math classes I took in college. My professors gave me Ds just so I could graduate.

"Right. Well, effective next week. Thank you for your time and service. Clark will have details about a severance package. Good luck."

"But ... I'm blue." Tears sting my eyes. Real tears. Springing from the panic that comes from thoughts about making rent, student loan payments, paying for food, buying ink remover ...

"Indeed you are." Brant Cole nods, grabs the umbrella from his shorter and very silent second cousin, twice removed, and stalks off.

"Did that just happen?" I ask Mr. Clark. He shakes his head yes. "Okay. I'm going home. As soon as I can get my keys. I will be taking the rest of today off."

He doesn't protest.

7

I DON'T WANT to go home.

Gretchen sort of offered to give me a ride, although she spent so much time looking through the lost-and-found for something to cover her white leather seats that I left without saying goodbye. I need to walk, despite my cobalt hue. I don't even care that people might think I just robbed a bank. Maybe they will fear my wrath.

When antisocial sentiments spike, I go to Powell's. The world's greatest bookstore. In the many blocks between the *Register* and the bookstore's front steps, I practice Dr. McCoy's breathing exercises. Everything smells and tastes like dye.

How am I going to face my family tonight, blue skin aside, and admit that I will soon be unemployed? Did this all just really happen? But I'm good with obituaries. Grieving families email to tell me how my words eased their pained hearts. Except for that one where we misspelled her dad's name but that wasn't my mistake. And she got a cool pen out of the deal.

A woman in front of Powell's is strapped with babies—one on her chest, one on her back, a third in a narrow stroller, a diaper bag heavy on its handles. She needs help navigating the few steps. I grab the footrest across the front and hoist.

"Oh, thank—you're blue."

"Yeah, accident at work."

"You work at a bank?" The baby in the stroller stares at my discolored face and bursts into tears. The woman stuffs a cookie-like thing in his hand. He shuts up. "He might smile if you talk like Cookie Monster or Grover."

I am not going to do this.

I know that ratty brown sweater. "Hey, aren't you in Gretchen's writers' group?"

She squints at me for a sec and then smiles. "You're her friend—" She can't remember my name.

"Jayne."

"Right! Jayne! Sorry. Baby brain. I'm Suzette." Her handshake is sticky. The chubby bundle on her back squeals. "Are you going inside?"

I hold the door for her, momentarily glad that this haphazardly groomed human female with three babies in her care is more of a spectacle than I am. The baby in the stroller holds out his mushy cookie in my direction.

All of a sudden, Suzette's sexy-time writing efforts seem heroic rather than icky. How in the world does she have time to do *anything* with three children under the age of twenty?

I have no real direction, so I follow her, making small talk, noticing every plop of slobbery cookie her child leaves behind. Like a soggy, germ-infested *Hansel & Gretel* breadcrumb trail. We end up in the coffee-colored section (Powell's is color-coded by genre) where bursting bodices and edible abs are on display. Not a Thomas the Tank Engine to be had.

"I call it Me Time."

"I'm sorry?"

"Reading and writing smut. It's the only time I get to be someone ... else. Don't get me wrong—I love being a mom." She pauses. "Okay, that's a total lie. This gig sucks." She leans closer. "The plan is to sell enough books that I can hire a nanny and a plastic surgeon. Triplets *destroy* your belly. It's like a roadmap of Los Angeles here now." She squishes her lower abdomen in her hands.

This is terrifying.

"Do you have a publisher?" I ask.

"Just myself."

I have to play dumb here. I sell Jaina Jacen's sci-fi stories online, but this information, once out of my mouth, could easily make it into Gretchen's ears and then so on and so forth. Best keep quiet.

"E-books are big business, baby," she says.

"Really?" Okay, what marketing is *she* doing to sell books? I'm lucky if I sell fifty a month of three different titles.

"Hell yeah. If you can get yourself an audience, you can make serious bank. That's the only thing keeping me from losing the few marbles I have left." She taps her skull with a fingertip that wears long-forgotten remnants of nail polish. "Gretchen should be selling her work online. What she read the other night?" Suzette fans herself. "That was goooooood."

A little boy in a yellow raincoat tugs on my sleeve. "Why are you blue?"

"Because she didn't eat her broccoli. Shoo," Suzette says. It's sort of weird to have this little kid standing so close to book covers boasting bursting breasts. "Anyway, Gretchen totally surprised us. Between you and me, she usually writes half-baked pieces about skirts and shoes that cost the same as a year's preschool tuition. She really outdid herself."

She outdid herself because it was not her work. All Gretchen did was steal my journal. I cannot admit that those were my words, though—not only would it make me look like a needy jerk, but I cannot confess to owning *that*. You know. S. E. X.

"Anyway, my grand plan is to get my stories out there—tons of them, wham, bam, thank you, ma'am—and get the bathtub ready to bathe in my dollars. And Gretchen's a smart enough girl. She's got the funds to hire someone to do all the heavy lifting—editing, cover art, marketing." Suzette wipes greenish boogers off the face of the baby hanging from her front. "You know what, on second thought, don't tell her about this. Please. Gretchen doesn't need the money." She laughs. "And I don't need the competition."

I end up serving as the human shopping cart for Suzette's acquisitions—she can't carry the books with so many members of the next generation hanging off her wilted frame, so I oblige. One romance novel after another, the shock of their garish covers waning, each offering little variety or room for imagination: bad cop with cuffs, stud cowboy with a whip, hot businessman with a dog collar. Thank heavens I'm blue so no one will recognize it's me under this growing stack. Then again, all the people I know are at work, gainfully employed, earning money for their rent and student loans and car insurance.

The knife Brant Cole jammed into my side turns again.

Among the stacks in the gold, rose, and purple rooms, I learn more about Suzette's plans to take over the publishing world. She name-drops authors like I should know who they are, talks about publishing platforms, how agents get involved, how movie deals are being made.

How people write under pen names so no one knows who they really are.

"I've heard people do that," I say, narrowly avoiding stroller baby's outstretched, very gooey hand. I hope I sound convincing. Gretchen's friends wouldn't be interested in Illyria and Mooney and their intergalactic quest for a perfect love.

But the journal locked in my tiny closet safe—the finished Dr. McCoy-prescribed story, and the almost-finished sequel currently cloaked in *Pride and Prejudice*'s skin—those might fit the bill.

No. No way. How could I let anyone know I'd written ...

My cheeks warm. I wonder if the flush of red now means I'm purple.

But bills need paying. I will have to find another job, certainly, but if I can hide behind a pen name, no one will know the difference. Right? Hell, no one close to me has figured out that I've written the sci-fi stuff. Why would changing genres be any different, especially if it means I can make a little money and maybe find a way to spend more time writing?

As Suzette talks, my thoughts cycle around the pros and cons and what-ifs and *what kind of jobs am I even qualified for these are tough times post-Recession hey maybe selling these stories could help a girl out.*

When we finally head to the cashier, Suzette's mouth still moving, the clock tells me that two hours have passed and despite the fact that four little kids have asked about my blue face, one security guard asked if I was okay, two of Suzette's three progeny have pooped their diapers, and my pants are smeared with whatever the stroller baby didn't eat, I feel less disgusting than I did upon entering.

Jaina Jacen has a plan.

EIDER: CHAPTER 4

by Jaina Jacen (September)

"You have to help me find the way out."

"My Sovereign, if I—if we—get caught," Taisa says. She need not finish the sentence. If something untoward happens outside the compound, we won't have court guards to protect us. We're on our own. And once we return—if we return—my father will have me locked up. I cannot bear to imagine what will happen to Taisa.

"It is my Twelvemonth. I'll not stay locked up in here and breathe the same air as these people who so fear my father's wrath that they bow lower than a parasite. Life is bigger than this, Taisa," I say, spinning with arms outstretched. "It's bigger than we are. I don't want to wilt. We go tonight."

"Where? What life is to be found amongst the lowerclasses that you don't see here?"

I laugh. "All the life."

I want to see the market. I want to mingle among the other classes, to try foods still smoking from the spit and fresh produce plucked from trees and tilled fields. I want to listen to players and take in the dancers ... and maybe dance a little myself. Such scandal it would be!

"We need a weapon." Quickly, I disrobe and pull on a lighter tunic, some pants, a pair of light slippers. This formal garb is too oppressive. I need to move with stealth.

"Illyria," Taisa puts her hand on my wrist, "no. Don't do this."

"It's going to be fun. I promise."

I know my way to the armory. I only need a small sidearm, something I can conceal under a hooded cape. I've seen the soldiers practice marksmanship when Father thought I was studying with Master Imre. Lady Livia made the mistake of teaching me how to make a fragrant tea with the handy side effect of inducing somnolence—it's safe to say that Imre has drunk his share in the last few months. How else am I to escape his boring lectures about starcraft mechanics and lunar engineering?

I'm down and back before the ladies bring the afternoon meal. "We wait until dusk. Then we go."

Taisa tries in vain to talk me out of it, reminding me the way will be well lit with both moons in full shine. When I ignore her, she shoots me dark looks from her place across the room. Once the ladies have retreated to the kitchen quarters, I bind my hair tightly with drab scarves and hand Taisa a cloak stolen from my brother's cache.

"I'm to wear this?" Her lip curls in disgust.

"No one will pay mind to you in a man's cloak. With the hood low, your face will be obscured from the bright moonlight." A necessity as Taisa's hair and skin tone would make her instantly recognizable as a handmaiden.

I start down the back stairs skirting the galley. "Where are you going?" she hisses.

"Out the back."

"It is guarded. You'll never get out that way."

"I've been watching, Taisa. I know when the guards take their leave."

She sighs heavily. The nerves are obvious in her furrowed brow. I lift my cloak, exposing the sidearm.

"You're going to get us killed," she mumbles as I grab her hand and drag her out of the corridor.

8

"HEY, SMURFETTE." Luke grins and locks the door behind him. My skin under the three layers of foundation is raw and screaming at me about the abuse from alcohol prep pads, lemon, and olive oil. The ink is stubborn. Most of it washed out of my hair. The brown is again brown but the blond stripe courtesy of a wine-infused Gretchen playing beautician is now a weird greenish color. First-world problem.

"Gretchen came by for lunch. Said you had a rough day." He hands me a small paper bag. Inside, fresh oatmeal-chocolate-chip cookies. I shove my face into the opening and inhale.

"Mmm, these will make it all better." I open his car door for him.

"Why, Miss Dandy, chivalry is not dead."

"Actually, this handle—it jams. But, Sir Luke, I would've opened the door for you regardless. I'm a well-mannered lady."

Seat belt clicked, I stuff a cookie between my lips and pull into traffic.

"What are you going to tell your family about ... this?" He swirls a hand in front of his face.

"That I'm starting a new career as a performance artist. I'm hoping it embarrasses them enough that we can leave early."

"What, and miss listening to your father go on about Reagan? No way. We're staying at least until the second course."

Hanging out with Luke reminds me why Luke is so awesome to hang out with: conversations with him are like a party with a free open bar and no one there to make fun of your outfit. We always talk about the good stuff. Geek stuff. *Star Wars* stuff. New comic books and new movie adaptations and awesome recipes and his favorite music stuff. He knows that Senator Palpatine is Darth Sidious, and that General Grievous hates being called a droid. Or if we're *Star Wars*-weary, we can talk about Middle Earth or the Seven Kingdoms of Westeros or Craigh na Dun as if they were real places, places we could find if we were to get lost while wandering the forests and fields skirting Mt. Hood. I never feel uncomfortable or weird or *Omigod is he going to try to touch my boobs*. It's never like that with him.

He just ... is.

"Soooo, you want to tell me about today?" he says.

"Other than the fact that our angry restaurateur is still angry?"

"Gretchen said you might have encountered an unexpected career change."

God, she has a big mouth. "Yeah. The Evil Overlord offered me a position with the bean counters, but since I have absolutely zero experience in the realm of accounting, I'm jobless as of next week."

"You don't count beans?"

"Not unless they're in one of your salads," I say.

"What are you going to do with all your spare time?"

"I was thinking of pole dancing."

He laughs loudly.

"What? I couldn't be a pole dancer?"

Luke clears his throat. A quick glance at him—is he blushing? "No. Yes. Absolutely. You could pole dance. I have to be careful how

I answer this—could be a trap." He laughs again, shaking his head. "Jayne Dandy, I think you would make a fine pole dancer."

"Thank you, Luke Piewalker." Shit, now I'm blushing. *Hey, Mouth. Maybe aim before firing.*

What I *don't* tell Luke as we make our way along Portland's wet Friday-night streets is that after following Suzette and her progeny around Powell's, I went home and pulled out the journals. Maybe did a little research into some inexpensive cover art. Perhaps considered shoving these little minxes out into the world to earn their keep.

If no one knows it's me, and my already pathetic salary sort of got kicked in the girly bits today ...

But I'm not sure if I should tell Luke about this. Now, or ever. What if he looks up Jaina Jacen? He would totally know those names, where they came from. Or what if he wants to *read* something I've written? What, if in reading the first book—*Resist Me Not*—he realizes that a certain hero with unruly dirty-blond hair and a lovely dimple and chocolaty-chocolate eyes and nice man hands with just the perfect amount of dark-blondish forearm hair that tapers off at the wrist joint ...

He will recognize himself. He will see that I've borrowed from him for the better part of a year and turned him into a character who woos and wins the woman of his dreams. A woman who, naturally, is a much more gorgeous and confident form of me. Duh.

No way. No way I can tell him. I'd rather die first.

"I'm not sure. I guess I have to find another job."

"Welllll, I could use some help at the food truck."

I look at him, lingering too long at a newly green stoplight. The car behind me honks. "Me? Have you seen me cook?"

"You'd be doing me a solid. I'm trying to help Leia, but she's too busy sharing herpes with her tongue-bath buddies. And she wants to spend more time with her band. Or something. Anyway, you wouldn't have to cook very often. Just little stuff."

"I don't know. Can I think about it?"

"Absolutely. Or you could just say yes and start Monday."

Working alongside Luke ...

"Think about it I shall."

"Cool. It'll be fun to have Yoda slinging pastries." He pats my upper arm and I almost crash into the curb.

As we pull into the US Bank Tower, the anxiety-ridden butterflies who live and fret in the folds of my stomach remember how much I don't love high rises.

I'm relieved there's no valet—even though I cleaned out the car, it still smells like it's been forgotten in the parking lot. Because it has. I prefer taking transit to work because traffic stresses me out and parking downtown is expensive.

Luke opens my car door this time. I step out and immediately spill my purse. Anyone need a tampon?

"You okay?" he says, helping retrieve dull pencils and dead mints and lipstick I actually thought I'd lost.

"Yeah. Sorry—I always get this way before I see my family."

"You're prepared for the apocalypse here," he says, handing over my pocketknife and the trial-size bottle of Purell.

"You'd be surprised how often I use these."

He stands and plops a few sticky coins into my palm. "I'm right here for backup, Smurfette."

As we move toward the elevator banks, I flinch when he places a hand against my lower back. I watch my feet so I don't have to make eye contact with anyone.

Thirty floors up, my gut persists in its angst. Though I'm glad when Luke and I are standing in the middle of the building and I don't have to linger too long near windows. How the hell would I survive a fall that far?

The maître d' shows us to my family's table. Of course, we're the last to arrive. My brother, bent over his phone, ignores his girlfriend who prattles on about something—sounds like shoes—my mother nodding attentively. Maggot's mouth drops open.

"What. Happened. To your face?" My sister always speaks too loudly.

"Hi, I'm Luke." He reaches across the table and shakes Maggot's pointed finger.

"Rogue dye pack. Long story."

"One that involved bank robbery?" Frankie adds, looking up long enough to laugh at himself.

"Where's Dad?" I ask.

The table is quiet. "Held up," Maggot says. If staying at his office to watch his nubile secretary walk back and forth to the copy machine defines held up ...

"Anyway, we've ordered. Sit down so people stop staring," my mother says. A waiter sidles up to the table. Luke orders two Street-cars. I can go with that. Leave the wine for the lightweights.

"Luke ... Jayne's never mentioned you."

"Because he's a *boy*, Mother," Maggot says behind her hand.

"How are you two acquainted?" my mother asks. Her lipstick leaves a thick reminder of itself on the rim of her glass. I notice the bottle is already half gone.

"Oh, Jayne and I go way back."

"Is that so?"

"Luke owns a food truck near the office. We've been friends for a few years," I say.

"A food truck. How quaint. What kind of food?" Insufferable. You'd think Sheila Dandy was born sucking on silver spoons and not food-bank juice boxes in some Podunk Oregon backwoods. Which is the truth.

"Luke Piewalker's," he says, smiling. I think I like watching this. Sheila's not getting to him.

"Dude, I've heard of you!" Frankie says. "'*May the Course Be With You*' on your truck—right? One of the gals in our office is addicted to your turnovers."

"Then she has excellent taste," I say.

Sheila turns her gaze on me. It always feels like the Eye of Sauron searching for the One Ring under my elven cloak. "So, Jayne, how are things at your little newspaper?"

"Fine. They're fine."

"I picked up a copy the other day—they have 'em for free at the newsstand," Frankie says, "and I looked for your name. When are they going to let you write some real stories, Jaynie? I saw your friend Gretchen's name—"

The girlfriend interrupts. "She's the girl who writes the fashion column, right?"

"Yes." I sigh.

"Oh, she's great. Has a real pulse on the local fashion scene. Did you know that Portland has had four designers win 'Project Runway,' more than any other major city?"

"I did know this," I lie. "Gretchen's very good at her job."

"Jaynie, they should set you loose to uncover Portland's seedy criminal underbelly. I could help you—we have some really shifty clients coming through the office," Frankie says.

"Thanks, Frankie. Yeah, I'm just waiting for the right story to come across my desk."

"I thought they had you writing obituaries and classifieds," Maggot says, swirling her wine.

Luke intervenes. "What do you do, Margaret?" He knows, but I am grateful for the diversion.

"I'm a dermatologist."

Luke shudders. "Wow, I'll bet you have to have a strong stomach for that line of work."

Maggot stares him down. "I enjoy helping people look their best."

My mother's phone buzzes against the table. A look at the screen and then she silences it. "Jayne, I am concerned that you are not meeting your full potential at this little newspaper job. And are you still giving your paychecks to those farm animals?"

Jesus, here we go.

As if on cue, the waiter squeezes between Luke and me to deposit our drinks. I guzzle half in one swallow.

"I could get you a job at the office. You're good with secretarial, right?" Frankie says. Of all my family members, Farting Frankie is the least awful. His biggest crime is that he's sort of an airhead. As smart as he is to have survived law school and make partner by twenty-eight, he's still that dumb loner who tagged along with my friends and me when none of the other neighborhood kids would play with him and his stinky colon.

Maggot interrupts. "Well, I propose a toast. Tonight is about our little man Frank who is now big man at his law firm. Cheers to Frankie!"

Glasses are raised and tapped. Dinner arrives. Lamb, which I refuse to eat—and they all know it. I gnaw on the salad and half listen to their excruciating conversation by focusing on Luke's cookies waiting for me in the car.

My mother's phone buzzes, and is silenced, regularly. Frankie's girlfriend talks about celebrity gossip—as if she knows Brad Pitt and Angelina Jolie personally. Maggot whines about office politics and doesn't blink when sharing gross details of a sebaceous cyst gone awry or how she's seen more cases of cystic acne in her teen patients and that leads her to believe there's something malevolent in our water supply.

"Jayne?"

Oh God.

"Hey, Food Critic."

"Holden," he says, raised hand offered in greeting to the whole table. Forks have paused en route to mouths, I'm sure frozen because my family cannot believe two boys—*men*—would know my name. "How are you? Looks like you got most of the blue off." He repeats the twisty-hand-in-front-of-face thing everyone keeps doing.

"Yeah. A little elbow grease and olive oil. I'll live."

Holden reaches in front of me and shakes Luke's hand. "Great lunch today, man. That lentil soup was top notch."

Luke smiles; a faint blush pinks his cheeks.

"So, Jayne, I heard you got laid off."

Shit.

"What?" Sheila and Maggot speak as if one mouth.

"Oh. Wow. Sorry." Holden looks truly embarrassed and speaks to the table. "I heard it's only temporary. Right?" Too late. Damage done. "Okay, well, I have to get back to dinner. Uh, I guess I'll see you Monday? Oh—don't eat the lamb. It's not quite right," he says, sliding past our table.

"Laid off? Now what are you going to do? You know, we repurposed your room at the house a long time ago, so you're going to have to talk to your father if you need to—"

"Sheila, I don't need to move back home. Relax. I'll figure it out."

"Don't call me Sheila. I am your mother. If you'd only gotten a *real* degree instead of that flimsy liberal arts thing. Next thing you know, you'll be wearing broom skirts and singing *Kumbaya* with the Democrats at Pioneer Square—"

Luke suddenly stands, his phone in hand. "We hate to be spoilsports on this festive occasion, but we're going to be late."

All eyes are on Luke. Including mine. *Late for what?*

He slides money to Frankie and winks. "Thanks for inviting me tonight. Jayne?" He pulls my chair out.

"You're not even going to wait for your father to arrive?" Sheila says.

"We've been here for an hour and a half, Mom. Dad's not coming," Frankie says quietly. He looks at me and smiles quietly. We both know our father is a philandering cad. But being married to Sheila Dandy would drive any man to extremes. It's their battle, not ours. "I'll email you about the secretarial job. I'm sure we can get you in."

"Thanks, Frankie." I squeeze his shoulder and grab my coat and purse, eager to get away from the death glare my mother is layering on Luke's face.

Inside the elevator, Luke exhales. "How can you be related to those people?"

I should feel defensive—they're my family—but he's right.

"Lucky, I guess."

"You got the lion's share of cool genes."

I smile. "Well, I'm not a lawyer or dermatologist, so I clearly didn't get the lion's share of smart genes."

"Sure you did. Just because you chose a different path doesn't make you dumber."

"The fact that I write obituaries for a living—and the fact that I will now be unemployed and no longer writing said obituaries—that makes me dumber."

"I'll bet none of them spend their weekends feeding rescued beasts, though. That is pretty cool."

"My family feeds on each other. They're beastly enough."

"Speaking of, you've told me about this magical farm in Tigard. When are you going to introduce me to your feathered friends?"

"Owen and Beru," I say. "Any time you feel like getting a little duck shit on your shoes, I'm your girl."

Luke wraps an arm around my shoulder. I stiffen as the elevator doors ding open.

"So, uh," I step away, "did you have anything else planned, or are we just ..."

"Oh, you're not done with tonight. There's an all-night sci-fi movie fest thing going on at the Bagdad. You're gonna get your geek on, if it's the last thing I do."

"But—I'm still blue."

"That makes it even better." He takes the keys from my sweaty palm and opens my car door for me. I stare at the worn fabric of the passenger seat. "Resistance is futile, Lady Jayne. Get in." Luke winks, and I obey.

And me without my lightsaber.

9

PORTLAND'S BAGDAD Theater opened its doors on January 14, 1927. Nearly a century later, the theater continues to shine with stripes of her original glory intact thanks to the loving care of the famous McMenamins family of brewpubs, historic hotels, and theaters.

Sounds like an advertisement. Maybe they'll hire me to write their marketing collateral.

Tonight, however, is not about being jobless. This evening's unexpected turn of events—exchanging Sheila Dandy's vitriol for the pleasure of Luke Walker's company—is about the splendor of the brilliant green neon, the red of the vertical signage hugging the building, and how it burns brighter than I remember. The Bagdad underwent major interior renovation last year—lush carpet, a massive new screen, cushioned seating. Despite all the modernism, stepping into this place, with its high arches and vaulted ceilings and stately columns, harkens back to a simpler time when a new entertainment, the talking picture, was a fresh and exciting prospect.

"The event started this afternoon with *Metropolis*. Made the same year the theater was opened," Luke explains as he pays for our tickets. "We've just missed the end of *Planet of the Apes*—"

"What a shame. Charlton Heston does nothing for me."

"Not a fan of damn, dirty apes?"

"Apes are great. Heston, not so much."

"The next seating is in about fifteen minutes. Let's get food and drink that will clog our arteries."

"Wait—what's the next film?"

"Princess Organa, prepare to depart for Tatooine."

My smile is so big and dumb and goofy. We're seeing the original *Star Wars*, the 1977 masterpiece that started it all, on the big screen with full surround sound. And I said I wouldn't cry.

Once the *Apes* moviegoers trickle out, we find seats, our hands clutching bags of butter-slathered popcorn and pints of microbrewed beer. (If you ever find yourself at a McMenamins establishment, the Ruby Ale is a particular delight.) I've seen *Star Wars* a millionty times in my life, but never here, and never with Luke.

Have I mentioned how ridiculously excited I am?

"So when was your *Star Wars* cherry popped, if I may be so bold?" The low lighting hides my blue-tinged blush incited by his cheeky innuendo.

"At a slumber party. Gretchen's house. We were eleven, maybe? Her parents are loaded so Gretchen's parties were always a huge affair. Invited all the girls in our class. I wasn't into painting finger-nails and swooning over Justin Timberlake, so I snuck out and watched *Episode IV* with her little brother. It's safe to say that my life changed that night."

Luke smiles. "You were late to the game, young Padawan. Eleven years old?"

"You've met my family. Anything science fiction in *our* house? Are you serious?"

"Not even for Farting Frankie?"

"He was into Transformers and Teenage Mutant Ninja Turtles. Or something. I think. But no *Star Wars*."

"He has terrible taste, then."

"You saw his date tonight."

Luke laughs again, sips his beer. "Yes. Yes, I did."

"Not everyone has cool parents who initiate them into the club at birth."

"More like at conception. My mother loves to tell the story about how she cried at the ultrasound when she found out she was having twins—she was going to get her Luke and Leia all in one fell swoop."

"Good thing you weren't both girls. Or both boys."

"I think she still would've named us Luke and Leia, gender be damned."

"Your mom sounds awesome."

"Is it terrible for me to admit that both my parents are?"

"Absolutely not. But it doesn't surprise me."

"Oh, really? Why's that?" Luke's smirk turns mischievous. I'm in danger of flirting here. Saved by dimming lights.

Within seconds, the opening crawl that changed movie history flashes across the screen. "*It is a period of civil war. Rebel spaceships, striking from a hidden base, have won their first victory against the Evil Galactic Empire.*"

Shivers. The good kind.

A hundred and twenty-five minutes later, Luke Skywalker and Hans Solo have rescued Princess Leia, and while all is not right in *their* world, it seems to be pretty spectacular in this one.

As we exit through the incoming moviegoers, Luke pulls his buzzing phone from his pocket. His expression changes. Not for the better. One pin to the balloon, and the air is out.

"Everything okay?"

"Yeah. And no." He stares at the phone for another second before answering the text. "I—I have to go."

"Okay. Do you want me to drop you at your house, or ...?"

"No, no, I'll get a cab. You go ahead."

"Luke, I'm not going to let you take a cab. I can drive you wherever."

"Honestly, I just have to deal with ... this." He leans over and kisses my cheek, though its haste says *friend*, not *you're awesome and I can't wait to spend more time with you.*

Why does my heart feel lessened?

"Yeah. If you're sure," I say. "But I don't mind giving you a ride."

"It's cool. At least let me walk you to your car," he says, his hand cupping my elbow as we turn down the block. "So, Monday—you can come by and we can talk about you working at the truck?"

"Yeah. Absolutely. That would be great."

"You'd be helping me out."

Too soon, we're at my car. "Thanks for tonight. For suffering my family. And for the movie, of course."

Luke smiles softly and in the moment between me exhaling and his phone chiming again, I swear he looks at my lips. I'm trying not to look at his. Because this is not what I do. I can't. It's too weird. Luke is my friend. I shouldn't want to kiss him.

Should I?

Jayne Dandy, you have got to get a handle on your crazy.

"See you Monday?" he says, squeezing my arm.

As the door seals me in, Luke walks backward long enough for a final wave, and then the phone is at his ear. Whatever—whoever—was on the other end of those texts, they must've been more important than I am. Because duh, we're just friends. This wasn't a date. He was doing me a favor by coming to dinner. He went above and beyond by treating me to the movie.

What else did you expect, Jayne?

EIDER: CHAPTER 5

by Jaina Jacen (September)

The marketplace is everything I knew it would be: loud, crowded, overwhelmed with wares and raucous debate. The air lies heavy with the aroma of meat over open flames. Ales poured from huge silver casks make quiet men loud. We're careful when we walk past to tuck our heads; our double moons make midnight like noon, and the silvered surface of the vats reflects every passerby.

"This way," Taisa whispers.

"Where are you taking me?" I say, slowing my step.

"Somewhere safe."

"I don't want safe." I yank my arm free of hers. "It is my Twelve-month. Which means I get to be in charge."

Upon turning away, I slam into the side of a man whose shadow darkens everything.

"Little lady, watch where you're stepping," he slurs and burps, the air above me fouling. I squeeze past, beyond bays of grandsheep and trihorses and horned swine. Taisa is not far behind, hissing the name I gave her to address me—Sella, a lowerclass name.

I burst through the human thicket and into the wide square, its watchtowers extending far above the business below. Music pulsates from across the space, and my heart forgets its own rhythm when I see him.

Taisa finally catches up, panting and looking about nervously, tugging on the edges of her hood to preclude the view of our fellow citizens.

"He's there," I say.

"I know," she says, looking down. "I told him to meet us."

I turn on my heel. "You did what?"

Taisa laughs behind her hand. "I've known you since before you walked. I know you better than anyone, better than I know myself. What power do I have to keep you from getting what it is you want most?"

I should be angry at her bravado, but instead, I throw myself at her and kiss her cheek.

"But wait—" I straighten my arms, still clutching her thick sleeves —"he doesn't know who I am."

"He does. And he's waiting for you." Taisa winks and looks toward the young man.

Who is now quickly closing the distance between us from his place across the square.

10

JUST BECAUSE A GIRL rescues and then names a couple of Mallards and contributes money to their food fund doesn't mean said ducks are going to curl up and play cozy. The farm's owner teases me that it's because my clothes smell like the mean non-duck at home—if Quack only knew that her invisible presence is scaring the feathers off Owen and Beru. She'd probably smile. If cats could smile.

Today, as with most Sundays, the farm buzzes with my bleeding-heart urbanite comrades in denim and khaki. After checking the barn job board, I shovel horse poop and rake leaves until my arms burn, followed by seed for the chickens and ducks and the new geese who aren't interested in playing fair. For the record, geese do not have teeth but the serrations in their beaks, called tomia, can still make a misplaced finger bleed.

Beru surprises me by settling alongside on the bench while I throw back a midday snack, but that's likely because she wants a bite. Still, she lets me pet her. So soft. Her partner gives the typical male Mallard call, a raspy, two-note holler, from across the yard and she quacks back but doesn't move. Within a few moments, her eyes soften and close. Call me the Duck Whisperer.

If Friday night hadn't ended so abruptly, I would've asked Luke to join me today. Introduced him to Beru. Asked more about his sci-fi stories, though carefully—I cannot let him know what I, or rather what Jaina Jacen, has done or what my alter ego plans to do as soon as I'm home and scrubbed clean of duck doo-doo.

Which happens sooner than later, thanks to a late-afternoon downpour. Welcome to fall in the Pacific Northwest. Don't bother removing your coat. Also, dump the puddles in your boots on the welcome mat before entering *thank you very much.*

"Hey ... you're home," I say, kicking aside Gretchen's Vuitton bag near the front door. She spent Friday and Saturday night at her parents' house to dog-sit.

"You smell like a barnyard," she says from the couch. Her toes are splayed in a foam separator; the apartment reeks of nail polish.

"What, no pedicure this week?" I hang my soaking coat over the heat register. Quack yowls from the kitchen sink.

"I'm applying a protein coat. The esthetician says my toenails are thinning."

"I hear that's a real problem nowadays."

She sits up, grinning. "How are *you?*"

"Fine." My voice is muffled, head buried in the sparse fridge. I'm hungry and I swear I had an éclair in here from the other day.

"How was your date, dummy?"

"It wasn't a date."

"It was a date."

"Gretchen, we went to dinner with the Dandys. Not a date."

"YES, but according to exhibit A, the grease-stained ticket stub left on the kitchen table, you also went to a geek movie where maybe geek popcorn was shared, followed perhaps by the exchange of geek germs." Her freshly reshaped eyebrows waggle at me.

"No germ sharing happened, unless I picked something up from the theater toilet seats." Finding the fridge devoid of éclairs, I settle for a beer and a yogurt cup—it's either that or very questionable hummus. I don't think hummus is supposed to be green. Or fuzzy.

I stop briefly at the sink to let Quack get her fill of post-duck aroma. If I don't, she will pee on my feet later. Don't ask.

"I brought your stuff home. From the office," Gretchen says, pointing with her knuckle at a banker's box on the table. I lift the lid —it's very full. I didn't realize how many rubber ducks I'd brought in over the years. And books. And notepads plump with article and story ideas Clark wouldn't let me write.

"Thanks. I don't much feel like going back in there tomorrow. Not after ..." I gesture to the remainders of the blue dye.

Upon plopping on the couch, I spy a gift bag printed with rubber ducks sitting on the floor near the coffee table. "What's that?"

"Oh. Food Critic dropped that off for you about an hour ago. Said he may have stuck his foot in his mouth Friday night at the Grill?"

"Yeah. Little bit."

"Said he felt bad. So he brought you a prezzie."

The note taped to the outside says, "Humblest apologies for my loquaciousness. Let me buy you lunch? ∼ Holden / P.S. You didn't eat the lamb, right?"

From the tissue paper, I extract a do-it-yourself paintable duck kit —very clever. Five points for the Food Critic.

"So tell me why you didn't show Luke your birthmark?"

I have a weird birthmark along the inner slope of my right boob. A light-brown stain shaped like Australia. You can imagine the jokes that have come out of Gretchen's mouth since the infection known as puberty took hold: "Take him Down Under, Jaynie." "Show him where you keep your kangaroo." "Maybe if you show him Oz, he'll let you play his didgeridoo." *Et cetera.*

"Showing Australia to Luke would imply that we are something beyond friends. Which we are not." I don't mention how Luke brought our non-date to a hasty end. Although it's still bugging me. Who texted him? Why did he leave so suddenly and with such a pronounced mood shift?

Oh God. He has a girlfriend—she texted. Or maybe he's married and he leads a double life and keeps her and their four-point-two children a secret from the world.

This doesn't matter. I have no claim over him.

"When are you going to see each other again? Maybe you guys could share some Mountain Dew and window-shop at comic book stores."

"Tomorrow. Looks like I'm going to be working at the food truck for a while." I can definitely figure out if he has a girlfriend if we're working together. Right?

"Ohhhhhhh, Jaynie, that's hot." Gretchen mutates into a porn star. Panting, groping herself as she speaks. "You can get it on with your boss. Oh God, whipped cream. Yes! Right there!"

A dirty look accompanies my beer bottle cap launched across the room. "Leia has reliability issues. As such, I'm going to fill in until I can find something full-time."

"I cannot believe Cole let you go on the same day you got attacked by the restaurateur."

"Tell me about it." This beer tastes good.

"Clark was in a terrible mood all afternoon. Oh man, and when Mrs. Clark made her regular Friday afternoon cookie drop, you should've heard her. She's super pissed that Clark let Cole fire you."

"Downsized. Not fired." Mrs. Clark was the reason I got the job in the first place. And by association, she's the reason Gretchen has a job because I convinced Mr. Clark to hire Gretchen when her marketing degree resulted in a famine of job offers due to a glut in the market. Plus Gretchen is the sole person who can make Brant Cole stutter—I think Clark recognized the power that could wield.

I slide my ducky art project on to the table. "I'm gonna take a bath. You going out tonight?"

"I am. New guy."

"Named?"

"Eric."

"Have I heard of him?"

"Not yet. But you might hear him later ..." Gretchen puckers her lips.

"Don't forget to light your carnal candles."

"You need to get *your* carnal candles lit, Jaynie!" I close my bedroom door before she finishes.

When Gretchen and I agreed to cohabitate—the logical, fiscally responsible choice because we were always at one or the other's post-college apartment—we had to find a place with individual bathrooms. And mine had to have a tub. Because I like to soak and think.

On tonight's lavender-bath-bomb-infused mental agenda: Jaina Jacen's foray into the business of naughty.

This is all very hasty, and I realize that—but if I don't do this now, I will talk myself out of it. I bought a premade cover from an artist online whose sister does interior book formatting. They're both just starting out, so poof! No waiting. I sent it off yesterday morning; upon checking my email this afternoon, it's here.

Oh my God, my words have been shaped into a book.

All I need now is to find my courage to press *publish.*

Said courage is aided by the bottle of Bull Run Distillery's Aria Portland Dry Gin, gifted by a local club as thanks for a successful *Rose City Register* ad campaign. I may not have a job there anymore, but by God, I will drink Brant Cole's gin!

One beer finished. Two shots of gin.

I can do this. Bravery, thy name is Jayne Dandy!

What if someone finds out what I did?

They won't. Jaina Jacen is a pen name. It's not traceable back to me. No one knows about Petra and Conall, or Callisto and Beckett, or Jentry and Amedeo from my sci-fi/fantasy stories. How will they ever know about these latest star-crossed lovers, Miranda and Alec?

I should text Luke. See what he's doing. See if he's okay, you know, after the text that ended our otherwise awesome non-date. Maybe confirm that I am coming in to work tomorrow.

What if he forgot?

I should text him.

Terrible idea. None of my business.

Just one text? A quickie?

Stop delaying, Jayne.

This gin is very dry. The bottle says juniper and lemon zest. I think I taste the lemon.

Put the phone down. Focus on the task at hand!

What is the task at hand?

The little button in the author dashboard, the one that says PUBLISH? Click it.

Now.

Do it.

Slurp. Exhale. Click.

Done.

11

"YOU SEEM IN A GOOD MOOD TODAY." Dr. McCoy opens the box I've brought from the food truck. It's the end of my second week working alongside Luke and although I've set the grill alight three times, he hasn't fired me, which means I've gained five pounds. But he also taught me to make the perfect over-easy egg without tearing the yolk, so we're even.

And as yet, my sleuth skills have not detected the presence of a girlfriend.

"So much has happened since I last saw you," I say.

"Well, you have fifty-two minutes to fill me in." She bites into a small glazed cherry turnover.

I rattle off the boring stuff—the dye-pack incident, getting laid off from the paper, Luke offering the food-truck gig, the ridiculous dinner with my family but how Luke saved the day with *Star Wars*—oh, and my father moving into the corporate apartment so he and my mother can "reevaluate their options." Like we didn't see that coming.

But this is all *et cetera* news. Boring, second-page stuff. I want to get to the headlines.

I'm nearly bouncing out of my chair by the time I pull the e-reader out of my bag.

She chews while I power on and scroll to the desired page.

"This." I hand it over.

"*Resist Me Not*, Temptation Series #1, by Jaina Jacen." Her expression is confused. "If you're reading erotic fiction, this is definitely a step in the right—"

"I wrote it."

Her eyes widen. "This is your work?"

I nod excitedly.

"How ...?"

Which requires another explanation: about my earlier sci-fi and fantasy stories being self-published under Jaina Jacen, how I therefore already have a small amount of name recognition, about meeting Suzette and triplets at Powell's, about how I figured it was a win-win situation and no one in my life knows it's me, so if I can make a few bucks, then sweet.

"I can't believe you did this so fast," she says.

"Well, the material was finished. I just needed to put all the pieces together, and that was easy enough. Lots of people are doing it nowadays. And some are apparently making crazy money."

"What made you decide to take this step?"

"I will be out of savings in less than two months. The sci-fi stories only bring in a hundred or two a month, if that. And I cannot go back to living with Sheila Dandy—I'd rather be homeless—so, desperate times call for desperate measures."

"Does anyone in your family know you've done this?"

"Oh my dear God, *no*! And they won't. Not ever. No one knows about any of it."

"Not even Gretchen?" I shake my head no. "But isn't she your best friend?"

"Yes." That little guilt mouse bites me again. I throw cheese at it.

"Don't you think she's going to figure it out eventually?"

"Not if I can help it."

"This is a brave step, Jayne. Very resourceful of you. Is Jaina a play on your name?"

"No," I say. "Um, Jaina and Jacen are the twin children of Hans Solo and Princess Leia."

She chuckles. "Clever! As you know, I'm a Trekkie." She nods to a Phaser II prop in a glass case on the bookshelf. "Limited edition replica from *Deep Space 9*."

"Very nice," I say. She's shown me this before, but to each geek his own.

"You know, Jayne, I think publishing these stories could be a powerful tool for you to overcome some of your issues. You're okay to write about sexual behaviors and put them out there for the world to see—"

"But that's why it's so perfect. No one knows it's *me*."

"Yes, but have you considered how empowering it could be if you were to offer these titles under your own name?"

I'm nauseated at such a thought. "No one can know."

"Is there a reason other than your general embarrassment?"

I take a deep breath. "The main character—Alec—he's ... basically Luke."

"So you are fantasizing an interaction with him." Hearing this spoken out loud by someone other than me sends a humiliated flush from head to toe. "Jayne, don't be ashamed! This is terrific progress."

"But that's why I have to use a pen name—if he found out ...," I say.

"You know, the author of *Middlemarch* was a woman—Mary Ann Evans—she wrote under the name George Eliot so her work would be taken seriously."

"I can assure you—this is no *Middlemarch*."

"So because it's not 'high literature,' but rather fictionalized sexual fantasy, it's somehow less important? I'm assuming you've still put in the time and effort to build a story. You shouldn't diminish what you've accomplished here. The fact that you're able to fantasize and then articulate people engaging in sexual behaviors is a huge step toward overcoming your fear of intimacy. And it's especially potent that you are using Luke as an example of your ideal."

"We're just friends," I say. She smiles knowingly. "Hey, people write about interplanetary travel too, but they're not building the Millennium Falcon in their garages." I thought she was going to be proud of me for doing this, not lecture me about it being an opportunity for growth.

"Jayne, don't misunderstand. My point is twofold: one, you can keep this identity and occupation secret forever if you want. But I'm saying it could be a positive step toward claiming your sexual self. Two, if you can imagine other people engaged in romantic scenarios, it might open the door for your own experiences. Athletes use visualization to improve their game—this could be your form of visualization to break down those walls you've built around yourself. Sort of like a test run."

I'm not a voyeur. It's not like I'm hiding under my covers with a flashlight pretending to watch other people going at it—

Oh God, that's exactly what I'm doing. Even worse, I'm using real people as fodder for my not-real characters.

Should I be embarrassed that it's so fun?

"And the idea that you're using someone you know—I'd say this is excellent progress."

"But humiliating if he finds out."

"Why? What's the worst-case scenario? Ever consider that he might be flattered?"

"I just ... I don't know."

"Jayne, I think you're on the brink of an important breakthrough, but you need to get clear with yourself—does your interest in Luke stem from your truest feelings for him? Perhaps even love? If we pull back even farther, is it that you want to fall in love with someone or do you just want to be okay to experience sex, love notwithstanding?"

"I just want to be normal."

Dr. McCoy laughs quietly. "You are not abnormal, my dear."

What do I want? Really? "Falling in love would be the ideal, but with that comes the expectation of sex."

"Usually, yes."

"I *want* to have sex. I do. Preferably with someone I love. But as you know, the whole thing freaks me out."

"We know you aren't, by definition, afraid of the mechanics—bodily fluids, touching, what have you—so this is purely psychological, rooted in fear."

"I want to feel safe. And protected. And not ridiculed or laughed at."

Dr. McCoy smiles. "Thank you. Excellent."

I think I just made progress. Because we're both smiling.

"Now, I must say that I am rather surprised, and impressed, that you published this story before allowing me to read it—"

"But you're the only person I've told about it. Wait—you're not going to buy one, are you?"

"Do you want me to?"

Shit, do I? "Can I think about it?"

She nods. "I'll wait until you give me the okay. But this really is a big step. Part of addressing your neuroses is realizing that habitual fantasizing is just one piece of who you are. And that it's okay. Think of all the books and beautiful works of art that would've never seen the light of day had their creators not been habitual fantasizers."

So being neurotic isn't bad. It's good?

"Finishing a whole book is a remarkable feat. Be proud of yourself," she says.

"Even if it's borderline pornographic."

"Do you tell a story with a beginning, a middle, and a satisfying end?"

I nod. "Satisfying end" is a nice euphemism for the end Alec and Miranda meet.

"Well, then, congratulations, Ms. Jacen. You've taken this neurosis and made it your bitch."

I like that.

EIDER: CHAPTER 6

by Jaina Jacen (September)

"It's you," I say.

"It's me." His eyes sparkle with the light of a thousand stars. I shouldn't stare, but his face will not let me go. How can this be the product of a Class II union? The sages say only Class I citizens are beautiful, based purely on careful engineering of their genetic composition.

This young man's beauty is beyond scientific interference. And yet he possesses a boyish charm evident in the clever twist of his smile, the dimple in his cheek. His hair is lighter than I remember, and the earlier wayward curl against his forehead has its wavy companions back.

"Why are you here?"

"When a highborn lady asks to see me, I am not one to disappoint."

"Oh." So he's only here because of my station?

"I'm just teasing. I wanted to see you in real life, outside of the strictures put upon us by your position."

"You did?"

"Of course. You spoke to me earlier like we were longtime friends. No one ever does that, especially not a Class I," he says.

"So it was the fact that I treated you like a human being that made you want to come here to meet me, to risk a terrible fate if you are caught?"

"I like my chances. It's not every day that someone with your chemical composition comes along."

Now he's taken it a step too far. "You've examined my composition?"

"Call it a privilege of my employ."

"That's illegal. I could have you executed."

"You could ... but you won't."

I snort at him and cross my arms. "And why is that?"

"Because in your composition, the data revealed a high concentration of desire for adventure, thirst for rebellion, and lust for life."

I quirk an eyebrow at him. "You can tell all of that from a blood sample?"

He laughs and offers me an arm. Bold one, he is. "No. Not at all."

"Then why dare say such things?"

Before I know what he's doing, his hand is under my cloak, at my hip, dangerously close to my skin. "Because you're here. In public. At the double moon, carrying a sidearm, with Class II and Class III citizens. You're a rule breaker."

"Ssshhh, not so loud," I say, stifling a smile. "And get your hands where they belong or I will shoot you."

He stands before me, again bold enough that he touches my dangling fingers. "I don't know why I am risking such foolishness, but I had to see you. One visit was not enough," he says.

Taisa chuffs under her breath. "Be mindful of this one, Sella, or he's going to sell you a trihorse and tell you it's a fish." I'd probably believe him.

"No, I mean it. You probably don't remember, do you ...," he says, eyes wistful.

"Remember what?"

"The reason you said you knew me. At your sample collection?"

I scrutinize his face. A faint memory floats to the fore. He pulls the collar of his shirt down and exposes a light brown mark, what the elders call nature's paint, in the shape of a bird.

"Think hard ... Lyrie."

The paint—I remember this.

"What is your name?" I whisper.

"My second name is Mooney."

It does not register. I know no one named Mooney. But that painted mark—I've seen this before.

And it wouldn't be so strange. Young children have no need for second names, especially among their lowerclass playmates.

"Pollux?" I whisper.

"Pollux Mooney, at your service, My Sovereign."

12

"BEFORE WE CALL this meeting to order, a wee round of applause for our dear Jayne for this lovely box of ridiculously fattening treats that we will all live to regret tomorrow when we have to add three hundred crunches to our morning workouts," Gretchen says.

She might have to add three hundred crunches; I have a small Piewalker box hiding in our fridge for my morning workout.

Though this is only my second foray into Gretchen's Tuesday-night writers' group, it's clear that a pattern is followed here: wine, snacks, more wine, a little writing stuff, and then wine.

They should rebrand themselves as budding sommeliers rather than wishful wordsmiths.

Suzette did change her sweater from the last time I saw her—this one's red—but a moth has made dinner out of the lower edge. After seeing stroller baby mangle that cookie-ish thing at the bookstore, I'm pretty sure the crunchy blob on the sleeve is food.

Not like I'm one to talk—this week's activities include a trip to the lingerie shop for more underwear thanks to Quack's latest attack on my laundry basket. Yes, my demon cat eats panties. That's why you never let Quack lick your face.

"So, news first. Anyone have anything to share?" Suzette asks.

Beth, the hostess, shows a small check received for an article accepted at a knitting magazine. I'm guessing the multicolored infinity scarf around her neck is her handiwork. Another gal got a request from a small publisher to see the first thirty pages of her manuscript. Beyond other members sharing recent acquisitions of signed books from unknown authors, news is quiet this meeting.

"Well, *I* have something interesting to share." Suzette looks directly at Gretchen when she speaks. In fact, it's sort of unnerving how she only takes her eyes off Gretchen's face long enough to cast a half glare at me, and then back to Gretchen, even as her hands move to power up her e-reader.

"As you guys know, I've been working to self-publish some of my work. As a consequence of that, I keep my finger on new releases on a daily and weekly basis so I can check out the competition and see what they're doing to sell books. This title I found has had an unusual surge in sales considering it's only been out a short time. The chatter is calling it 'lightning in a bottle.'"

The woman with hemp, clown-style pants and equally clownish hair taps her rather dirty bare foot impatiently. I sort of want to hold her down and wash her feet.

"See if this sounds familiar." Suzette reads from her screen.

The sipped wine creeps up my throat, my cheeks so hot, I might faint.

Thud thud thud. My heart kick-boxes my sternum.

Gretchen is oblivious to what's going on. She has no idea what's about to happen.

Suzette lowers the e-reader. "Jaina Jacen? Is that your pen name, Gretchen?"

"What?" Gretchen's wine glass freezes en route to her mouth.

Oh God oh God oh God.

"This story—this is what you read for us at our last meeting. And then you went and published it without telling anyone? You knew I'd been talking about doing this—I wouldn't have minded having a chat about your plan and strategy."

I tip my glass on purpose. Wine tumbles down my shirt and splatters on to the hardwood floor. "Oh! I'm so sorry!" I say. Beth jumps up, smiling, to grab towels. "No, Beth, let me clean this up. I'm so sorry. Gretch, can you help me, please?"

I grab her arm and pull her into the kitchen before she has a chance to protest.

"Ow! What in the hell has gotten into you?" Gretchen yanks her arm from my pinch and dabs at her blouse. More wine spillage from my manhandling.

"Listen to me very carefully: the story Suzette is talking about—it's *mine*—I ... I published it online. Under a pen name. Jaina Jacen. Suzette thinks it's your story, the one you read last time we were here."

Gretchen's mouth hits the floor. "*Pride and Prejudice?*" she whispers. Then, slightly louder, "YOU PUBLISHED A PORNY STORY?" Her face lights up like Vegas neon. "Oh. My. Sweet. Baby. Jesus. The apocalypse is nigh."

"Shut up. Listen to me," I hiss. "Go with it. Whatever she says. Deflect. Just pretend you know what you're talking about."

"I have zero idea—I know squat about online publishing or whatever it is you people are talking about. Jayne, what is going on?"

"Everything okay in here?" Beth says, squeezing between us for the tub of Lysol wipes sinkside.

"Oh, yes. Sorry again about that, Beth."

"I'm just glad for your shirt that it was the Sauvignon. I almost pulled out the Cabernet Franc tonight." Her giggle reminds me of a happy chipmunk.

Gretchen waits for Beth to clear the kitchen. "So what do I tell her? She clearly wants details."

"Say this: you had a friend at the newspaper help you with copy editing and the cover. You found a company online to do the formatting—"

"What does that even mean?"

"You have to have the book taken from a Word document and made into an e-book format."

"God, this sounds like nerd talk."

"Gretchen, *listen*."

"Fine. What if she wants the name of that whatever-you-just-said company?"

"Tell her you can't remember and you'll email it to her."

Her expression changes from amusement to hurt. "Why didn't you tell me?"

"I'll explain later. Let's—let's just get through the next sixty minutes and then I will tell you everything once we're not here."

"Jaynie wrote sexy vagina funtime. Today should be a national holiday."

"God, please stop saying that."

"Vagina, vagina, vagina," she whispers far too close to my ear.

I refill our wine glasses and turn her toward the living room. "Remember, you're Jaina Jacen."

"Rooooowwwrrrrrrr." Gretchen claws at the air.

Gretchen, surprisingly, manages to hold Suzette's rather aggressive questioning at arm's length, offering short answers. I supplement where I can, under the guise that I helped research the process. As we're pulling on our shoes to leave, Suzette gets in my face.

"I told you not to tell her about this. Thanks a bunch." Her fake Uggs have a hole in the big toe. I feel bad that I stole her thunder, but my feet need to stay warm too. I pet my guilt with a reminder that Suzette wants to pay for a nanny and plastic surgeon with her book earnings; I really just want to stay out of my repurposed bedroom at Sheila Dandy's house.

A girl's gotta do what a girl's gotta do.

But something she said earlier makes me anxious to get home: "unusual surge in sales," "lightning in a bottle." I haven't checked sales since I uploaded. I figured it would only make me crazy to stalk statistics that have no context yet—only the few sci-fi "fans" I have know who Jaina Jacen is—and what if they're pissed that I'm not writing about deep space but deep throat instead?

When Gretchen shuts her car door, she does not press the go button right away.

"E'splain, Lucy."

I repeat the kitchen conversation, slower and in more detail, including the part about the sci-fi stories under Jaina Jacen. We sit in front of Beth's house long enough post-meeting that Beth waddles out in her ratty terry-cloth robe to make sure we don't need a tow truck.

"So, are you selling books?"

"I don't know. I haven't checked."

"You just put it up there and wait for the money to roll in?" She turns the car on to defrost the now-fogged windows.

"I guess."

"Why did you do this without telling me?"

"Because ... I was embarrassed. I ran into Suzette at Powell's on dye-pack-let's-fire-Jayne day, and she told me about her grand plan to publish her erotica stories. I already had the fantasy stories out there, so I thought maybe it was worth a try. I really do not want to move back home."

"You're never moving back to Sheila Dandy's. I won't let you."

"Still, I need money."

"Right. No, I get it. And what I read was great, Jayne. Way better than Suzette's stuff."

"Well, regardless, I figured if she can do it, so can I."

"What does Dr. McCoy think about this? Oh my God, what will Sheila Dandy think if she finds out?" Gretchen throws a hand over her astonished mouth.

"Sheila Dandy is never going to find out."

Gretchen clucks.

"Shut up. Just because I don't want anyone to know this is me does not make me a chicken."

"Yes it does."

"No, it does *not*."

"Chicken."

"You're a jerk. I thought you would have my back on this." I face forward and stare out the windshield. Gretchen laughs and places a hand on my shoulder.

"You're the jerk for not telling me. Even about the sci-fi stuff."

"I knew you'd make fun of me. And I have enough people in my life doing that."

"But Jaynie, when I make fun of you, I'm only doing it because I love you. Not because I want to hurt you."

"Still ..."

She turns my face to look at her. "I know the layoff was unexpected. I'm really proud of you for doing this. Way to take the bull by the balls."

"Horns."

"Right. Horns. Because you would never touch a bull's balls."

"Gross! Would you?"

"Depends on the bull." Gretchen laughs and gives my cheek a grandmotherly pat. "Everyone in there," she thumbs toward Beth's house, "thinks I'm Jaina Jacen."

"I know. I'm sorry. I didn't mean to put you on the spot like that."

"Are you kidding? I write about *shoes*. We both know I'm just wasting time to get free Louboutins."

And yet she's the one with the full-time job.

"Jaina Jacen sounds like a girl who likes it rough. Maybe even doggie-style."

"Gretchen!"

"What?" she laughs. "You do know that you're writing about SEX, right?"

"We need to go home before this devolves any further."

Gretchen cackles like a madwoman. "I think once we break down these invisible walls of yours, we will find you are a woman of hidden talents, Jayne Dandy."

Precisely.

13

AS I TIE on the rubber-duck apron Luke specially ordered for me, my mood is remarkably buoyant.

"Good Thursday morning, Miss Dandy. What's with the smile?" I cannot tell Luke that it's because Jaina Jacen has sold almost four thousand books in the short time *Resist Me Not* has been out, and her online reviews from readers are ... amazing. I cannot tell Luke that I stole his charming persona and arrhythmia-inducing smile and wrote "sexy vagina funtime" and people are, quite literally, eating it up. Or, to quote Gretchen, they are "slurping, massaging, and moaning" their way through the book. Ew. Okay. Good. Isn't that nice.

In whatever form the readers are enjoying it, I cannot tell Luke that I'm excited about something for the first time in years.

"Just glad to be here, I suppose."

"How refreshing to come to work to your smiling face every day. And no Leia drama! I think you need a raise," he says. "But Jayne, seriously—I don't want to create a wedge between you and your brother. You know, about the job."

Farting Frankie, true to his word the night of dinner at the Grill, found me a job, though not secretarial. Full-time, in the mailroom. At minimum wage. The mailroom? I'm twenty-six years old. I don't want to spend my days with first- and second-year law students who are hoping they can kiss enough ass to land themselves post-grad jobs.

"What, and miss this?" I blob whipped cream on the end of Luke's nose. Though he smiles, he looks surprised.

I flirted on purpose.

Jaina Jacen knows how to flirt—why not Jayne Dandy?

Of course, Sheila Dandy doesn't understand my unwillingness to cooperate when "Frankie went above and beyond to make this happen for you." Mind you, Sheila Dandy has never worked in a mailroom. She hasn't worked since she was twenty, when my father scooped her out of the shitty department store where she sold bras to overweight, middle-aged women on income assistance. Throughout our formative years, she would then use her tales of employment woe —"You have no idea how hard it is to stand on your feet all day and pretend to be happy when you know you're going home to ramen and cockroaches"—to guilt us into, well, everything.

"Oh, before I forget," Luke says, handing me an envelope. The front is marred by a thumbprint of what is likely fruit topping. "Your first check. With tips."

"Hey. Thanks."

"And this." He gives me a paper bag, the top stapled shut, a large number "1" Sharpied across the front.

"What is it?"

"A surprise."

"Like a grab bag?"

He laughs. "Sort of. Only you're not allowed to open it until you have all the bags."

"There are more?"

"Mm-hmm."

"How many?"

"I think twelve?"

"Luke, what is this?" I hold it up and sniff it. Shake it. Squeeze it. No idea. "Food?"

"No. Not food. But you can't open it until I give you all the bags. Deal?"

I'm not a cheater. If I leave this out for Gretchen to find, she will open it. She's the kid who knew all of her Christmas presents way before Santa left the North Pole. The one year Gretchen snooped for *my* Christmas presents, Sheila Dandy got so mad, she donated everything to the Giving Tree at the mall.

In fact, I do believe Gretchen still owes me some blue and purple Rollerblades and a Tamagotchi from the Christmas of Despair, 1999.

"Okay. I will wait until all bags have been gifted."

Luke offers a hand—we shake on it.

WITH THE LAST TURNOVER SERVED, garbages emptied, chairs stacked, and the awning tucked away under oppressive cloud cover, Luke pulls his apron over his head and blocks the rear door.

"What are you doing tonight, Miss Dandy?"

My neck and face heat up.

"Because my buddy has a costume shop and he just got in a load of new pieces in prep for convention season—he needs people to come over and try things on so he can photograph them for his website."

"Like, model the costumes?"

"Yeah. I guess. Here's your chance to show Gretchen what real intergalactic high fashion looks like."

"Are you ... going to try stuff on?"

"Totally! He does this every year. Invites his closest friends. He'll have drinks and appetizers. We try on shit and get our photos taken and it's a blast. And I told him I'd bring you along." He reaches into the subzero and pulls out a tray of small éclairs. My weakness.

"You're bribing me."

"I will not confirm nor deny." Luke scoops a pastry off the tray and deposits it into my hand. Definitely bribery. "So yes. You'll come along and play dress-up and eat and drink things recreated from Chalmun's Cantina?"

Spoken like a true Jedi.

14

FOOD TRUCK PARKED at his house, Luke invites me inside so he can change into clothes that don't smell like food. He offered to take me by the apartment so I could freshen up, but this is as fresh as I need to be for now—I'm nervous about Gretchen's loose lips and the Jaina Jacen jokes she might "accidentally" drop on to the carpet.

His living room is remarkably clean for a bachelor. The space is an advertisement for IKEA, from the red sectional to the pine coffee table and matching media cabinet, but the six glass-front bookcases—absolutely stuffed with *Star Wars* memorabilia—are dusted and organized. And he has more books than I do.

I must say, I appreciate a man who reads.

In the corner stands a life-size Stormtrooper and R2-D2. I cannot imagine how much these cost. When I raise my hand before R2's domed head, he chirps and whirrs. I nearly jump out of my skin.

"Motion sensor in that one," Luke laughs, towel drying his dampened hair. Oh my God, he's shirtless. *Shirtless*, I tell you. And he looks yummy. Not overly muscled, surprisingly fit given his line of work. Tuft of light chest hair. Leftover shadows of a summer tan.

Stop looking, Jayne.

"R2 is my dad's. They moved to San Diego so they could volunteer for the San Diego Comic Con every year. They live in a condo complex occupied only by sci-fi and comic geeks. It's awesome."

Eyes on the droid. "It's cool you all have this stuff in common."

"It's kinda hard not to like it when you're surrounded by it. But look at Leia. She hates all of it. She tells people our parents are dead so no one ever finds out where we come from."

"That's terrible."

Luke chuckles as he pulls his shirt on. "That's Leia. She's ... confused. She came into the world pissed off that I was the twin born first."

Through the glass, I admire the Mace Windu action figure Luke showed off a few weeks ago. "I love that your parents are sci-fi fans, though. My mother makes fun of everything I like."

"Why not encourage your kids to like what they like? And there are far lamer things to idolize than *Star Wars*."

"I got good at hiding things. So she wouldn't make fun of me."

"Did she do that to your siblings?"

"Not really. You've met them. Margaret is my mother's clone." Luke's brow furrows. It might be pity.

I don't need pity. It's not like I grew up in an abusive environment or was locked in closets or deprived food.

"Anyway, we should go, yes?" I move to the front door, before he has an opportunity to say anything further.

We take his rickety pickup across town to his buddy's costume shop. The old glass of the storefront windows shudders slightly from the music pumping inside. A handful of people in various states of costumed glamour stand out front, their smoking plumes smelling very un-tobacco-like. Luke shakes hands and shoulder bumps a few guys, introduces me to friends whose names I won't be able to put faces to because they will always be Chewbacca, Imperial soldiers, or Captain Kirk for the rest of time.

Inside, flashes of blue and red and green from spinning party lights enhance the dimmed overheads. Classic rock pounds out of speakers that vibrate the floor if you stand close, and the place smells of new plastic and old building. Costume racks in the main room have been pushed against the walls. People dress one another in feather boas and hold up space-inspired hats and vests and pants; two girls with remarkably bright hair help one another into boots that probably should be used with scaffolding and warning signs.

"Joe!" Luke hollers and waves. An older guy with a bleached fauxhawk waves back and weaves through the crowd, careful not to spill the blue drink in his hand.

"Good to see you, Pie Man," Joe says, clapping Luke's shoulder. "Who is this divine princess you've brought along with you and where can I get one?"

"Joe, this is Jayne Dandy."

"I'll say she's dandy." He winks. The British accent excuses him for giving me the once-over, and although I would never admit this out loud, it's sort of nice to be the one getting the ogling. Usually it's Gretchen. My average height, average weight body topped with B-cup boobs doesn't get me the glances when standing alongside Gretchen's *look at me I'm a fashion czarina* bod.

Still, I should act offended.

"Thanks for the éclairs. Drop them with the bar kids." Joe points toward the back. "Care for a beverage? Offerings of every ilk. Then grab some costumes—the new stuff is on the racks near the change rooms. Renegade is set up in the warehouse when you're ready." Joe sips from his drink. "Good to meet you, Miss Dandy." He leans closer, his breath hinting that he's had the Jedi's share of the blue juice tonight. "Watch this one—he might try to show you his pocket droid." Joe winks.

"Ignore him, Jayne. And my droid doesn't fit in my pocket."

He's talking about his ... yes. Of course he is. Cheeks, burn accordingly.

Luke places a hand against my lower back, less awkward than it was the first time he did it at the restaurant the night of Frankie's promotion dinner. Instead of pulling away, I lean into him a little. Hey, lots of people in here. I don't want to take up too much space.

Luke leaves me against a bulging rack of spacey costumes while he drops off dessert and fetches us blue drinks.

"Trouble on Tatooine," he says upon return, handing me a cup printed with a Sith lord.

"I'm sorry?"

"The name of this drink—Trouble on Tatooine. As in, you drink too many, and you'll find yourself waking up next to a Jawa." I laugh. Oh man, if Gretchen were to hear us geeking out, she'd start screaming "vagina" again just to refocus the spotlight.

"So—costumes—who do you want to be tonight?" Luke asks.

"No idea. I guess we should see what's here."

We clink our cups and head toward the rack of "new to be modeled" near the change rooms. Through a wide door, people in crazy and cool get-ups wait around for their turn in front of the camera. I'm guessing Renegade is the photographer—a tall, well-muscled woman, a cross between Elvira and Lisbeth Salander. The sides of her head are shaved and she has so many piercings along her ear, it's a miracle she can hold her head up to look through the viewfinder.

But her set-up is legit—lights, umbrellas and soft boxes, backdrop, a camera that I'm sure Gretchen's fashion friends would slobber over. And Renegade's not yelling at anyone. In fact, everybody seems to be having fun. The few times I've trailed Gretchen on fashion shoots, the participants are always stressed out and crabbing at each other. I made the mistake of taking a club sandwich in once—three models sitting across the room in makeup chairs stared at me, pinpoint pupils, mouths agape, like a zombie looks at a freshly tossed bowl of brains. If those models hadn't been held down by hairdressers yanking on their scalps, I might have died.

Luke takes our cups and tucks them on a lower shelf out of harm's way as I flip through the hangers. Lots here for the boys, and the stuff for the girls is, well, revealing. I could be a medieval kitchen wench, but that seems awfully close to real life. There are already a few *Star Trek* minidresses walking around. I'm not really into the Japanese manga scene, so other than *Sailor Moon*, I'm not even sure who these characters are. I switch over to the rack for the guys because I'm not in the mood to display my reproductive units.

"Okay, got mine. Close your eyes. I don't want you to see," I say.

"No hints?"

"Nope."

"Okay. I think I have mine too."

Ten minutes later: "Are you ready?"

"I am. Are you?" I say over the dressing room wall.

"Yeah. On the count of three, we open the curtains and present ourselves to the world."

"One ..."

"Two ..."

"Three," I finish, sliding the curtain aside. And then the laughter. "Really? A Spartan?"

"Don't I look like Gerard Butler?" he says, turning sideways and patting his midsection. Second time in under an hour that I'm seeing his delightful upper half sans apparel. Aaaand I'm staring too long. Again.

"And you! No Princess Leia slave bikini?" he laughs.

"Dude, Loki is powerful—I feel so ... Norse." I run my hands along the ridiculous horns protruding from Loki's famed Marvel-era helmet. "Honestly, I feel sorry for Tom Hiddleston. Like, these actors —don't they feel totally weird when they have to go on set and act like they're saving the world when really, it's a green screen and they're fighting guys in motion-capture leotards?"

Luke is only half listening. Instead, he's twisting and turning in front of the mirror. "Does my butt look fat in these Spartan panties?" He smiles and buckles on an arm gauntlet. "And they get paid outrageous amounts of money to act like weirdoes. That's why they're called *actors*."

Once his own helmet is in place, he looks pretty decent.

"I think you're ready for your close-up," I say.

"After you, Lady Loki."

As we descend the concrete stairs into the warehouse, I'm instantly glad I made this costume choice. The room is filled with flesh, cleavages bulging through peekaboo holes, lots of leg squeezing through fishnet tights, thigh-high boots that cause the girls to tower over their drink-bearing boys.

Luke, though, reveals himself to be a total gentleman and talks only to me while we wait in line. The couple next to us, it's clear that the male half doesn't have Luke's polite tendencies. His female friend is yammering on about all the things wrong with the new *Spiderman* franchise but his eyes are busy groping every female curve in the room.

Once it's Luke's turn in front of the camera, my stomach is a twisted knot. This is so far out of my comfort zone, calling attention to myself and purposely having a photograph taken. But watching Luke flex and squeeze his biceps and legs behind the Spartan shield, I relax a little. He's not Luke the food truck guy on that blinding white paper—he's a Spartan, and he is eating it up.

After his sequence of shots and a few jokes are shared with Renegade, he hollers my way. "Loki! Come! Show the Greeks some love. Join me in conference." He bows.

I step on to the paper, and Renegade clicks a few shots of Loki and the Spartan.

I haven't had this much fun in forever.

Luke steps away and then I'm in character, channeling my inner Norse god, posing with my staff and cape, trying to keep the horns balanced. This costume is for a guy, so the fit isn't snug, but when my ten minutes expire, I do feel slightly more badass than I did when we walked in tonight.

I owe Luke thanks.

And I would give it to him, but he's talking to a very leggy, very busty, fire-engine-red-haired woman fondling the forked tail of her devil costume. Her footwear makes her taller than he is; the intimacy of their conversation makes me uncomfortable.

He points in my direction. She turns and looks. A cold, polite smile, the kind you give to the IRS agent auditing last year's return. Luke waves me over.

"Jayne, this is—"

"Tiana. I am Luke's girlfriend."

My heart splatters against my ribs. *Girlfriend?*

"Ex-girlfriend," Luke corrects, straightening his broomed helmet.

"A technicality." Tiana's harsh accent lends bite to her words. "Who are you, Jayne?"

"Loki, the Norse god."

"Not what I mean. I know this Loki. I mean, who are you? How do you know my Luke?"

"Jayne works with me at the food truck."

"So you are hired help," she says, turning to face me head-on.

"What do you do, Tiana?" I ask.

"I am a movie star. But if you were anyone, you would know this."

"Tiana's father is a Russian film producer."

"And Russians make excellent films," Tiana says. "Especially the ones starring me."

"That sounds like an interesting career," I say. I imagine Tiana running through an alleyway in high heels, state secrets tucked in her too-tight bra. "Have you been in anything we would know?"

"I only work with Russian filmmakers. Do you speak Russian?" She looks down her nose at me. Oh, too bad Gretchen's not here. A worthy adversary at last.

"Sadly, I am monolingual."

"What?" Her lip curls. I'm afraid she might melt me.

"English only."

"Yes, well, that is what will ruin America. The arrogance of its people who think English is the only language."

Wow. Okay.

110

What the hell did Luke see in this girl?

"Well, good seeing you, Tiana. Take care," Luke says, cupping my elbow to move me toward the stairs. I only need to turn once to confirm that the burning in my back is from her eyes lasering angry Russian holes in my flesh.

"Go ahead and ask."

"What?" I say innocently, hoisting my heavy coat as we ascend back into the main shop.

"How did I end up with her."

"Oh. Uh, she doesn't really seem like your type."

"She's an actress—she can be anyone she wants to be." He tips forward and catches the helmet before it hits the floor. "She was a friend of Leia's. We hung out and then she moved into our house, until she and Leia got into a fistfight over who ate the last of the Polish pickles. This was a couple years ago, but she still tells people I'm her boyfriend."

"Sorta creepy."

"It would be, but she gets bored of boy toys really fast. She dated another friend of mine after me—"

"I'll bet that was awkward."

"It was, but she has a thing for geeks. Once Bart realized Tiana was a nutter, he bought me a framed, production-used storyboard from *Return of the Jedi* as an apology."

"Nice."

"I thought so." Luke hangs up the sword and shield. "I just don't want you to think—you know—that Tiana and I are a *thing* or whatever. It's old news. She's just weird."

"Hey, totally not my business." But I so want to know if she was the one who texted that night, if she is the reason he left so quickly in a cab.

None of my business.

Luke's eyes hold mine for a sec. "We should get changed, then, yeah?"

I nod and tuck into the change room. "Uhhhh ... hey, Luke?"

"Yeah?"

"I think someone took my clothes."

"Really?" The metal rings of his stall curtain slide across the bar. "Are you decent?"

I open my curtain. He helps me by looking in the other unoccupied stalls. My clothes are definitely not around. "Let me ask Joe. Be right back."

Luke disappears into the throng. I retreat into my change room and look again, under the bench, just to make sure I didn't somehow kick them out of sight. Now I'm glad I kept my small handbag with me. I can handle missing a pair of jeans but a wallet and cell phone—ample reason for panic.

"Anything under there?" Luke asks behind me.

"Nope."

"I asked Joe—he said one of his gals may have accidentally cleaned out the room. And apparently the lost-and-found is huge right now with so many people here."

"Can we look? I don't really feel like buying a Loki costume tonight."

I follow Luke into a very small side room that is—as promised—overloaded with clothes. None of which belongs to me. Joe pops in to mention that I'm welcome to anything in here, although wearing someone else's clothes that have not been washed ...

"You look cute as Loki, if it's any consolation," Luke whispers while we're standing at the register. Instead of buying Loki tonight, twenty-five bucks gives me a week's rental. Lucky me.

The cashier, dressed as Rainbow Brite, offers me a plastic bag for the helmet.

Despite the fact that I will be moving out of the store, into the public realm dressed as an angry Norse god, I realize I don't want the rush to be over. This was way more fun than I expected. And we're in a part of the city where I don't know anyone, so whatever. I can let my freak flag fly until I get home if it means hanging out a little longer.

Truth be told: I don't want to go away from Luke yet.

Saying goodbye, Joe doesn't miss an opportunity to pinch my ass on the way out the door.

"Charming," I say to Luke.

"He's an ass man. Leia refuses to come in here anymore because he's always trying to get her to try on Queen Amidala's one-piece battle costume." Said costume is all white, skin-tight, and at one point in the film reveals that the actress, Natalie Portman, has great abs. The entire ensemble doesn't leave much to the imagination. I'd never be able to pull it off. Refer to aforementioned turnovers.

"Soooooo, are you tired, or do you want to grab a nightcap or a coffee or something?" he asks. Flutters. Like little feathery wings brushing against the backside of my sternum.

"Yeah!"

"Yeah, you're tired, or ...?"

"No. I mean, I'm not tired. But—I'm a little overdressed, wouldn't you say?"

"I always wondered what it would be like to get coffee with Thor's brother."

"Okay, then. But whatever Asgardian secrets I share must remain between us."

"Deal." He loops my arm through his.

I let it happen. I'm okay with this. We're just friends, right? He's sort of my boss. Well, not really because the food truck is just a friend helping a friend and I will have to find a real job eventually unless I sell a lot more books and speaking of books I should be home writing instead of out playing dress-up but Luke is so cute even though he's not dressed as a Spartan anymore and the fact that he's walking so close to me down this street toward the coffee shop is okay because technically he's my friend and there's nothing weird about him touching me—

"You okay?" he says.

"What? Yeah. Fine."

"You look a little deer-in-the-headlights," he says. "Maybe too much Tatooine for you?"

"Maybe." I smile. "This costume is hot." I fan myself with my free hand.

The café is quaint, so Portland with its reclaimed chandeliers and cozy seating and diner-style bar seating.

We order cappuccinos and settle in at the counter. "So, again, I'm sorry about Tiana." He sips, foam dusting his upper lip.

"No, it's cool. Don't worry about it."

"I just don't want you to think I'm 'that guy'—she's a handful. But we tend to run in the same circles, depending on her latest conquest."

"She sounds dangerous."

"Nah. It's the accent. She plays it up," he says, laughing. "When Tiana isn't the look-at-me-I'm-an-actress girl, she's fun and silly. Unfortunately, her wild imagination tends to leak into her tongue, and much of the time, it's anyone's guess how much of what she says is truth."

"That could complicate things."

"I'm glad I figured it out sooner rather than later. I couldn't deal with her lying and head games. Although she gets points for creativity, I'll give her that."

"How so?"

"When we first met, she would work afternoons and evenings. She told me she was touring with a troupe that performed at retirement homes. Sounds cool—very thoughtful, caring sort of gig. Yeah, turns out they were pole dancing and stripping for hire—"

"At the retirement homes?"

"Yup. They had a few regular places they'd go. The nurses would arrange it for after the administrative staff left for the day, and these old geysers were getting the show of a lifetime."

Okay, he's right. Tiana gets points for creativity.

"I didn't care so much that she was stripping—I just don't like being lied to about it."

"Maybe she was embarrassed."

"Tiana? You saw her, didn't you?" He's right. She doesn't seem like the embarrassed type. "Anyway, lying is a huge pet peeve. Leia was a terrible fibber when we were growing up and that made my parents crazy, so now I have a zero-tolerance policy for it."

I swirl my coffee to cool it down.

"So what about you, Jayne Dandy? Whose unlucky heart did you break?"

I laugh. "Now there's a short story."

"Seems your boy Holden is working hard to get your attention."

Holden. Since I've started at the food truck, he's there every day, sometimes twice, trying everything on Luke's menu. "Holden is addicted to your food, me thinks. As he should be."

"Hmmm ... I see how his eyes twinkle when you serve his lunch." Luke smirks.

"Holden's a nice guy, but I hardly know him. He was hired right around the time I was laid off."

"But he hangs on your every word, Jayne. Keep an eye on that one."

Does Luke *want* me to think of Holden beyond just friendship? It's so awkward to talk about another guy—especially when it's not Holden's attention I desire.

Before I can respond, someone behind mentions my name.

"Jayne? Jayne Dandy?"

I turn. My innards tilt.

"Heyyyyyy! It's me, Lisa Davenport. Well, Davenport-Richards now. And you remember Rachel," she says, looking to her right. *Oh dear baby Jesus why do you hate me so.* How could I forget perfect Lisa who stole everyone's boyfriends right out from under their noses, or darling Rachel who wiped me clean in every election event from grade seven onward, whose mouth was the megaphone that shared the failed make-out party debacle with the entire school?

Oh my GOD. I am dressed as Loki. In public. In front of people I haven't seen since we parted ways after the high school graduation all-nighter a million years ago.

"Hey," I say weakly. "How are you guys?"

"Omigod, we're so good. I just got married—" Lisa thrusts a mighty diamond into my face. "You might remember Martin Richards—he was a senior when we were sophomores. Anyway, he's an accountant with a huge firm downtown and we live in Lake Oswego. And Rachel is just here in town visiting. She has a big job on Wall Street."

"Wow. That's great." I feel Luke's hand squeeze my elbow gently. "What are you guys doing in the city tonight?"

"We were at a gallery opening for a friend just down the block," Rachel says. She scans my costume from head to toe, that trademark wicked smile pulling at the corner of her narrow mouth.

"What about you?" Lisa says. "Are you still living at home, or ...?"

"No, I have my own place. With Gretchen. You might remember her."

"Really? You guys are still friends?" Lisa says. "Isn't she involved with fashion stuff?"

"Something like that," I say. I am so not going to explain anything to these people. High school died a long time ago. I'd like to leave its rotting corpse buried.

"Did she dress you in this tonight?" Rachel says.

"No—we went to a ... costume party. My other clothes were stolen."

"Halloween's still two weeks away."

I nod nervously.

"Well," Lisa shifts her weight, "introduce us to your husband." Her gaze slides to Luke.

"Oh, he's not my husband. Just friends. This is Luke Walker," I say. "Luke, this is Lisa and Rachel." He politely shakes their limp hands.

"What do you do, Luke?" Lisa asks.

I answer for him. "He owns Luke Piewalker's."

Rachel rolls her eyes and checks her phone, but Lisa squeals loud enough to scare the neighborhood dogs. "Oh. My. GOD! The food truck? You're, like, famous! I *love* your turnovers! The strawberry-rhubarb ones are my favorite. Oh, my sister and I always hit your place after we've ravaged the shopping district," she says. "Oh, you should totally marry this one, Jayne Dandy. You will never go hungry."

Rachel holds up her phone—*click*—and chuckles to herself. Shit, I think she just took my picture. I hate you, technology.

"Luke, you have to know, our Jayne here—she was always talking about going off into the wild blue yonder to become the next big literary thing. Always the English teacher's pet."

"Yeah, Jayne, did you ever get that Great American Novel written?" Rachel snipes.

"She's working on it," Luke says.

"Oh, do you remember that time she tried to convince Ms. Lindy that a 'concubine' was actually a flower her mother had in their front yard?" Lisa says.

Rachel joins in. "*Col-um-bine*. Remember that, Jayne?"

Gosh, Rachel. How could I forget with you here to remind me?

"Oh, oh, wait—Luke—poor Jayne. She had a hard time with boys when we were younger, so everyone called her Jaynie Prudie because she wouldn't make out with that kid—what was his name?" Lisa says, giggling at herself.

"Robert," Rachel adds, daggers pointed at my neck. I notice that her hips are definitely wider than her shoulders now and she needs her upper lip waxed. Small, petty consolations.

"Right! Robert. God, that was hilarious. 'I am not going to touch tongues with that kid!' Jaynie screamed. The whole party heard her!" Lisa can hardly stand upright with her own amusement at this point.

I cannot believe this is happening. I cannot believe they are telling Luke these stories. If I could just bring out Brave Jayne, but getting sucked back into this vortex of my adolescence has cut me off at the knees. Lisa's married; Rachel has an important job. I serve pastries out of a truck and write lame stories.

"Well, I'm glad she doesn't have problems touching tongues

anymore," Luke says, wrapping an arm around my shoulders. "It was nice to listen to you two self-important cows make my girl Jayne feel like shit, but if you'll excuse us."

Lisa's laughter breaks off. Rachel looks freshly slapped.

Luke slides off his stool, bumping Rachel backward, and hoists me to the ground around my waist, straightening my long coat, and plants a kiss against my head as we bulldoze our way through the twosome and their dumbstruck faces.

I would high-five and chest bump him *right here* if I didn't feel so humiliated by what just happened.

Luke opens the truck door and offers me a hand as I climb in.

"Thanks," I say.

"Some people just never leave the past where it belongs, Jayne," he says.

The rest of the drive is quiet, and for that, I am so grateful.

Though the feel of his lips against my temple and his arm around my shoulders stays with me until we pull up in front of my building.

"Bacon chowder for the lady tomorrow," he says.

"Wouldn't miss it for the galaxy."

He waits until my key is in and the door opened before he drives off, but I don't think he sees that I watch through the glass doors as his taillights disappear around the corner.

EIDER: CHAPTER 7

by Jaina Jacen (October)

I throw myself into his arms, not as a romantic endeavor but as a grateful hello to a friend who meant so much to me during a time before propriety consumed our day-to-day lives.

"Illyria, be careful," he whispers, setting me back on my feet and readjusting my hood.

"It's you! Where have you been all this time?"

"Learning. Growing. Working. Not unlike you, although very unlike you."

"Oh, how I miss those days of our childhood when we were free to be friends."

"As do I, My Sovereign."

"Stop calling me that," I say, "especially here." I look around us and realize Taisa has stepped away.

"Your handmaiden is at a stall. Retrieving refreshments, I believe. After all, it is your Twelvemonth, is it not?"

I smile widely. "It is." And what a Twelvemonth to remember. "I'm of age now."

"Which means your father will have suitors lined up outside the compound walls."

My smile fades. "Don't remind me."

"You don't want a husband?"

"One of my own choosing, please? We have the ability to fly to distant planets, cure and prevent diseases and malformations, manipulate the weather—and yet, I am not trusted to choose my own husband?"

"Who would you choose? If you could?" he says, flashing his teeth.

"Have you heard of the chimpanzee?"

"The what?"

"A primate species indigenous to the Dead Planet. They would show their teeth as a sign of aggression."

Mooney laughs loudly. "You spend too much time reading about the Dead Planet."

"I want to know what killed it—so that those in charge here do not damn us to the same fate."

"You always were ambitious."

Taisa is moving toward us, her face bright with excitement. In her hands she clutches tall vessels of ale. We are never permitted ale inside the compound. This is a big night indeed.

"I knew when you didn't recognize me at the compound, I had to convince Taisa to smuggle you out," Mooney says.

"You're an enterprising devil," I say.

"On the contrary, it appears that it is you who is enterprising." He nods toward my hip again.

"Yes, well, a girl can never be too careful."

"Do you know how to use it?"

"Well enough. Shall I demonstrate?"

Mooney laughs again. It sounds musical.

"So—what do I call you?" I ask.

"I'm known as Mooney. No one remembers my first name. If you call me Pollux and someone overhears ... It could be a giveaway."

"Then you must call me Sella."

"A Class II name? I couldn't."

"If you don't, it could be a giveaway."

A yell echoes across the square. "STOP!"

The mirth on Taisa's face dissolves as her hood is pulled back and the ales slapped from her hands, splattering to the ground. Our eyes meet. Without uttering a word, she urges me to run.

Before I can move in any direction, though, hands clamp my arms and Mooney is thrown to the ground, a boot pushed angrily into the side of his face.

I throw my hood back and the hands on me release. Everyone drops to his or her knees.

"Remove your foot from his head, or I will remove your foot from your body." The soldier obeys. I help Mooney to his feet, but a soldier pushes him to a knee. Mooney dusts himself off but he's not allowed to get close to me.

Our eyes meet. This cannot be goodbye.

He coughs and throws something toward me. I reach down and retrieve it before anyone can beat me to it, thrusting it into the deep pockets of my cloak.

"Your father, My Sovereign," the soldier next to me says, stretching an arm to the southernmost watchtower.

The look on Father's face tells me this could be my only foray into open territory until he marries me off.

"Nothing happens to him." I gesture to Mooney. "Am I understood?" The soldiers bow their heads in deference. Taisa is dragged alongside me. "And let go of her, you animal."

We are escorted into an armed carrier waiting outside the square's towering walls, overkill given the proximity to the main compound.

Upon reaching the arch that will carry me hence, I turn to get one last look at Mooney.

And find him doubled on the ground sustaining blows they didn't dare level in my presence.

15

"WHAT ARE YOU WEARING?" Gretchen's face is slathered in green mask and the apartment looks like a bomb went off. Quack is stretched out on her pile of old *Rose City Registers*. We bring home extra copies so she can eat those instead of our books. She sees me and lifts her ratty head before realizing, "Oh, it's just you," and moving to clean her butt.

"Long story." I plunk down on the couch. A headache hovers undecided behind my eyeballs. "What is all this?"

"First, why didn't you answer my texts?"

I pull my phone out. It's been on silent all night and I didn't realize it. I find many missed texts from Gretchen:

OMG u need to see this.

Jaynie, the book is selling!

WHERE R U

COME ON I'm starting to worry

R u nekked with the Pie Man? Is he showing u his sword?

WTF WHERE R U CALL ME.

R U HAVING SEX?

"So?" she says.

"So what?"

"Sex?"

"God, Gretchen, no. Perv. We were at a party. A loud party."

"Loud party with terrible fashion sense," she says, thrusting her laptop on to my legs. I need to change. The pleather is sticking to my skin. "LOOK at this."

I made the mistake of showing Gretchen how to navigate the sales site for Jaina Jacen's e-books. When she scrolls down the page, I sit up rod straight.

"There has to be some mistake."

"I've been watching it all night." She clicks to the Jaina Jacen Facebook and Twitter pages. I have hundreds of new followers, a boatload of comments and tweets.

How did I miss this all happening? Probably because I rarely check in. A handful of new readers a month doesn't exactly scream "social media firestorm."

But that's exactly what this is. A freakish, Asgard-worthy firestorm. Maybe Loki brings me good luck.

I move back to the sales page. "I have to call someone ... this can't be right," I say. But the rankings are there to support these numbers. There are five digits in the sales column.

"Seventy-six *thousand* books?"

"I did the math on this, Jayne." She hands me a calculator. I stare at the screen. There is *no way* I've earned that much money. There are too many digits in that equation. No way.

No way no way no way.

"You're going to need to hire an accountant," she says. Before I can respond, Gretchen has me off the couch and we're dancing around the living room like freaks—her in the gooey avocado tightening mask and me dressed for battle—who've just won the lottery.

Because we sort of have. *I* sort of have.

We scream and dance and bounce until the hippie couple with the new baby downstairs slams on the ceiling with their organic-fiber broom. Quack hisses at us.

We fall on to the couch, out of breath and giddy. "Oh my God, I cannot wait to see the looks on Sheila's and Maggot Dandy's faces when they hear about this."

"NO." I sit up straight. "Gretchen—no one can know this is me."

"What? Why not?"

"Because—they just can't. Please."

"Babe, you're going to have to get past these weird hang-ups. I've spent the entire night checking out your competition, and those people travel. They go to book signings and they give public readings and they do all sorts of shit that *you* are going to have to do if you want to keep your fans."

"I don't have *fans*."

"Like hell you don't!"

"Gretchen," panic grips my throat, "there is *no way* I can do this. I—I can be one of those recluses, you know, those writers who refuse to leave their house ever. Salinger hardly ever made public appearances."

"This is the twenty-first century, Jayne. Salinger never sold eighty thousand books in under a month, either."

I grab both her hands. "Gretch, please—no one can know. I can't tell anyone that this is me."

A sly smile creeps across her face as she stands and opens her arms wide. "Which is exactly what I thought you'd say. SO ..." She moves over to the wall to some haphazard drawings that look like a kindergartner got hold of a sixty-four box of markers. "These are Jaina Jacen's outfits." She moves to a flow chart she's created on taped-together copy paper. "This is her brand itinerary."

"A what itinerary?"

"These are all the things we will do to make sure Jaina Jacen is a brand. I've spent the whole afternoon and evening on this. We need swag—bookmarks, pens, bags, T-shirts, kitschy shit the fans love so you can continue to build the Jaina Jacen name. I have a whole list of conferences and signings we need to look into—"

"How did you do all this just *today*?"

"Slow fashion news day?" She moves to the kitchen table and picks up another page, holding it against her chest. "And hear me out with this next thing. I know you don't want anyone to know that this is you. The gals at the writers' group already think I'm the hand behind the handiwork. Soooo ..." She tapes a photograph—of herself, one of her many—to the wall. "I can be the face of Jaina Jacen."

I stare at her charts and drawings and finally stop on her professionally done headshot.

This is a solid plan. I can keep writing the words, and Gretchen can take the credit because I never got into this to be famous. I got into it because Dr. McCoy thought it would be good for me. And so I wouldn't have to move back to Sheila Dandy's Hall of Terrors.

Except ... money. Whenever money and friendships tango, tangles follow. And this is a lot more money than I have ever seen.

"How are we going to work out the cash, is your next question. I've already thought about it. And here's what I propose: I'm just the face. I will, of course, have to familiarize myself with every Jaina Jacen book you write—how many do you have?"

"There's a handful of sci-fi stories."

"Fine. I'll suffer through those, but they're not the ones selling. In terms of future property in the erotica department, what have you got?"

I blush when I think of the *Pride and Prejudice* journal in my closet safe.

"Jayne, how *many*?" Gretchen knows my face too well.

"One more almost finished—the sequel to the first one. That's the one you read part of. Plus notes for the third book."

"Got any ideas for more?"

"I don't know. Maybe." *Yes I do but I'm a chickenshit and this is embarrassing.*

"Brilliant! Okay, you need to finish the second book as soon as possible and then get on the third so you have something to go after that—maybe by Christmas or New Year's. I didn't know if you had more stories so I didn't look too far into strategy yet. But you're going to have to commit to this—like, writing every single day." Duh, I already do that. "Work part-time at the food truck or whatever if you want. But with these numbers, you can probably afford to quit."

"I don't think I get money from the books for at least sixty days from publication."

"That's only ... what, three weeks from now? Whatever. We'll work it out. Jaina is going to need more books, and that means you're going to be busy."

Part-time at the food truck? Will that put Luke in a bind?

How did this happen so fast? Obituary writer to novelist in mere weeks?

Gretchen tapes up another string of paper, this one scribbled with numbers and arrows. "I know that writing the books is most of the work, but me getting up in front of an audience," which she loves, "is still sort of hard. So perhaps you pay me per appearance. Or, if you want to do it on a percentage basis, like how you would pay an agent, then we could work that out too. I could manage the marketing, online stuff, event organizing, whatever needs doing. Like I said, I still have to figure out how best to market this brand. Which should be easy enough because I'm a natural salesperson." Gretchen could sell ice to Eskimos, among other politically incorrect maxims.

"Okay. What percentage were you thinking?"

"Most agents charge fifteen percent. That's what my modeling agent took. Managers take another ten, but you don't need a manager or outside publicist if you have me. I think if you want me to do appearances and handle publicity and marketing, then twenty to twenty-five percent is a fair deal. What do you think?"

Twenty-five percent. That sounds like a lot. But how much is it worth to not risk the world knowing that it's *me* behind all this?

"How about twenty-five plus expenses? But you have to promise to never leak a word of this to anyone."

"Not even Luke?"

"Oh my God, especially not Luke. Gretchen—when you read the books ... Alec, the main character ... he's sort of modeled after Luke."

Gretchen's smile stretches across the room.

"Please. Not a word. To him, or to my family. No snide comments, no joking around when we see them. If you're going to do this, you have to commit a hundred percent to being the face of Jaina Jacen—and being discreet about our arrangement. I'll write the words, but you have to take on the persona. And that means reading smut in public."

Gretchen poses in front of me, hand on popped hip, boobs perky underneath her nightshirt, white teeth gleaming against the green of her crumbling mask. She flips her blond ponytail.

"Bring on the sexy vagina funtime, you saucy minx."

16

ELEVEN DAYS UNTIL HALLOWEEN. Which means Luke wants to decorate the food truck. Unfortunately for me, said decorations are in his rented, second-floor self-storage unit, and the building's elevator is toast. Hence I take the stairs. While normally this wouldn't pose a problem, in the few days since our official agreement was inked, Gretchen, now "the face of a publishing diva," has experienced a sudden spike in vanity.

Vanity means exercise.

Exercise means pre-dinner yoga alternating with one disc from a set of DVD workouts led by a Nazi-esque woman with frightening eyebrows and abs my granny could've washed her delicates on. If I'd had a granny. With delicates.

And all of this sweating and stretching of sinew, Gretchen refuses to do alone. She says I have to be in top physical condition to keep my brain healthy and the endorphins flowing so I can write more books. Already a slave driver.

As such, these stairs conspire with the unwieldy Rubbermaid bins to burn through my flesh. One stair at a time, my butt muscles scream at their thigh cousins who in turn wrench on irked calves and don't even ask about my poor, overworked tummy. My various muscle groups were happy with being shapeless and average.

En route back to Piewalker's, my mother texts that she has canceled my father's birthday fête because he's a lying, cheating bastard. She has cc'd this text to my siblings, my father, and his secretary. No one should've ever introduced Sheila Dandy to the magic of text messaging.

And the sickest part—beyond looping your children into your marital woes—is that my mother cheated on my father years ago. Twice. So cliché—the gardener the first time and then the pastor at the Church of Damnation they went to when I was a kid.

Wow, Jayne, why do you need therapy?

When I make it back, sweaty despite the outdoor chill, I spot Gretchen and Holden at one of the small tables, hands cupped around steaming mugs. Weird—it's a bit early for lunch yet.

"Jayne!" Gretchen shuffles over to my double-parked car. I'd ask for her help with the bins but the heels on her new boots and the sheen of her nails say I'm on my own.

"What are you guys doing here?" I grunt.

"You're not going to believe it. The restaurateur—he came barging into the office screaming profanities and freaking out. Poor Holden almost peed his pants. But Mr. Crazy Chicken had an animal carrier with LIVE SKUNKS in it. Mr. Clark called the police but Crazy ran up to the roof and tried to parachute off the top."

"It's only four stories!"

"Yeah! So he smacked into the roof of Clark's Sebring—smashed it right in."

"Oh my God, is the guy dead?"

"I don't think so. Lots of broken bones, if his screams were any measure. But they cleared out the office because the cat carrier definitely had skunks in it. Thank GOD they didn't spray us." She follows me back and forth, talking as I drop off the first and second bins. I have to unload quickly. Parking devils lurk in darkened corners searching for their next motorlicious meal.

"Why do I always miss all the fun?"

"Anyway, I needed to come over and talk to you in person—there's something else."

"Better than a skunk-toting lunatic parachuting off the newspaper building's roof?"

Gretchen stops me as I pull the third bin out of the back seat. "Last night, after the thing at Anne Bocci's studio—you should see the beautiful pieces she has planned for spring and summer—I went with a couple friends to the Copper Horse. Luke was working again."

"Yeah ... and?"

"And there was a woman there. A tall, mouthy redhead. She had a foreign accent."

"That's his ex."

"Wellllll, she didn't look very ex-like last night."

I stop, the third bin heavy against my sore legs. "What do you mean?"

"I mean she was grabbing at him and kissing him every chance she got."

Heart deflates.

"Luke told me that she's not taking their break-up very well." My voice doesn't want to add conviction to my words. I want to believe that Luke—Mr. I Don't Abide Liars—is not jerking me around. Although, whatever. He's not my property. He can kiss whomever he chooses.

"Holden!" Gretchen yells and snaps her fingers, pointing at the bin I've now deposited on the sidewalk. He jogs over.

"Hey, Jayne. Let me give you a hand with that."

I smile weakly.

He carries one side, which is great—they're not so heavy as bulky—but my arms are shaky. Especially now.

Holden helps me stack the four bins next to the awning, out of the light afternoon drizzle. Luke pops out the trailer door and hands me water. "Look at you, all sweaty and working hard. You'll be glad to know you've got Thanksgiving and Christmas covered now too."

I look at his face, searching for I don't know what. Shifty eyes? A devious grin? Tiana's leftover lipstick?

Gretchen shoos Holden away, back to the table, and pulls me out of view of customers. "This might cheer you up." From her huge bag, she pulls out a paperback book. *Resist Me Not, A Novel*, Temptation Series #1, by Jaina Jacen.

"What is this?" I hastily look around to make sure no one's listening in.

"I ordered paperbacks. That night after the writers' group—when you showed me how to log into the system, I figured it out. I wanted to surprise you. This is the proof copy, so you need to go through it and make sure there are no mistakes."

"Oh. Wow." I can't help but smile. It's cool to see it in real life, in my hands, in paper and ink. "Wow."

"You already said that." Gretchen gives my cheek a light pat. She's excited for us too.

I shove the book back into her bag. "Keep this hidden. You *promised*." Gretchen's eyes blaze with mischief. I don't know why I'm so uptight about it. Even if someone sees this in her hands, they have no way of linking this identity to me. And it's not like we're doing anything to keep Gretchen's tie-in to Jaina Jacen a secret. That was the whole point of bringing her in as the face of our brand.

Gretchen, looking over my shoulder, grabs my arm. "Oh God. Jayne." She spins me around.

Sheila Dandy is standing in front of the food truck. With a rolling suitcase.

Seriously?

"Mother. What are you doing here?"

"You turned down the job with Frankie for *this*?"

Ah, shit. "Mom, you remember Luke, and Holden, from the Grill that night." She bobs her head coldly.

"Hello, Gretchen. Are you working here too?" she says. I find it interesting that my mother treats Gretchen with such contempt when Gretchen's father could buy my parents a hundred times over.

"Hello, Sheila. Love the coat." Gretchen air-kisses my cheeks. "Holden, we should go. Whatever is about to go down, you do not want to watch." He doesn't have a moment to protest but instead looks over his shoulder as Gretchen drags him away.

I'm grateful—except Gretch didn't drag Luke away. I'm relieved there are customers to keep him safe from whatever avalanche is about to befall me.

"Why are you here, Mother? And what's with the suitcase?"

"I'm cleaning out your father's office at the house."

"Sooooo, you brought me office supplies?"

"No. I brought things that belong to you—notebooks of your stories and school projects that he kept over the years."

"Oh." *You don't want them, Mom?* "It would've been easier for you if I'd come to the house and picked up a box."

"I didn't want to wait for you to have time off from—your 'job.'" Her phone rings in her purse. She silences it. "Anyway, I have an appointment for a massage. So here." She scrapes the suitcase across the sidewalk. "And call your sister. My birthday is coming up and I'm assuming everyone will want to get together for dinner."

With an invite like that, who can resist?

She stops three steps down the sidewalk and points. "Jayne, isn't that your car?" I spin around.

Indeed, my car is now attached to the ass end of a tow truck. When the parking devil and I make eye contact, her clawed wings unfurl behind her and the hiss of her exhale carries across the distance.

I sheath my verbal sword, although removing the demon's tightly coifed head would make me feel so much better.

Dejected, I saunter over so she can hand me the ticket and skitter away to track down more malfeasance on Portland's infested streets. It doesn't do any good to argue with these folks. As such, I watch my poor little car bounce her way down the street to have an afternoon rest among a lot full of other cars whose owners have misbehaved.

I don't know if Luke sees me before or after his hand lands on

Tiana's ass, but he certainly sees me when her tongue is halfway down his throat.

Ignoring their obviously happy reunion against the back of the food truck, I step quietly up the tiny stairs and move into the kitchen. Apron on. Hair pulled back. Phone turned off. Hands washed. Eyes stinging with tears.

Words that don't sound altogether friendly are exchanged, sneaking through the crack in the screened window above the sinks. This is none of my business, and yet I cannot pull myself away.

"You need to leave," Luke says.

"But Tiana wants to stay."

"Please, I have customers waiting."

"That is what your girl is for. I am for fun. Tiana needs love too."

"This is over. This is not happening. We are not together anymore."

"Why you not love Tiana? Look at this body. What is not to love?" Slurping. They're kissing again. "Please, Pie Man, let me show you my pie."

"No. You need to go, now." Luke sounds angrier.

"Or what? What will you do?"

"I'll call the police and file harassment charges."

"You are a liar. And the police will not believe you. You have my lipstick on your face. And I can say that you hurt me." *Slap! Slap!*

Luke moves into frame of the window, his hands hoisted. I slink out of view. "You're a sicko."

"I will keep slapping my beautiful cheeks to make them red like Soviet flag if you don't kiss me again."

"Don't come back here, or I will file a complaint."

"What, so you can go back to your little mouse in there? Is that who you want? Mouse girl with mousey hair and mousey face and no boobs who likes to wear boy clothes?"

Me? I'm not mousey. And I don't like to wear boy clothes ... at least not all the time.

Something splats against the trailer's side. "Take your stupid pie!

My father hates your pie anyway! Says he's had stale borscht that tastes better!"

The sound of high heels stamping away precedes Luke opening the door. He's covered in what used to be a banana-chocolate cream pie, filling and whipped cream oozing down the side of his head, plopping on to his shoulder and the formerly pristine floor. Such a waste. I resist the urge to scoop some off with my finger.

"Hey ..."

"Hi." I grab paper towels and start to clean up.

"Your car got towed?"

I nod.

"I'll pay for it. It's my fault. You were double-parked because of me."

"It's okay. I got sidetracked with my mother showing up."

Luke pulls me up from the floor. "Don't clean. I'll do it. This is sort of her thing."

"None of my business, Luke."

"It's not what you think—"

"I don't think anything. You're allowed to kiss whomever you want."

"But I don't want *her*. We're over—she knows that—but when she sees me hanging out with another woman, she gets weird."

"Luke, honestly, you don't owe me an explanation. I know we're just friends."

He nods and holds my eyes for a second. "Right. Okay."

"Oh, hey, I, uh—I have weird news." Might as well get this over with while the stinger is still lodged in my throat. I stick to the vague script Gretchen and I came up with—she insists that I have time to write, so I have to make it happen somehow. "I've been offered another part-time job." *Be careful, Jayne.* "For an online thing—it's flex-time, either mornings or afternoons from home, so I can be here when you need the most help."

"Wow. Sounds like a great opportunity. When do you start?"

"Any time. But I was thinking maybe next week."

"Hey, whatever you need to do. You've really helped me out, so that's great."

"But can you manage alone in the hours I'm not here? What about Leia?"

"Yeah, I'm sure I can get her to come in and help for a little while."

"Thanks for understanding."

"Anything for a friend," he says, wiping the pie filling out of his hair with more paper towels.

The ding of the silver countertop bell interrupts further conversation.

Holden's back.

Wait—Holden's back?

"Couldn't stay away, hey?" Luke says.

"You have such great service, I cannot resist," Holden says, smiling at me. "Actually, Luke, I meant to talk to you earlier but you were busy. I'd like to do a piece on the food truck. For our holiday issue. I'm working on a round-up of the best eateries in the city, and of course, Piewalker's has to be on that list."

"Sure. That would be great."

"Sweet. So, maybe I can buy you a drink after work one night this week and we can have a proper interview?"

They shake on it. Holden steps to the side so Luke can help the customer waiting behind him. "Jayne, before I go," Holden says. He lowers his voice and beckons me closer. "You okay? Gretchen was telling me a little about your mom."

"Yeah. I'm fine. It's nothing." It's not nothing but I'm not going to talk about this right now, not here. And not with him.

"So ... I was sort of wondering if maybe I could take you to dinner."

"Someplace new to review?"

"Uh," he chuckles under his breath, "no, I mean, you know, like dinner. Like a date."

When Luke's hand freezes midair clutching a customer's money, I know he's heard Holden's request.

I can't make eye contact with either of them. I feel like I've done something wrong. I honestly have never been in this situation, and I don't know how to handle it. Shit, where is Gretchen when I really need her?

Luke doesn't care what I do. He doesn't feel the same way about me that I feel about him. He had his hand on Tiana's ass not ten minutes ago. Remember?

I'm a free woman. Luke doesn't like me. And maybe Dr. McCoy would be proud of me for branching out.

"Yeah. Yes, okay. That would be fun."

"Excellent. So, Friday? Say, 7:30?" That's four days from now. I have time to back out if I suddenly develop Ebola.

My heart thumps with guilt. *Say something Jayne he's staring at you. They're both staring at you.* "Sure. See you then."

I smile quickly and then turn away from the counter under the guise that I have something sticky on my hands. I hold them under the hot water until the steam reaches my face and Luke's voice calls me back to the present.

"Two large bowls of pumpkin butternut squash to go, please," he says over his shoulder. While he's not rude, the coldness of the words sucks the air out of the room.

What have I done?

EIDER: CHAPTER 8

by Jaina Jacen (October)

My father waits until the following morning to level his sentence.

"Your Twelvemonth was ruined, secondary to your abject disregard for rule and order. I am mortally embarrassed, Illyria. Suitors have been sent back to their compounds without the pleasure of your acquaintance. Food was wasted, never a wise choice for any man—"

"You could have given it to the Class IIIs. The feast would have fed legions."

Father's face burns. I should quiet my tongue.

"You are expected in the meeting hall and for lessons with tutors, but you are not to venture off this floor except under my orders." My father doesn't shout when he's angry. He doesn't need to. The vehemence in his voice causes the polished granite under his feet to tremble. One can imagine what it does to the nerves of the people around him.

"Pollux Mooney and I were childhood friends. We were merely talking! Nothing nefarious or illicit was happening. Please tell me he is okay, that your brutes didn't hurt him."

"He was given fair punishment for his crime."

"His crime? Talking to me? Since when did talking to me become a crime?"

"Interclass fraternization with a member of the ruling elite? It has always been a crime."

"Yours are ridiculous rules."

"Tread carefully, dear Illyria."

"Or what? You'll call your henchmen to kick me senseless with their boots?"

My father grunts and moves across the room. He's added more bodies to the watch outside my chamber. Taisa, her face purpled with the lasting effects of her own sanctions, stands with head bowed as my father slams out of the room.

"This will not stand," I say. "I'm getting out of here."

"Illyria, please," Taisa says quietly. "Let's go into the meeting hall. Your friends are here."

"My friends? Those vapid gossips in fine gowns stitched by the hands of Class IV children are not my friends."

"Can we have no conflict for one day? I can't suffer any more bruises."

I pause and walk to her, wrapping an arm around her shoulder. "I am so sorry. This is all my doing. I will call my nurse. You will be fixed in no time." I move to the panel along the wall where I can summon any number of compound staff.

"No. She won't help me. They've been told not to. As a reminder ..."

"This is so unfair."

"Illyria ..." Taisa approaches and bows her head. "Please. The meeting hall. Your father will return even angrier if you don't make the required appearance."

Reluctantly, I agree. Because she's right. Just as she always is.

And as expected, the hall buzzes with sordid speculation about my "attempted escape."

"I heard the soldiers arrested her."

"Well, I heard she was with a lowerclass man. That they were planning their elopement."

"I heard she was drunk off ale."

These are just the conversations overheard before my so-called friends realize I've arrived.

"I did not sustain an arrest. I did not get a sip of ale, although I very much wanted one. And the lowerclass man is a friend—"

Gasps consume the room.

"—from my childhood. We were merely catching up." How romantic would it have been to be planning my elopement, however.

The Dead Planet is said to have allowed people to marry for love. People of all nations and colors and stations were allowed to intermingle and marry as they saw fit. Occupations were chosen rather than assigned. People were allowed to have friends wherever they went.

Of course, this is the romantic version of things, delivered through an old sage tutor who died last season. Her replacement told me to unlearn such fantasy, that the Dead Planet is dead for a reason, and that Eider's strict rules serve a very real and very important purpose: to sustain humankind against a universe of unhuman rivals with technologies and intelligences far greater than ours. We are simpletons among the stars, but giants among men.

Eider lived. The Dead Planet did not.

I could tattle on these immature girls for their verbal indiscretion; I could have them subjected to punishment for their deplorable treatment of our Class III handmaidens and most especially for the vitriolic banter about my whereabouts.

But that's boring.

Let their mouths move. Soon they will be paired and carried away by men of equal status to go live in distant compounds, their lives consumed by activities that will do little but provide more fodder for gossip, their abdomens soon swollen with the next generation, their heads empty of anything useful to pass along.

While I listen to the idle chatter of my agemates, the sudden memory of Mooney's gift, tossed at my feet, hastens my steps.

As long as I retreat to my chamber, no rules have been broken. I made an appearance in the hall—that was all Father asked of me.

I'm so relieved to find it still hidden in the deep pocket of my cloak. It is a paper tightly folded that once opened reveals a message that stills my breath:

Three sunrises hence, we leave.

17

"YOU LOOK VERY NICE," Holden says, holding the car door open. It's a newer model Volkswagen, the Zipcar logo on the side bolstering Holden's hipster reputation.

"You too." It's a reflex response—he actually looks the same as he always does, which isn't bad. More corduroy. Another vest. He does have lovely curls and a nice smile. His pants are too loose to really get a fix on his physique, but I'm not one of those women who has to date a cover model for *Men's Fitness*. In fact, I'm not one of those women who dates. Period.

Anxiety like a tongue against a 9-volt makes me want to chew down my fingernails. But they're freshly painted, thanks to Gretchen attacking me with her beautifying routine. The nails feel weird, though. Like my fingers can't breathe. I'm sure I will have the Blushing Pink picked off by night's end.

I would've invited Holden in for a drink or a chat so I could feel less crazy, but the cat—she's not a fan of men. Or women. In fact, most beings with a pulse are a target. And although she's had her rabies shot, it's not worth the risk. Rabies is the deadliest viral pathogen facing mankind; fewer than ten people diagnosed with the full-blown disease have survived. I don't want to be responsible for contributing to those statistics should Holden's hand find itself near Quack's mouth.

On top of the I'm-going-on-a-date nerves, I've got Gretchen's latest news running through my head: Jaina Jacen has her first public reading. At an independent bookstore in St. Johns. A romance writers' group has invited Jaina to come in given the crazy success of *Resist Me Not* #1. And the second book, *Tempt Me Softly*, is slated for upload next week. The cover isn't exactly what I wanted, but I have to let go—"In Gretchen We Trust"—as she keeps reminding me.

And she's ecstatic about doing the reading. Has her outfit already picked, has booked herself a mani-pedi for the day of. I suppose I can put on clean jeans and hide behind the stacks. Make sure people titter and pant at the right moments.

Holden pulls into the restaurant lot and even springs for valet parking. The ever-present fall rain is annoying, but the second valet is quick with an umbrella. Perfect as maybe now my coif won't wilt before dessert.

Oh. God. Dessert. I have yet to be seated or see a wine list. But dessert will eventually arrive, signaling a near end to the evening. And then what? What if he wants to kiss me goodnight? I should've said no. I should never have come out with him. I should've stayed in tonight to work on Illyria and Mooney and watch *Clone Wars* reruns in my pajamas while feeding mouse hearts and the blood of virgins to Quack.

What am I doing here? Do I even like Holden? Do I want to like Holden?

You are here because you need to stop hiding in your apartment. And Holden is a lovely young man. Look how clean his fingernails are and how nicely pressed his shirt is.

"Jayne? You okay?" Holden stands with the front door open, waiting. I'm frozen. *Wake up, dummy.*

"Yes. Sorry. Trying to remember if I turned the curling iron off." I step through the door and wait alongside Holden as he addresses the maître d'. We're seated in the back of the restaurant, a quiet, cozy table for two with candles and a red-checkered tablecloth. If they bring us a plate of pasta and ask us to reenact *Lady and the Tramp*, I won't be surprised.

The waiter, who happens to be a friend of Holden's, shares the specials. I allow my date to order for us both because I'm out of my league here. My dining expertise doesn't extend much beyond specialty burgers in places where they clap and stand on chairs to sing "Happy Birthday" or the Thai place near our apartment where we order the same thing every weekend.

We wine. We chat. He asks about my history with the *Rose City Register* and how I'm enjoying working at the food truck. We spend a fair amount of time on ducks, my favorite, and domesticated exotic birds, his favorite. I tell him about Beru and Owen and the Tigard farm, and he invites himself to come with me one weekend and help out. He admits that he's watched the *Star Wars* franchise a time or two, though he's nowhere near my or Luke's level of geekdom.

Small talk over decadent breadsticks dripping with warm butter, rosemary, and baked garlic cloves. Holden's not a bad conversationalist. Witty. And his eyes sparkle when he smiles. I do appreciate a good eye sparkle.

When the pasta-prawn scampi-shallot plate arrives, the waiter serves me first, divvying up the prawn equally between two plates. A plate of beef short ribs and tiny beef medallions braised in red wine with vegetables alongside appears—as Holden thinks I should "diversify" and sample the best this place has to offer.

His are informed culinary choices that don't fail to disappoint. I think I have a new favorite with the scampi.

He tells me about his parents, growing up in northeast Portland, how he shares his love of birds with his grandmother. As he talks, I'm trying to ignore the itching that has started along my bra line and across my back. Until I can't anymore.

"Will you excuse me for a sec?" I feel flushed—not the kind that I get from being embarrassed but maybe like I've had too much wine. I won't finish the glass he's just topped up. In the bathroom, I scratch like I need to get to the bone. The *itching* is insane. I wait for my fellow diner to exit before I pull up my blouse.

And see what the hell is going on not only on my back but around the front, across my abdomen, crawling up my neck. Slowly—actually, not so slowly—one giant, pissed-off hive is eating me alive.

I will not panic.

I dampen a towel and blot at my skin, but the inflammation grows before my eyes, coalescing into a red swarm of itchy torture.

If I calm down, maybe sip some water and breathe deeply, I should be able to turn this hive train around. Right?

I've lingered too long. Holden's going to think I've ditched him.

I keep the folded, wet paper towel with me to hold against the growing welts along the back of my hands and wrists. A quick search through my purse reveals nothing even close to an antihistamine, and rightfully so. I have no allergies to anything. Except perhaps the treadmill.

As I walk back to the table, the itching travels down my legs. The backs of my knees feel too fat, like someone has inserted a garden hose and my bendy parts are filling up with hot water. So hot—my entire body is under the influence of an invisible blowtorch.

"Sorry," I say, sitting to gulp my ice water.

"Jayne, are you all right? You're very flushed."

"You know, I'm actually not sure. I'm feeling really weird." My throat feels ... tight. The water almost doesn't want to go down the tube.

His eyes widen as he stares at me. "Your cheeks are blotchy. And your lips. Oh God, do you have any food allergies?" He signals for our waiter. "Something's wrong. We need to get help."

"No. I'm fine. Really. Just give me a sec." But as I speak, my tongue thickens against my palate and I am feeling a little wheezy. And my lips—when the reflection in my very shiny butter knife scares me, I yank a compact out of my handbag.

This is not good. I am not supposed to look like I was ambushed by a psychotic aesthetician bearing a demonic collagen injector.

Within just a few moments, Holden and waitstaff whisk me out of the dining area. We sit in the front of the restaurant, cold towels pressed against my neck and forehead, the restaurant manager adjusting a folding, three-paneled screen so no one can see the Oompa Loompa from table four. "No need to scare anyone," he whispers to Holden.

The ambulance's sirens wail down the block and I think it's probably for someone else—surely Holden can drive me to the hospital for some Benadryl. After all, he has his Zipcar tonight. Only when the front doors to the restaurant open and the blue-clad EMTs hurry in do I realize the sirens were all for little old swollen me.

This is why I don't date. Well, among another four hundred and twelve reasons.

The medics assess my vitals and ask a bunch of questions. I am feeling quite lightheaded at this point and my tongue, so thick in my mouth, makes breathing an interesting challenge. Holden answers when they ask my name as the female EMT cannot understand what I'm saying.

"Miss Dandy, do you have any allergies to medication?"

I shake my head no and try to tell her that I don't have any allergies to *anything*, but she can't understand me. And given the state of my flesh and face at this very moment, it's obvious that I am definitely allergic to something.

A stab in my thigh is followed by the grossest rushing-thudding-barfy feeling I have ever experienced. Thankfully, they do it in the back of the ambulance out of sight of the other patrons who've become increasingly curious with the commotion in the restaurant's waiting area. When I roll around like a whiny toddler, I don't even care if Holden sees me. I just want this feeling to go away.

Satan, thy name is epinephrine.

"I feel like I'm dying," I whisper to the medic. She laughs quietly and pats my hand as she takes my pulse. She makes sure I'm holding on to the paper basin in case I do indeed throw up. Which I might. God, I hope I don't choke to death in the back of this ambulance with Holden waiting right outside the ambulance doors.

"You'll feel better in a few minutes. We're going to transport you to Emmanuel and get some fluids going. Let the docs look you over. You've got a great reaction going on here." She smiles.

Great for whom, exactly?

I keep my eyes closed during the short journey. Fabulous. My first date in forever ends in an ambulance ride. The rocking motion of the truck teases my unsettled belly. When my darling EMT (I think she said her name was Rebecca or Renee or Randi) chatters via the radio and gets the okay from hospital staff to give me something for the nausea, I consider kissing her on the mouth. Which would be big thanks coming from Jaynie Prudie.

The next two hours go as well as can be expected. I'm swollen like a tick and while they don't give me any more of that terrible epinephrine, they won't let me go home until the swelling retreats. Holden sits rigid against his chair back, his eyes wide and darting about as we listen to the moaning, sad, sick people in adjacent curtained-off beds.

He stands long enough to squirt more hand sanitizer from the pump on the bedside cart. "I hate hospitals," he whispers.

Gosh, I love them.

I've tried calling Gretchen about nine times—no idea where she is tonight but I really could use her here instead of Holden. When he's pumped enough Purell to sanitize a Marburg outbreak, he dozes off. At least he followed me to the hospital, though. Not every guy would do that.

Just as another nurse comes in with more ice and to check the swelling around my face, Holden's phone rings. He jolts awake and holds up a hand to excuse himself through my curtain, though his absence is short-lived.

"Jayne, I am so sorry. I have to go. That was my nana, and her budgies got out—the neighbor cat has the birds cornered in their apartment laundry room, and if I don't go ..."

He's going to leave me here to go rescue some birds?

"Oh. Okay. Sure."

"You gonna be okay?"

I hoist the glass of ice chips.

"I'll call and check on you." He smiles and gives my knee an awkward pat, and then poof. Gone.

To save budgies.

Delightful. He takes me to a restaurant that almost kills me, and then bolts to save some stupid birds.

I call Gretchen again. Still no answer. What is the point of having a best friend if she is never bloody around when I need her?

"Your friend left in a hurry," the nurse says when she comes back. She has cotton balls and Band-Aids in hand. "We're going to go ahead and take the IV out and see how you do." She holds up a blister pack with two pills in it. "Benadryl, extra strength. Take one in two hours and then another four hours after that."

I nod.

"And take it easy this weekend. No work. Dr. Cates will give you a note if you need it. The epinephrine and other medicines we gave you tonight will make you feel crummy for a bit. You should sleep tomorrow. Do you have someone you can call to come give you a ride home?"

My eyes burn with tears. I do, but she's not answering my calls. "Yes. I can call someone."

Thumbing through my contacts, my finger hovers first over Sheila Dandy's number—but I really don't want to call her. It's late and I do not have the mental fortitude to deal with her drama right now. I could call my dad, but according to Sheila's latest text, he is now out of the country with his "whore secretary."

I call Maggot. It goes to voicemail.

Same with Frankie.

Where is everyone in my life and why do they suck so hard?

And then I see his number. It's after eleven. I could let it ring four times, and if he doesn't answer, I'll call a cab. I think my credit card has enough space on it for cab fare. I hope.

It's ringing.

Two.

Three.

My thumb hovers to disconnect.

"Hello?"

"Luke? It's Jayne."

"Hey ... hi. How—what time is it?"

"It's a little after eleven. Did I wake you?"

"Yeah, but that's cool. Are you all right? You sound stuffed up."

"I'm actually, uh, at the hospital."

I hear shuffling in the background. "What? Are you okay? Did you get in an accident?"

"Well, funny story. I was having dinner with Holden and I had an allergic reaction to something we ate, and here I am, at Emmanuel, doing my best Angelina Jolie impression."

"Oh my God, that's terrible."

"Yeah. I'm sorry to be calling but I can't seem to find Gretchen, and my sister and brother aren't answering."

"Wait—where's Holden?"

"He ... had an emergency. He had to go."

"He had a bigger emergency than you being hospitalized for anaphylaxis?"

Now that he mentions it, it does sound pretty ridiculous that Holden left me here. But I don't want to get into a deeper explanation.

"I was just sort of curious if I could get ... a ride home."

"Sure. Yeah, absolutely. Let me throw some clothes on and I'll be there in twenty. You still in the ER?"

"Yeah," I say, surprised by the sudden surge of tears in my throat. "Thank you, Luke."

"See you soon. Don't die before I get there, okay?"

I smile through the tear tumbling down my cheek. It disappears into the white sheet and I realize the evening wasn't a total loss—I still have the fingernail polish in place.

Score one for Jayne.

18

WHEN I FINALLY PASS FINAL inspection by the ER doctor and am released, poor Luke has been waiting in the reception area for over an hour. And yet his smile gives no indication that he is anything other than happy to see me.

"Hey, Jayne Dandy. You're looking well," he says, offering an arm for my still unstable shuffle. The heels are tight around my puffy feet, but I just need to get to the truck and then I can take them off.

Luke drills me on the ride home about what I ate at dinner, trying to narrow down the allergic culprit. He tags the shrimp as the most likely offender—same as the ER doc—but given Luke's experience in the kitchen, he doesn't rule out oils or spices that could've been added to the dish, especially considering I've never had shrimp issues before.

"I'm just glad Holden figured out what was going on and they called for help," he says. "Food allergies are dangerous."

He's glad I lived. As stupid as it sounds, that makes me feel warm and fuzzy. In a good way. Not in a scary, I-need-more-epinephrine way.

Luke helps me up the stairs and unlocks the apartment. I'm

drowsy and I really just want bed. I need a shower, but the nurse said to wait until morning so the hot water doesn't aggravate the hives.

I almost forget about the Jaina Jacen stuff plastered all over the place.

"Wait!" I turn on Luke, practically shoving him into the still-open door. "Um, Quack—my cat—she's a bit unstable. You can't come in."

"What?"

"Like, I'm afraid she will attack you." I put my hand against his chest to keep him just far enough back that he can't see the drawings or flow charts or the shiny new 20x24 poster of *Resist Me Not*'s cover taped to the far wall.

"My tetanus shot is up to date," he says, smiling.

"Right, I know. Uh, Gretchen's last boyfriend had to have part of his finger sewn back on after one of Quack's temper tantrums." This is totally a lie. I must remember to tell Gretchen so she can just nod and say *Oh yes it was terrible so much blood poor fellow.*

"Okay, well, I'll have my phone nearby. Call me if you need anything else," he says, backing into the hall.

"Luke—thank you. So much."

"Anytime, Dandy. I'll call you tomorrow and check in."

"You don't have to."

"I want to." He pauses and his lip tugs a little. "I'll look forward to seeing you when you've let the air out of your tires." He points to my swollen feet and then turns with a small wave and leaves.

I feel like a jerk for not inviting him in, but I'm not ready to explain The Wall of Sexy Vagina Funtime to anyone yet. And he, of all people, would totally recognize the origins of the name Jaina Jacen. But to explain how non-geek Gretchen came up with such a name—I'll have to concoct something about how I made up her pen name for her and hope that Luke buys it.

I make up stories all the time, right? Telling a few little white lies isn't really lying—I'm simply storytelling to protect myself from total humiliation.

Luke hates liars, Jaynie. Liar liar pants on fire.

Shut up, mean voice. Take your Benadryl and stop picking on me. Besides, he's one to talk, isn't he?

The door to Gretchen's room opens. When I see the flicker of light against the darkened walls, I know she's got the candles going. The heady smell of fake fruit confirms it.

Carnal sleepover.

A tall, dark-haired man in a wrinkled button-down stands partially bent over while Gretchen's long, bare arms wrap around his neck. The slobbery sounds of smooching follows.

Oh, come on. She couldn't help me tonight because she was getting her girly bits massaged?

I clear my throat.

Surprised, they look in my direction.

"Hey, Jaynie," Gretchen coos. "This is Eric."

"Hi, Eric."

"You—you look kinda terrible." Gretchen steps out of Eric's embrace and moves toward me. I stop her before she can flick on the hall light. "What the hell happened?"

"Don't you ever answer your phone?"

She smiles and looks over her shoulder briefly at her post-coital companion. "I was *busy*, so I turned it off."

"Well, I had an anaphylactic reaction to dinner and have been at the hospital all night. I tried calling you but finally had to call Luke for a ride home."

"What? Where's Holden?"

"Budgie emergency."

Eric snickers.

"I don't know if I want to know what that means, but I am so sorry." She wraps an arm around my shoulder. "Eric, darling, good seeing you. There's the door. I'll call you, 'K?" The smile drips off his face like melting wax, and he slowly steps toward the front door, as if unsure if she's kidding.

She blows him a kiss and shepherds me into my room, closing the door behind us. A growl vibrates from under the bed.

"It's your mommies, Quack. Chill out," Gretchen says. "She tried to kill Eric so I locked her in here." Gretchen helps me out of my clothes, spinning me around to have a look at the red patchwork on my back. "I don't know what it looked like before, but this is something else."

I pivot for a view in the closet mirror. "It's definitely better," I say as Gretchen shimmies the jammies over my head. "And I got to go in an ambulance."

"Was that fun?" she says, smiling.

"Not fun."

"Did they at least give you a lollipop?"

"No lollipops." I climb into bed and Gretchen tucks my rubber-duck-printed fleece blanket under my chin. Sheila Dandy's suitcase full of my childhood literary efforts sits in the corner laughing at me. I looked through it a couple days after her appearance at the food truck. As I'm already feeling sorry for myself, I indulge in wallowing further—my mother doesn't love me enough to hang on to figments of my youth.

Gretchen sees where my teary eyes have landed. "I'm sorry I wasn't there for you," she says, patting my hand.

"It's fine," I say, wiping an errant tear. "So ... Eric ...?"

"He has a beautiful body. His wiener is kinda on the small side, but he's good with his—"

"That's enough."

"You're an enigma, Jayne Dandy. You can write about it but you don't want to hear about it in real life?"

"You're like my sister, Gretchen. Hearing that someone has his hands on—or in—you is ... weird."

"Oh, and he had his hands all over me." Her grin is wicked. "Sleep now. I'll have my phone on. And tomorrow we can spend all day strategizing how to take over the literary world."

"Will there be cookies?"

"I will get you cookies."

"Thanks, G." She moves toward the door. "Don't forget to blow out your sex candles so we don't burn down tonight," I add.

"Good night, Stay Puft."

"Oh—Gretchen—if Luke asks you about one of your boyfriends having his finger sewn back on post-Quack attack, just nod and agree. 'K?"

"Yes, Madame Storyteller. But you do know that getting Luke Piewalker into your bed would do wonders for your complexion."

I lob my stuffed Yoda at her and let the Benadryl carry me someplace soft, where Calamine lotion tumbles in frothy waterfalls and Luke Piewalker stands atop the bridge, fluffy, cherry-topped cupcakes in hand.

EIDER: CHAPTER 9

by Jaina Jacen (October)

Three sunrises from last night?

That means two more after today's.

Where are we going? What does he know that I do not? How will we get away?

Taisa is slower to return to the chamber than I am, but she still catches me with the small, creased paper clutched in my fingers.

"What is it, My Sovereign? Your face is colored."

I cannot show this to anyone, not even Taisa.

Her stealth, while usually undervalued, will not get me out of the compound undetected. Not this time. I need blood from a Class III's finger to unlock the bioreaders on the compound's exterior doors. Taisa's blood will not work—surely they'll be watching her closely. But I have coins to spare, and underpaid allies who work in the compound. Surely one of them will help me.

"Nothing. Just a silly note," I say, hastily refolding it.

"In the passageway, one of my cousins stopped me. With news."

Her eyes are wide, bordering on frightened. "Continue ..."

"*Your friend Mooney—*"

"*Is he hurt? Is he dead?*" *My mouth and throat parch against the coming revelation.*

"*No, he's in detention but is expected to be released without additional charge. Thanks to your father.*"

"*Ohhhh, that is a relief.*"

"*But that's not all.*"

"*We were only parted for a few moments, Taisa—how could you possibly have gathered so much news?*"

"*My Sovereign, he is to be married.*"

19

WHY AM I SO NERVOUS?

Gretchen's trunk is packed with our first-ever order of paperback books, Sharpies, the swag and promotional items she ordered, the book-cover poster, and some ginormous cookies she picked up at Costco. Her nails and hair and outfit are perfect, and she is calm and unruffled while I run around the apartment, making sure we haven't forgotten anything and hiding any exposed cords so that Quack doesn't electrocute herself again.

"Jayne, everything will be fine," Gretchen says, blotting her lipstick in the hall mirror. "They're going to love us."

"What if they don't?"

She turns and showcases her immaculate self. "Darling, your words have never had a truer, more devoted fan than the one standing before you. I promise to do you justice."

"Right. Okay."

"Also, the cat." She points above me. "You should move."

I look up, and sure enough, Quack is poised on the edge of the tallest bookcase, her one eye assessing my skull like it's a rib-eye steak seasoned with catnip.

"I'm taking you with me to see Dr. McCoy, you beast," I say, stepping aside.

"After you, Miss Jacen," I say. Gretchen curtsies and tiptoes down the stairs. I lock the deadbolt and give the door a solid tug, although for a brief second, forehead against the cold wood, I consider unlocking and sneaking back into my room. Gretchen can handle this thing on her own, right?

Dusk comes early in the Pacific Northwest autumn. Surely there is nothing as beautiful as a twilight unsure of what to do with itself—thick white and gray clouds obscure only part of a purplish-blue sky that continues to put up a fight. And the trees? Like someone spilled paint and it splattered reds and oranges and deep yellows against oaks and vine maples and ash and poplar and birch and Washington hawthorns.

The rain is sporadic and noncommittal as we unload the car, or rather, as *I* unload the car with the help of one of the bookstore clerks. Gretchen doesn't want to get dirty or ruin her newly styled hair, so she disappears into the back room to hang out with the store manager and sip tiny cups of espresso until her adoring fans arrive.

By the time the display and chairs are set up, swag is arranged, cookies plated, I'm sweating under my light sweater and am ready for a nap. I've suffered no lasting effects from last week's charming allergic experience, although Holden is so embarrassed about how the evening turned out, he delivered a fruit basket—certified organic, no allergens!—with a bouquet of tiny rubber ducks dressed in scrubs and stethoscopes. He also made a coupon that is redeemable for "One Ginormous Want or Need," as in, I say the word, he's at my beck and call. If I happen to lose a budgie in the next little while, this will come in handy.

Luke even surprised me by calling both Saturday and Sunday to check in, and he's been easy on me all week during my afternoons at the food truck, making sure I take breaks and drink plenty of water. Working at Piewalker's isn't physically demanding necessarily, although it's not uncommon to work up a sheen serving food and doing dishes.

And while Tiana hasn't shown up in the last little while, it still niggles at me. Are they together? Are they not? Is he really still interested in her and therefore, my unrelenting attraction is all for naught? Should I ask him about it? How does a person even meander into a conversation like that?

"Jayne, right?" the store manager says, pulling me back to present. "You can wait back here with the staff in case we need more chairs." She talks to me like I'm on her payroll, which is fine—I'm here to support Gretchen because she is supporting me. But it does feel ... weird. Those people are shuffling into the fold-up chairs to hear my words. They're Instagramming and tweeting pictures of themselves next to the book posters because I spent the hours hiding under my covers with my *Star Wars*-inspired flashlight to make my imaginary couples court, copulate, cohabitate, and commiserate. My pretend people have lived only in the space between my brain and my hand's ability to write down words for so long, and now they're out in the wild. Frankly, I'm having a hard time wrapping my head around it. Especially when I'm adding more chairs to the back row while Gretchen stands backstage applying another layer of lip gloss.

This was your choice, Jayne.

Yes. I realize that.

And as the crowd of two turns into thirty-two, the dampness in my underarms and across my top lip makes me so glad that Gretchen is the one who has to stand before this audience in her fancy shoes and freshly waxed legs and read the sexy vagina funtime words *out loud*.

I hate myself for being such a chicken.

Speaking of chicken, my stomach growls. Loudly. A woman in front of me turns in her chair and smiles tightly at my midsection.

I tiptoe backward to the refreshments table and stuff a cookie into my sleeve. Between the rows pertaining to architecture and Roman art, I inhale deeply—who doesn't love the smell of a bookstore?—and watch as Gretchen takes her place on the makeshift stage, says a few introductory words, and flips open the paperback.

We're going to have to work on her reading technique if this becomes a regular thing. Gretchen is a great flirt, though, her subtle hair toss and necklace fondle charming to men and women alike.

A group of four in the third row—one of them looks familiar. I know that hair, that head.

She turns her face to smile and whisper to her friend.

Oh my dear God, my sister is here.

What the hell is Dr. Maggot doing at a book reading, for a sexy funtime book? Margaret reads what she deems "important fiction" that wins awards and that people debate in columns and on boring Sunday morning television. She reads medical journals about the efficacy of salicylic acid on comedones and the best treatment courses for basal versus squamous cell carcinomas.

Oh no, no, no. She can't be here. She's going to hear these words and—

Wait. She doesn't know it's me. She thinks it's Gretchen. Which is the point of all this.

I've squeezed the cookie so hard, the chocolate chips have melted all over my fingers. I lick them clean, transfixed as I watch Maggot's reaction. Maybe she'll smile or giggle or snicker like she used to do when we'd sleep in one another's rooms and watch Disney movies all night (long live *The Lion King*) and she'd throw me a topic and I'd weave her the most ridiculous tale I could.

Gretchen makes it through the preselected pages. Gentle applause. People are smiling. Even Maggot is flashing her pearly veneers. Gretchen launches into our rehearsed speech about the next book—and how "it is now uploaded and ready for action!" met with excited tittering—where she "sees" the series going, and then she opens the floor to questions. My stomach knots. What if someone asks her something we haven't rehearsed? She said she can fake it. In fact, she told me she's very good at faking a lot of things. Which is why she hasn't returned the twelve calls on her voicemail from that Eric guy. Reportedly, she had to fake her way through that whole evening.

As long as she can fake her way through the next fifteen minutes —preferably without moaning or touching body parts—until I can throw cookies at people, we're golden.

The regular questions: *where do you get your inspiration, where do you write, do you listen to music when you write, do you have a boyfriend/husband/partner, and if so, what does he/she think about your books.*

Gretchen has these answers.

She doesn't have this one: "Your main character, Miranda, spends a fair amount of time studying endangered waterfowl and working to save threatened animals. Do you have a favorite animal that you want to help save?"

Our eyes meet across the distance. Gretchen failed biology in high school. She had to take an online biology course just to get the credits for graduation. Her brain, for whatever reason, does not hold on to animal facts like it does designer shoe and purse facts. She thought that Greenpeace was some new indie band, and that the World Wildlife Fund was a toy company that made adorable stuffed polar bears and monkeys. Which is sort of true, I suppose.

Frantic, I scan the shelves around me. Kids' section—a rack of plastic animal figurines. Meerkat—she won't know that one. Mandrill, nope. Otter, no—she won't know the difference between river and sea. Elephant! Perfect. It's big and she knows this one.

I hoist the figurine above my head.

"You know, with that part of the story, I really wanted Miranda to explore something I wasn't entirely familiar with, so I did a lot of research, but my own personal favorite animal is the elephant. I'd love to do more to help save elephants."

Smooth as silk, Gretchen stands and thanks the audience for their time and offers to sign books or e-reader covers after everyone has helped themselves to cookies and coffee.

My sister's eyes about pop out of her head when she sees me. I relish the smile inching across my lips.

"Hey, little sister," she says, fluffing her hair. "What are you doing here?"

"Gretchen's assistant," I say. "Better yet, what are *you* doing here?" Margaret's cheeks flame up.

"Girls' night out. I wanted to go to the art museum but it wasn't my night to choose." She casually hides the paperback book in her hand behind her back. "I'm surprised you're here when she's reading this sort of content out loud."

"Well, you know, gotta grow up sometime."

Gretchen approaches from our left. "Maggot! Good to see you," she says, air-kissing my sister's cheeks.

"It's Margaret, thanks."

Gretchen ignores her. "So did you enjoy the reading? I see you have a book there—shall I sign it for you?" She is positively radiant; my sister is trying not to be mortified as she hands over the paperback. "Who do I make this out to?"

"No one. Just your signature is fine." She looks at me. "Jaynie never mentioned that you were writing books."

"I was keeping it on the down-low, until I had books to talk about. And we—I—never expected these stories to take off like this!"

"They're doing well, then?"

"You're here, aren't you?" Gretchen smiles and pinches Margaret's cheek. When Gretchen hands back the signed paperback, she turns to me. "You are never going to guess what just happened."

She doesn't wait for me to guess. "See that woman over there, in the fishnets? She's the organizer and promoter for the second annual Spicy and Sweet Sexhibition at the Oregon Convention Center. It's a giant convention for sex! Like sex toys and sexy clothes and pole dancers and marital enhancement and sex doctors who come in and talk about improving your sex life and—"

"Yes, and?" I say. Gretchen is saying "sex" too often and too loud given the close quarters. Even my sister shifts uncomfortably in her Vuitton kitten heels.

"And they've invited us—me—to do a reading! At the convention!"

"Wow. Really?" I'm not sure if this is good or not. I think it's good? "When is it?"

"The Saturday after Thanksgiving. How cool is this? She said the minute she found out Jaina Jacen was a local author, she just had to have me read at the show. They're going to do a shit ton of marketing in the next few weeks because we're sort of late to the game, but she said she loved *Resist Me Not*, AND she downloaded *Tempt Me Softly* just now and says she has to go home this second and read in the bathtub. Isn't that so amazing?" Gretchen is bouncing up and down. Her boobs catch the eye of one of three males in the room as he waits to get his cookie.

"Yes. This is great."

"You totally have to come, Magg—Margaret. She said she'd give me free tickets, so I'll hold one aside for you."

"Oh, no, that's all right. Not really my thing. And Thanksgiving weekend, I think I'm skiing."

"You're not going to Mom and Dad's for dinner?" If she's not going, then I'm not going.

"We can talk about this later," Maggot says quietly.

"Well, you can always let Jaynie know," Gretchen interjects as the store manager beckons from across the room. "I gotta go. Great seeing you. Love the shoes. Send me your size and I'll get you some samples from fashion week." Gretchen kisses my sister's face again— which means she's kissed my own sister more in the last three minutes than I have in the past fifteen years—and flits off to meet her adoring fans.

"You look pale, Jayne. Have you had your iron checked lately? Oh, and call Mom," Maggot says, before rejoining her friends.

I move back to the architecture section where I left my melted cookie. Wiping chocolate off the wooden shelf with my sleeve, I watch as Gretchen soaks in accolades my fear has prevented me from collecting.

And try to ignore the clucking chicken echoing inside my head.

20

WITHIN THE FIRST TEN DAYS, the sales of *Tempt Me Softly*, Temptation Series #2, shoots us to the top of the sales charts. And the first book is selling like hotcakes as more and more people discover what is slowly becoming a series. Gretchen says we're receiving emails from agents in New York City, as well as publicists who want to "talk about our options" for future marketing efforts.

Gretchen is also nagging me about the third book. Which has paralyzed me and now I have writer's block or what I think might be writer's block because I'm totally freaked out that I have to write *another* book that people will be seeing and what if they don't love the third one like they're loving the first two and I may have used all my sexy funtime words and I'm having a hard time—excuse the pun —finding another word for "manhood" that doesn't sound weird and stinky and I think the performance anxiety is killing my mojo and I wonder if there is Viagra for writers.

The fretting consumes my mornings, the time I've set aside to write new material, establishing what I fear is a dangerous pattern. By the time I'm home from afternoons at the food truck, my brain is only capable of handling minute tasks: eat, shower, give Quack her kitty Prozac, stare blankly at the morning's pages, or lack thereof. Lately I've been spending more time with the folks of Eider—no pressure equals no writer's block.

But it's Tuesday, writers' group night, and Gretchen will not let me skip out. Says I have to be there to absorb all the positive energy because everyone's going to be "so effing excited" to see how well we're doing.

I hate to burst her bubble, but they're going to hate Gretchen, and by association, me, for Jaina Jacen's early success. Especially Suzette. I check her books now and again. Let's just say that if rankings are any indication of sales, she won't be hiring that plastic surgeon anytime soon.

"Don't let me forget to grab the pastries on the counter," Gretchen yells from her bedroom. Mmmm, she said "pastry."

"Did Luke do these?" I answer back, a twinge of jealousy biting at my jiggling thighs. I open the unfamiliar pink box and am greeted by—"Oh my God, Gretchen, *really?*" The pastries, in the form of white-glazed penises with cherry testicles, are definitely not from Piewalker's.

"Aren't they adorable?" she says, fastening her earring as she walks in. "Is that what you're wearing?"

"Jeans are fine."

"And the shirt?"

"What's wrong with the Death Star?"

"How can I be best friends with such a nerd?"

"I've been asking myself that for about nineteen years." Gretchen grabs a gauzy scarf from the back of the couch and wraps it around my neck.

"Less hopeless now."

Gretchen makes me sit with the pastries on my lap so the box doesn't shuffle across the back seat, claiming that the testicles will roll off their assigned members and then we will have balls all over the place. She then proceeds to tell me she was going to have little vaginas made to go along but that would've been an extra fifty dollars because of the short notice.

"I'm sure the ... thingies ... will be a hit," I say.

"Say it."

"Gretchen, come on, I'm tired."

"SAY IT."

"No."

"Come on, Jaynie, say the magic word."

"I'm sure the PENISES will be a hit."

"You did it!" A truck behind us honks when she swerves in her effort to high-five.

"Please, don't kill us."

"Especially not tonight. I have something extra special planned."

"More special than trying to guess Suzette's menu choices from today based on whatever is stuck to her sweater?"

"Oh God, I am never having babies if that's what they do to my clothes." She turns right without warning; I strain against the inertia. "No, I *mean*, tonight I have a special surprise lined up for everyone. Beth and I have been in cahoots. I think you'll like it." Evil glints in her eye. Surely Satan is looking up from his flaming compound, so proud of his naughtiest spawn.

"What did you do?"

Her grin widens.

"Gretchen Frances Marlowe, what did you *do*?"

"Your therapist will thank me. And I am saying nothing more until we get there." She pretends to lock her lips and cranks the stereo.

I should be nervous—Gretchen's pranks are always embarrassing—but I'm exhausted. In addition to the morning visits with my anxieties as I stare at the blinking cursor, followed by afternoons washing dishes and smiling for customers and trying not to think too hard about what Luke will be doing after work, Sheila Dandy has been plying more of her magic. She didn't stop at cleaning out my father's office—she also put all of his clothes in black plastic bags and tossed them on to the lawn. Apparently my dad came to the house to retrieve everything, a fight ensued, the police were called, and I was summoned to sit with my mother until she calmed down. Margaret was Mom's first choice; however, she was tied up excising fleshy moles so Darling Mother had to settle for me.

Fortunately no one was arrested, but that hasn't diluted the venom of Sheila Dandy's attacks. Her most recent text messages come all hours of the night, riddled with mistakes that tell me she's plastered, and the recipients' list has blown up to include my dad's closest colleagues and even his clients. She must've found a phone list while tearing apart his office. Last night's message included the drunken declaration that Dad has been formally uninvited to our annual Thanksgiving extravaganza. Then she texted me alone asking why Gretchen is writing porn.

Fun times.

But really, it's sad. All of it. Knowing their divorce is imminent is tough enough, but watching my mother's insidious implosion makes the situation so much more pathetic. And my efforts to sit and pet her hair and make her tea are met with spite and anger. Sheila Dandy's tongue is forked on a good day; with this latest turn of events, she's downright deadly.

And Holden ... darling Holden. He's texted me no fewer than four times in the last four days, every time asking for a redo of our failed evening, and every time I tell him that we'll figure something out. Honestly, I really need to be left alone to get my head on straight and write some words.

Gretchen pulls up in front of Beth's. Just in time. We were almost at the chorus for "Dream On," and my ears cannot handle any more of Gretchen's murderous musical stylings this evening. Poor Steven Tyler—if only he knew what Gretchen was doing to his masterpiece.

"Can you carry that in? I don't want to get anything on my jacket," Gretch says without waiting for my answer.

The second the front door opens, we're met with hoots and hollers and hugs. Beth and the woman with the too-tight ponytail and the other gal with the dirty feet (I really should learn their names) are so excited for Gretchen, cooing about her outfit and how they had no idea she had so much clever material up her sleeve and *why didn't you tell us you've been holding out you she-devil.*

I find Suzette in the kitchen, wine glass in hand, another stained sweater. Something orange. Squash? Carrot? I know when Gretchen dog-sits her mother's Pekingese, we have to feed her pumpkin so she can poop easier. Something about anal glands. Maybe the same is true for triplets?

"How are you, Suzette?"

"Fine."

"We brought pastries." I slide the box on to the counter, listening to the giggles moving from the foyer into the living room. "You might like 'em." I sorta feel bad for Suzette. I didn't mean to steal her thunder by publishing my books, and I can't even fess up and offer consolation. But the looks she's shooting in Gretchen's direction confirm that any words I might say would fall on deaf ears.

I lift the pastry-box lid. All the testicles are still in place. Scooping an intact piece out, I offer it to Suzette.

She looks at the tiny glazed wiener cake stretched across my palm. "I'm gluten-free, but thanks," she says, sulking past.

Well, shit. I can't very well put it back in the box now that I've touched it.

As the other gals are still preoccupied, I quickly shove the pastry into my mouth, but it's actually longer than I expected and the cherries are hanging against my lips when Beth comes into the kitchen.

"Well, well! Seems Jayne is having a party of one!" she announces. I chew as fast as I can and shove the cherries in, shame pinking my cheeks. She lifts the box lid and claps her hands. "If you think these are fun, just wait until you see what we have going on in the other room."

This is gonna be bad.

Beth hands me a filled wine glass and tucks her arm through

mine, practically dragging me into the living room. On the glass coffee table that wasn't here last time is spread ...

A ton of sex toys.

Large silicone penises in pretty pinks and purples, some with pearls in their, uh, shafts, with rabbit-shaped secondary heads and remote controls and smaller dongs in a rainbow of colors and frilled whips and multipronged things that I assume are vibrators and little bottles of lube and tubs of body chocolate and ...

I feel faint.

Gretchen moves to my side and eases me into a padded chair.

Beth stands before the group, wine glass filled to the rim. "In honor of Jaina Jacen, aka Gretchen, and her mad success with the Temptation Series novels, we're having an in-home party to celebrate! Like Tupperware without the stifling, '50s-housewife oppression. Orgasms for everyone!" She hoists her glass. Everyone—except Suzette—follows suit.

I put my head between my knees.

Yes, I know I'm being a hypocrite. I can *write* this stuff, I can think about it in the safety of my own head, I can take the money from people who read my words. I'm nothing more than a voyeur.

But that doesn't mean I want to think about all of the women in this room sticking these—things—into areas only partners and gynecologists should see. Dr. McCoy said I have to become more comfortable with the idea that an orgasm is a completely natural occurrence, but *seriously*, that doesn't mean I need to be in this living room, listening to these women talk openly about G-spots and whether they've tried anal and if they have, what it was like (what about ... poop?) and the best public places to get off and if anyone has had success with the little bullet thingie that you control with your smartphone.

Oh my God, too-tight ponytail lady launches into a story about how she uses the smartphone bullet during long meetings just to stay awake. How does *that* work? "This quarter's earnings are ohhhhhh ... yessssss ... earnings! Go, fourth quarter, goooooo!"

And then Beth decides that it would be best if we all touched the toys so we can get a real assessment of their battery power and "vibrational velocity." One remarkably virile toy has a demo mode with a simulated moaning. The crowd goes wild.

I need to leave. Before that ginormous dark purple penis makes its way on to my—

Aaaaand there it is. I hold my hands up as if at gunpoint, begging Gretchen with my eyes to take it off my lap. Like the biggest, hairiest, meanest tarantula you've ever seen, except it's not a spider—it's a purple penis. A huge, purple dong of frightening girth with scary veins sculpted into its length.

Whatever foreign country is responsible for making these— because I cannot touch it to check for a *Made in America* sticker—I am so sorry. Not all Americans are perverts.

Gretchen picks it up and passes it to my right. I'm up, grab my bag, coat on, transit pass in hand.

"Jaynie, it's okay, come on," Gretchen coos, stroking my upper arms.

"Yeah, it's fine. I'm just gonna go. I'm tired."

"I thought maybe you'd find this fun."

"Everyone seems to be having a lovely time." I pull on my second boot. "I'll see you later at home?"

"But it's a party. You should stay," she says, lowering her voice. "It's good for you. Like exposure therapy. Right? Isn't that what Dr. McCoy would say?"

My hand's on the doorknob. "Gretchen, sitting in a living room with a bunch of horny women playing with pretend dicks is not my idea of exposure therapy. I'll see you in a few hours."

During my walk to the MAX station, my anger rises—at myself for being so goddamned weird, at Gretchen for putting me in this situation, at the fact that if I don't figure out a way to get past this, I'm never going to be able to partake in what the rest of the adult population seems to enjoy. What is wrong with me?

That burning question has infected so many aspects of my life—

you don't have a boyfriend at your age? *What's wrong with you?* You have a college education but you ended up with such a crappy job? *What's wrong with you?* You say you like men but you're afraid to let them touch your boobies? *What's wrong with you?*

It was one thing for the kids in junior high to call me Jaynie Prudie, but why am I still hanging on to the bullshit those dumb old women spewed in that church basement? I am an intelligent, rational person—I know that no one is watching me in the darkness of my bedroom, except maybe the government, and that's because the government is creepy.

I don't even have a real reason to be so afraid. I've never been assaulted. No one has ever hurt me. It's all just the totally illogical crap that cycles through my ridiculous head.

The stories I write? That's how I wish it could be. Romantic and tender and understanding and safe. No one gets embarrassed, he won't laugh at the dimples in my thighs or tease because one boob is bigger than the other. There are no strange sounds or smells that will freak either of us out. I won't worry if some invisible entity is watching and judging me to burn for eternity in the fires of hell. Even Shakespeare said that lust itself is an act desired before and shamed after.

I can't win here.

The first and only sexual encounter I had was disastrous for both me and my poor partner who wasn't able to hang on to himself once he ... Right. Technically, therefore, I am not a virgin but that little encounter certainly isn't fodder for any of Jaina Jacen's stories, unless she's writing a tragedy.

Perfect sex is a fairy tale.

Rush hour over, I'm granted a seat on the train. A cute couple with matching glasses across from me cozies into one another; another guy with dreadlocks and one of those fold-up bikes stands bobbing his head to whatever tunes are spilling from his earbuds. An old woman in a plaid coat, wig askew, hugs her purse protectively, her wheeled fabric shopping cart frayed along one side, threatening to spill its contents. Our light rail system is a quiet ride, and after the chaos of today, I'm soothed.

I lean my head against the window and close my eyes, walking through everything I need to get done, wondering what new situations I can throw Miranda and Alec into that they haven't already overcome. The subtle vibration against my side suggests that my phone is going off in my coat pocket. I ignore it. I need a moment's peace.

Only the vibration doesn't cease. And then it's followed with a woman's voice.

Moaning.

Louder. Louder still. "Ohhhhhh, yesssssss. Ohhhhh God! Ohhhh GOD! Yes! Yes! Yesssss! Right there! Yessssss!"

It sounds like a porn is playing, muffled but clear enough.

A mother clamps her hands over her small son's ears and gives me a dirty look.

Holy shit, that sound is coming from me. From *my* bag.

No. No. No. This isn't happening.

I open the bag and it gets louder. The young couple across from me giggles. The old lady looks like she might stroke out. At least dreadlocked guy is oblivious, until he plucks an earbud out of his head and catches on to what everyone else is hearing.

All eyes are on me.

Someone has put one of those talking demo-dongs in my bag. *Where is the fucking off switch?*

The thing with the train, it's not a like a bus. You can't just pull the dinger and drop yourself off on any random street corner. You're stuck until you get to the next station.

Me, stuck with a moaning vibrator.

"It was just a party joke," I say sheepishly. I have to turn it off. The mom has now scooped up her son and is moving toward the back of the train. The old woman across from me waggles a finger and starts in about how society has gone to the birds.

I look around frantically for a garbage bin to dump it in or perhaps an unsupervised handgun so I can put myself out of my misery.

Dreadlocked guy closes the space between us and sits down next to me, his large tawny hand outstretched. "Let me see if I can turn it off."

The laughter around me, coupled with the lecturing granny, burns my eardrums. It might be melting what's left of my soul.

I slide a hand into my bag and extract the vibrating, rotating, moaning phallus. Jesus, it's huge. The hysterics intensify as more people up and down the train car hear what's going on. *Please, God, if you're going to strike me dead, right now would be good.*

My handsome savior slides a switch inside a tiny panel along the bottom. The moaning quiets. The train erupts in applause.

"Take a bow," he says.

This is so ridiculously humiliating, I have no other choice: I stand up and bow. More clapping. And then I'm laughing too.

He starts to hand the dong back to me.

"No. Please. I don't want it."

He chuckles. "Any takers?" He lifts the penis above his head. Too many hands to count fly up. He gifts it to the couple across the way. Cheers abound as the train doors open and my new friends drift back to their lives, giggling and high-fiving as they pass me on the platform.

EIDER: CHAPTER 10

by Jaina Jacen (October)

"How? So soon?"

"It was a condition of his release. Your father has had a hand in it."

My father is a monster.

"You must get Pollux a message," I say, breathless.

"Pardon me, My Sovereign, but have you seen my face?"

"Yes. I have. And I've apologized. We both knew the risks of leaving the compound, and yet, you didn't try very hard to stop me."

Taisa laughs. "Here we go again. Me try to stop you? You're a mad girl." She makes sure the door is sealed behind her. "If you give me a simple dispatch, I can get it to him. Of course, it has to be carried. Nothing through the System."

"How can you do this?"

She smiles and winks. "If I were to tell you that, My Sovereign, I'd have to poison your tea, now wouldn't I?"

"He cannot marry another. No one should have to marry someone they do not love." Unless he does love her. Whoever she is. Maybe they are longtime companions who have come of age and my father's

meddling is expediting their union. To keep him thus occupied and away from me.

But that's not how it happens. Not with Class I and II citizens. We are paired according to sophisticated algorithms that ensure the strength of our station. How I envy the lowerclasses who are often given freedom to choose their lifemates.

And Pollux Mooney doesn't even know me. Not the grown-up me. Sure, he knows the girl who chased him around the play yard as we conspired against our childminders, the girl who threw sand in his face and raced him to the top of the compound's lookout towers. That was when he was Pollux, and I was Lyrie.

But now he's Mooney, and he's a Class II collector. And I'm being queued and groomed for a silent role in my father's government. Father's heart won't beat forever, despite the medical interventions that promise a protracted life for elders.

It will then be my turn to take over—or rather, my husband's turn.

I don't want that husband.

And I don't necessarily want to marry Mooney. What if he growls and grunts and eats like a horned swine? What if his feet outside their boots smell like forgotten turnips?

No, not marriage. I just want to spend time with him. Why is that so horrible?

If he were in love with another, why would he give me such a note?

"I simply want to talk to him again. I have to see him. Before his marriage carries him far away and out of my life forever."

"Prepare your note ... and I will make sure he gets it before the moons rise."

21

GRETCHEN HAS TAKEN her role as Jaina Jacen very seriously. I don't want her to get in trouble at the paper, though selfishly, I love seeing what she's doing with the books. When I express my concern for what Mr. Clark will think of her frequent absences, she says everyone in the office believes she's shadowing some hot new designer freshly transplanted from Milan. The truth? She's getting situated with a new publicist about a campaign to boost sales of the second book and then plan a grand launch for the third—the one I have yet to write.

As it's a weekday, I should be at the food truck—alas, Leia is filling my shift as my feet presently are in stirrups while the nurse practitioner does her best to warm the speculum that's about to greet my ... yeah. That. I haven't had a Pap in four years. I read an article about cervical cancer being the silent killer. An article I found when I should've been researching my next book.

This tells you about my attention span lately.

Research Australia's indigenous duck populations? No problem! But hey, here's an article about the importance of regular Pap smears. LET'S READ IT.

In between questions about sexual partners—"None," I answer quietly—the NP asks me if I'm enjoying the new fall TV season.

What's a TV, Precious?

The Darth Vader theme rings from my bag. Luke!

I fumble blindly to extract my phone. "Hold still, Jayne," the nurse says. "Almost done."

Too bad. I'm answering this. "Hey!" I say just as the little scraper brush meets my cervix. Ouch.

"You busy right now?" He sounds funny—not *ha-ha* funny but rather *something's not right* funny.

"Um, no. Well, sort of. I won't be busy in about ten minutes, though. What's up?"

"I was calling to see if you were interested in today's hottest scoop."

"Uh, okayyyy." Excitement surges upon hearing his voice. Despite my efforts to the contrary, it does this every time. "Wait—are those sirens? Are you okay?"

"Food truck's on fire. Looks like you get the week off."

I HURRY the nurse to finish the exam. Yes, yes, fine, my boobs are lumpy. Too much caffeine. I'll cut back. Give me my pants—Luke needs me!

I might have run a few yellow lights. The tires only squealed once. Okay, twice. What I would give for a *Starsky & Hutch* police light for the top of my car.

Rounding the corner of his block, I gasp. Acrid black smoke billows into the sky. I pull alongside an empty meter, risking yet another ticket by ignoring the requirement that I feed said meter, and sprint down the block.

Yellow police tape holds back onlookers. Luke and Leia stand against one of the office buildings, talking to two cops. An EMT has Luke's hand cradled open, slathering it with clear gel. My heart tightens—he's hurt?

He sees and waves me through.

"What happened?" I ask. "Are you guys okay?" I ask both siblings but my eyes are on Luke's burned hand.

"His crazy Russian girlfriend is what happened," Leia snipes, wiping tears off her cheek.

"She's not my girlfriend," Luke says to the cop. He then looks at me. "We think it was Tiana. We have no proof yet."

"No proof? Except for the fact that she's Russian and bat-shit crazy and that was a Molotov cocktail—which is Russian—and we could have *died?*" Leia shrieks. She steps off to the side and lights a cigarette. One of her Mohawk'd male companions wraps an arm around her shoulders and whispers against her head.

"She was inside filling pastries when the trailer caught fire," Luke says.

"You're hurt," I say, pointing at this hand.

"Thanks for coming over so quickly. I know you had this morning off ..."

"No, I'm glad you called." Oh man, glad is an understatement.

Luke's hand wrapped, the EMT steps aside so the officers can finish their questions. The fire department makes quick work of extinguishing the food truck—it's devastating. Nothing but a smoldering husk of metal and melted tires. An officer tells Luke they'll tow the remains for evidence, in case it was a Molotov situation. Seems that could be a wee little felony.

Luke's eyes are sad, shoulders hunched, as he watches gallons of water drown his livelihood. When he stares at the curbside carnage, it's like watching his dreams crumble in real time.

"You want to get out of here?" I ask.

The nodding of his downturned head speaks for him.

"My car's this way." He gives Leia the keys to their pickup and a scorched laptop bag. He hugs her close, kisses her cheek. Says he will see her at home later. Such a good big brother.

I'm thrilled to not find a ticket tucked under my windshield wiper. But as he buckles in, I'm even more thrilled that Luke is sitting in my passenger seat.

This is so much better than a Pap smear.

22

WHITAKER NATURE PONDS is in a quiet pocket of Northeast Portland. I love it in the fall, the explosion of color from the trees, how those striking colors reflect off the still pond waters, how bugs flit in to sip and then thrust themselves skyward before a bird ends their journey, how the trails are littered with fallen leaves, and especially how the summer crowds have thinned. No dogs are allowed here, either, which is perfect for watching the colorful wood ducks paddle by. A solitary canoeist has the slough to himself. A busy beaver has recently felled a few small trees along the water's edge, upon which some Mallard couples have roosted to sun themselves in the surprise afternoon cloud break.

"You okay?" I ask, once we're seated on a bench on the observation dock.

"I don't know yet. Still kind of numb."

"What the hell happened?"

"I ran to the corner market to grab some milk and as I came up the block, I heard Leia screaming and saw flames climbing the back of the truck. She'd been inside working when something slammed the backside. She went out to see what was going on, and voila, fire."

"Thank heavens she wasn't hurt." I nod at his hand. "What about you?"

"I went back in to grab my laptop. All of our accounts, spreadsheets, recipes, everything, are on it."

"You got it, then," I say. He handed her the bag as we were leaving.

"Yeah. But I got this too." He lifts his hand.

"I can't believe that the one day I wasn't there, *this* happens."

Luke raises an eyebrow. "Hmmm, maybe that makes you a suspect."

I laugh. "Uh, I have an alibi."

"Oh, yeah? And what is that? Where were you between the hours of eleven and eleven thirty, Miss Dandy?"

I shake my head. "Oh, man ..." I cannot believe I'm going to admit this. "I was actually right in the joyous midst of a Pap smear."

Luke blushes slightly. "Yes. You're right. You definitely have an alibi." He runs a hand over a shy smile.

"Does it hurt? Your hand?"

He doesn't answer. Which means yes. If only I'd known, I could've grabbed painkiller samples from my chatty nurse.

"Everything will be okay. The most important thing is you guys weren't seriously injured. You're insured, right?"

"Yeah. It's just ... shit, what do I do now? And what about you? You're out of a job too."

"Don't worry about me, Luke. I'm just so glad no one was hurt. And for a little bit, you'll be doing paperwork. Making a lot of calls—then you'll get a new truck and we'll get Holden to write an exclusive about your rebirth, and citizens will flock to downtown to taste your wares and share their undying love."

Luke laughs quietly. "That simple, huh?"

"Like a phoenix from the ashes."

His phone rings. It feels so out of place, the jingling of electronica, in the quiet sanctuary of the park. "It's my mom." He answers and launches into reassurances that he's fine, it's just a mild burn,

"Yes, I will go see Dr. Blake" and "Leia's fine. I'll help her find something else to do to stay out of trouble" and "No, Mom, you guys don't need to come up."

Judging by the conversation, the Walkers are a close family, despite their geographic distance. With the next response, he looks at me and his eyes crinkle into a smile. "She's just a friend, Mom. Her name is Jayne. She's the one who's been working with me at the truck." Pause. He pushes the phone to the side. "My mom says hi."

"Hello, Mrs. Walker," I say.

"I don't know her feelings about giving you grandchildren, Mom. We're friends. That seems a little weird to ask at this juncture." Another pause. "Yes, she likes *Star Wars*." He pushes the phone aside again. "My mom says I can marry you."

My laughter echoes off the trees and startles a robin from the branches above.

"Tell Dad I'll call him later. I'm going to need help navigating the insurance crap." The smile drains off his face again. "Yeah, love you too, Mom. Thanks."

Call disconnected, his lip tugs into a half smile. "Sorry about that. My mother is eagerly awaiting new Padawans to add to her Rebel army."

"Hey, nothing says 'I love you' like pestering your adult kids for grandchildren." Sheila Dandy is repulsed by the idea, saying she will never answer to someone calling her "Grandma." Maggot, recently thirty-three, says her career isn't aligned with motherhood; Frankie says he's waiting for gene therapies to improve so he and his future bride can engineer the perfect child—"a combination of Clark Kent and Steve Jobs." Good luck with that.

"Mom means well. But she knows that any grandchildren will likely be my doing. We're all sort of waiting for Leia to grow out of her rebellious phase." He smiles. "Whenever I have a female friend, my mother starts in right away about the potential for conception."

The blush sears my neck and cheeks.

"I'm sorry—I didn't mean to embarrass you," he says.

"No. It's fine. I'm just weird."

He's quiet for a moment. A wood duck floats by, oblivious to our presence. "So, the obvious segue here ... what's up with Holden? Are you guys a thing?"

I chuckle. "No. Nice guy, but I'm not sure he's my type."

"What is your type?" Luke turns and pulls his knee on to the bench, careful of his swaddled hand.

"Better yet, what's *your* type, Luke Piewalker?"

"I'm not even sure anymore. I think I'll know it when I see it." My heart droops a little. "I thought I found The One when I was young. My high school sweetheart. Taylor was funny and she loved a lot of the same stuff I did and she didn't give me too much shit about the *Star Wars* thing. We used to talk about going to the same college and then getting married after graduation and opening up a café so we could be our own bosses and then our kids would grow up in the family business."

"Sounds nice."

"It was. Until she cheated. But isn't that the way those things always go? We were young and stupid. We had no idea what love was."

"Do we ever really know what it is?"

"I know what it is for me—honesty. I think I mentioned this before. Lying is such a turn-off, you know? The idea that someone could look me in the face and not be open? I need to know that I'm important enough in the relationship that my partner isn't afraid to tell me the truth. That's what hurt worst about losing Taylor. Even Leia knows that no matter what stupid shit she does, she always has to tell me the truth or I won't help her."

"Honesty is a biggie," I say, toying with the potential irony. No way to know unless I ask. "What about Tiana? Gretchen mentioned she saw you together."

Luke looks at me squarely. "At the Copper Horse, right?" I nod. He rests his knuckles under my chin so I can't look anywhere but into his eyes. "I swear to you, Jayne: I am not with Tiana anymore. I don't have feelings for her. Except maybe homicidal ones. And I'm pretty sure what happened today is because she finally got that message."

I don't know if the relieved exhale is as loud in real life as it sounds in my head. And when my face pulls back into a smile, I look down to not be so obvious.

Despite this relief, guilt nudges me. I should tell him about Jaina Jacen. Is omission still considered a lie? I'm not directly lying about anything—not like what Tiana or Taylor did—I just ... How can I tell him? It's about so much more than just writing a book. If Luke recognizes himself in Alec, I will never be able to look him in the eye again.

I cannot risk it. Not yet.

"In hindsight, I'm glad Tay and I didn't work out. The café was always my dream—she wouldn't have been happy chasing my dreams and not hers."

"Where'd she end up?" The strangest twinge twists within. Is that ... *jealousy?*

"She went on to graduate school and met her perfect guy there. I recently received an invite to her wedding. She looks very happy."

"Does that hurt?" I have zero context for this. My curiosity is hungry.

"Not anymore. It would've hurt if she were marrying the guy she cheated on me with," he says, his smile doleful. "But no. I'm glad she's happy. She emails once in a while to update me—he's an entrepreneur who installs water purification systems in ravaged lands, so she's been to Africa and the Middle East."

"Sounds like she traded your dreams for some other guy's."

"Maybe. But fate knows best," he says. "What about Jayne Dandy, though? Who's the one who got away for you?"

I chuckle. "I told you the last time we talked about this. There hasn't been anyone."

"I don't believe that."

"It's not so hard to believe. I had a brief boyfriend senior year in high school, but it didn't last."

"No one in college?"

"Not really. I've always had a lot of guy friends but no one serious."

"Your 'friends' at the bar that night ... they teased you. Called you Jaynie Prudie."

"Yeah." I'm so embarrassed to be having this conversation outside of Dr. McCoy's office. But Luke just said he values honesty. Let's see how honest he wants to get. "I have issues. With intimacy. I'm ... I'm afraid of sex and all that goes with it."

"Interesting." He doesn't move away from me. If anything, he leans closer. "Why do you think that is?"

"It's nothing terrible—I wasn't abused or anything—I just have these weird hang-ups about it." This is uncomfortable. "My therapist says I don't fit the technical psychiatric definition of what one might call frigid, but I just haven't been in a situation where I felt safe enough to give myself to someone else."

"Have you ever been kissed?"

My face hurts, I'm blushing so hard. "Yes."

"And what was that like for you?"

"Terrifying mostly." My heart pounds. I watch his face, wondering when he will stand and tell me our afternoon is over. He doesn't, though. He scoots closer. The wood of the bench is no longer visible in the space between us.

I like it.

"So, if I put my hand on your knee, will you run away in terror?"

I shake my head no. His hand moves to my knee. "I like you, Jayne Dandy. Is that okay for me to admit?" His face is so open, the depth of his long-lashed eyes urging me to trust him. To trust this.

I smile. "Yes."

"Do you like me back?"

"Yes," I whisper. *So much.*

"Are you okay with me touching your face?"

"Yes."

He rubs a finger against my cheek. I shiver.

His tongue wets his bottom lip. "If I were to kiss you, would you punch me?"

"I would never punch an injured man."

"Well, then, thank heavens for burns." He chuckles. "I'm going to try it. Are you ready?"

I nod. I am ready. I can do this. I can be brave. I've thought about Luke's lips many times before, what they would feel like against mine. *Don't wuss out, Jayne.*

He's slow on approach, and when his lips finally make contact, they're soft and gentle. This is nothing like the erratic, fumbled urgency of my last (failed) kiss. This is sweet and safe and delicious. I don't pull away when the kiss deepens or when his uninjured hand tucks under my ponytail or when his bandaged fingers touch my side or when he pauses and smiles against my mouth and teases my upper lip with his tongue.

"For an amateur, you're quite the professional," he says.

I think about the scenes in my books, where I've written this kiss a hundred times over with Alec and Miranda, where I've spent hours fantasizing what their perfect kiss would entail.

This pretty much sums it up. And this kiss is mine.

A loud clap of thunder overhead jolts us apart. The drenching rain unleashes as we sprint under the eco-roof gazebo, but once there, soaked and laughing, Luke pulls me into him and kisses me with greater vigor. I allow him to lean me against the gazebo wall, kissing him back, my fingers hooked around the belt loops of his jeans, and I feel so proud of myself for enjoying his hands on my body and his lips against mine and the way our hearts are slamming against each other like they're having their own conversation.

"Now *that* was an unexpected blast, wasn't it?" The canoeist. He's out of the water.

Our magical, movie-moment kiss is over.

Luke smiles politely and then whispers in my ear. "Are you hungry?" I nod. "Come on, then."

He drives this time. Boldly, I cup his sore right hand atop my thigh.

"Does it hurt?" I ask again, desperate to say something that doesn't sound stupid or silly or give any indication that I am nervous as hell.

"Not anymore," he says, a mischievous dimple punched into his cheek.

He pulls into the driveway of the house he shares with his sister, and I swear to God, I'm going to have an aneurysm. Once the car is off, he turns to me.

"I'm asking nothing from you. I am not taking you inside to tear your clothes off or make you do anything you're not comfortable with. I happen to have some excellent chicken breasts in the fridge that need cooking, and I could be talked into whipping up something for dessert." He smiles; my breath hitches. "And by dessert, I mean food. Lady's choice. This is a no-pressure situation, okay? Just you and me, hanging out, making a late lunch-early dinner thing."

"It sounds brilliant."

We scramble inside as the schizophrenic clouds continue their ranting and raving overhead. He lends me a clean sweatshirt to counteract the chill from the rain. It smells like him. I may never give it back.

Music on, gas fireplace burning, apron draped over my head, ingredients on the counter.

We talk about his growing up as one of a matched set, how he spent their childhood bailing Leia out of scuffles because she hated being "that nerdy *Star Wars* kid," how nursing a broken ankle earned in a high school soccer game changed the course of his future. "Food Network," he says. "All the cooking shows you never know you needed, twenty-four hours a day."

"That's how you decided to start the food truck?"

"Yeah. The idea was for Piewalker's to establish us and build the nest egg to get a down payment on opening a brick-and-mortar location."

"You're still going forward with that, I hope."

"I guess we'll have to see what happens with ... everything." I watch as he works his magic on two very pink chicken breasts—rubs them in olive oil, slices them open like pockets, and inserts smooth cream cheese, fresh crushed garlic, thinly sliced mushroom and red onion pan fried in basil pesto, and a combination of spices I'm absolutely positive we do not have in our ridiculous "kitchen" at home. When he pulls prosciutto out of a white-paper package from an actual butcher, my stomach growls her approval. All at once, I'm so glad vegetarian, gluten- and carb-free Gretchen isn't here to witness this beautiful scene in which we are engaged in such wanton farmyard slaughter.

Prosciutto-wrapped chicken?

Maybe I should call Mrs. Walker now and ask permission to marry her son. We can deal with that whole grandchild thing after I eat this meal.

Food in the oven, Luke wipes everything down and pulls out more ingredients. "Shall we make dessert?" His smile flirts for him.

And hence begins my first lesson in making pâte choux, the éclair pastry, from the parchment to the importance of monitoring the moisture levels of the dough and eventual egg-washed baked shells. I've never seen the éclairs made from scratch at the food truck—Luke always brings in the finished pastries and fills them on board, a skill he did teach me.

He backs me up against the counter. "I'm going to show you how to make the crème légère."

"Are you sure that's wise?" He's standing so close, and the hint of this morning's cologne is still evident, despite the day's traumas. My fingertips tingle with nervous energy.

"You try to sell yourself as a kitchen dunce, but I've seen you in action. I don't believe the front you're putting on."

"Yeah, I'm dangerous with a Lean Cuisine," I say.

Luke points at the ingredients, explaining their purpose one at a time. He stands behind me, supervising as the vanilla bean and seeds and milk come to a boil. While it steeps, he teaches me how to mix the sugar and egg until it's a pale yellow. In goes the flour and corn-starch. More mixing, his unburned hand swaddling mine, his body tight against my back because we're mixing like fiends and the air is short in my chest and it's the good shortness of breath and not the kind that comes before you faint secondary to an allergic reaction or after you fall on the crossbar of a boys' bike because even though girls don't have testicles, falling on the crossbar still hurts.

When I do breathe again, I can feel the shortness of his inhales too. He drops the spatula and turns me around. The blue gas stove flame flickers low behind him. A matching ferocity burns in his face that can only be described as electric.

This doesn't even feel real.

"With your permission, Jayne Dandy, I'd like to kiss you again."

I nod.

And then his hands are on my sides and he's shoving aside the crème légère ingredients and hoists my ass on to the counter and he's wedged between my thighs and his hands are on my neck and we're breathing the same breath and this is not like anything I've ever expe-rienced before that wasn't coming out of the end of my ballpoint pen and I like this but the panic horns are blaring in my head and I really should stop because what if someone is watching and I am being so bad—

"Ahem."

Luke pulls away as we both look behind us. Leia's home.

"I think your légère is scorching."

And just as happened with the canoeist at the park, Leia's arrival curtails what was undoubtedly my best exposure therapy session yet.

"I hope you've made enough of whatever's in the oven. I'm starv-ing." She plods down the hall. "And stop making out near the food. Gross."

Oh, the irony.

By the time the plates are cleared and our bellies are full of food that deserves its own TV show, I've learned plenty about the Walker twins. Leia, once she lets her guard down, is funny and self-effacing and totally proud of her "big" brother. She inspects his burned hand and nags him about calling their parents back. She and I finish filling the éclairs, and she doesn't even tease me when I overfill and the crème squirts out the second hole.

It's the most relaxing, enjoyable evening. And as we inch closer to midnight, I know I have to go home. Especially because Gretchen's phone calls and texts have gone ignored, as has work. Holden has texted twice to ask if I heard about the food truck and have I spoken to Luke and hey maybe do you want to grab a bite to eat later. Hmmmm, yes, yes, and definitely no, dear Holden.

Luke insists on driving me home—says he will have a cab waiting at my apartment for his return trip. He again holds my hand, bandages be damned, and takes the long way home. I can only hope it's because he's as reticent for the evening to end as I am.

I cannot believe this day. Yes, it's terrible the food truck burned down. But everything that happened after that? I couldn't have written this any more perfectly than it has played out.

Giddiness threatens—I may explode into a fit of giggles at any moment.

He pulls up at a quiet intersection and waits for the light to change. When he looks over at me, his attention is grabbed otherwise. "Is that ... *Gretchen?*"

Oh God.

The bookstore from the reading. They have Jaina Jacen in the front window, Gretchen's gorgeous, smiling headshot center stage, paperback books stacked and displayed in the shape of a big heart. Whoever dressed this window went all out—slinky negligee, wine bottle and glasses, glitter and sparkles everywhere.

"Are those her books?" He pulls around the corner and jumps out of the car. "Wow! Look at that! And the name—Jaina Jacen?—ha! I thought she wasn't a *Star Wars* fan."

Think fast, Jayne. "Uh, she's not. I helped her with that. She needed a pen name. I wanted a name that sounded cool but still sexy."

Oh shit, no. Don't make me do this right now. The red flags flap so hard in my ears, the alarms shriek so terribly: I'm lying to him. This is bad. So bad.

"This is really something else. You've been helping her with this?" He puts his hand over his heart. "And you didn't tell me?" At first, I'm worried he's mad because I didn't tell him but then he wraps his arm around my middle. "Maybe we could read one together. That might be a good way to ... break the ice." He kisses my cheek gently.

Oh man, oh man, oh man.

I pull my phone out. Check the time. Anything to divert his attention. "We should get going. It's cold out here."

Luke opens the passenger door for me, chuckling under his breath the whole rest of the way home. "Does anyone else know that it's Gretchen? And why didn't you tell me?"

"She wanted to keep it quiet until her big announcement. Just a few people know it's really her—my sister and mom. Apparently no one at the office has figured it out yet."

"Good for her. Man, that's sort of inspiring. I didn't even know she was a writer."

Me either.

"Hey, ask her if I can buy a signed copy." Luke smiles as he parks against the curb in front of our building. As planned, a cab sits idling up ahead.

Lights are still on in our apartment, and the sheer front-window curtains quiver with Gretchen's silhouette. I hope she doesn't see whatever comes next or I will never live this down.

"I'm so sorry about Piewalker's, Luke. But everything else after ... Thank you. For today," I say.

"Thank *you*. You saved me from myself."

"I don't know about that."

"Well, I didn't spend the afternoon staring at the ceiling and pondering the meaning of life now that I'm unemployed. Shit, we're both unemployed."

I'm not. Not really. "We're not unemployed. We're temporarily between gigs."

"That sounds so much cooler." He leans closer. "I'm glad you weren't there today—that you weren't in any danger."

"I'm sorry you were hurt." Our lips meet for a light kiss.

"Oh, hey, before I forget." He reaches into my back seat and pulls out another numbered paper bag. I didn't even see him throw it into the car. Sneaky. "Remember—you can't open 'em until you have all thirteen."

"Yes, sir." I balance the bag in my hands, curious about the contents based on weight. "Not even a clue?"

"Nope."

Awkward pause.

"May I kiss you goodnight?" he finally asks.

"Yes."

I'm grinning when his face makes contact with mine. I could so get used to this.

"Can I call you?" he asks.

"You will if you want your sweatshirt back."

"It's one of my favorites. Even though it looks way better on you." He kisses my forehead and hands me the box of éclairs I will likely finish all by myself. Tonight. As I lie in bed and think about how much amazing progress I have made and how damn proud Dr. McCoy is going to be of me.

EIDER: CHAPTER 11

by Jaina Jacen (November)

By morning meal the following day, my dispatch has been received—and returned.

"Meet me at the hydroelectric turbines just after moonrise. Bring what you cannot live without. ~ Pollux."

Bring what I cannot live without? What does that mean?

I hurry through the motions of my day, eager to again see the quiet ponds and beauteous nature that has taken over the defunct turbines. These old structures are no more than ruins today, efforts by the early settlers to harness the planet's natural resources. Advances in solar and plasma technologies, however, rendered the turbines obsolete. What man has taken from nature, nature will reclaim. The turbines among them.

At moonrise, they will be glorious with early evening fauna.

My late-day study session over, I rush to my chamber. Into a knapsack, I throw the few things I cannot live without: a tiny book given to me by my favorite tutor, a secret locket that holds a picture of Taisa and me, a spare shawl in case the turbines are cold.

I've asked Taisa to bring solution to alter my hair's color. Before she sets to work, she presents me with a small vial: blood for the bioreader, taken from one of her kitchen friends, a Class III whose in-and-out access of the compound would raise no alarm.

I again dress in tunic and pants. Hair plaited and tied around my head. No cloak for ease of mobility. Instead I don the longcoat that I might have "borrowed" from the armory on a recent trip—its fabric makes the wearer virtually invisible. It's all a trick of light.

"How are you going to get down to the kitchen, My Sovereign? Surely someone will see you."

I pull the longcoat's hood over and fasten the face covering.

Taisa inhales sharply. "You're—gone."

"Something else, isn't it?"

"I knew these existed, but I've never seen one up close."

I again reveal my face. "Go to the meeting hall. If anyone asks, say I'm resting. Everyone should be preoccupied with their preparations for the evening meal."

"And what about when they learn you're gone?"

"I've seen you participate in the play-acting with your cousins, Taisa. Pull on your dramatist's face." She blushes. Eider has actors and performers, but unless you're invited by the elders to perform, it is not something a compound servant should be doing. "You answer any inquiries with the answer that I am resting, dealing with problems of a feminine nature, and I have asked to dine in my room tonight."

"Good choice, My Sovereign. I don't think even your father would want to meddle with 'problems of a feminine nature.'"

"You can do this," I say. Taisa hesitates for a moment, but I break protocol and gather her into my arms for a tight squeeze. It feels heavier, more meaningful, than a simple goodbye.

I'm not sure if the embrace is to steel her nerves, or mine.

"Wish me the luck of the double moon," I say.

She bows before me and grabs my fingers. My chamber door open, she ushers me into the hallway. Before I fasten the covering over my face that will render me invisible, Taisa offers her smallest finger as a sign of our mutual confidence in one another. I lock mine around hers briefly, smile, and disappear.

23

"WELLLLLL, THERE SHE IS," Gretchen says. She's wearing the same clothes as when I left this morning. Hair knotted in a bun stabbed with a pencil; no makeup. She still looks like she could strut the catwalk.

"You didn't go in today?"

"Called in sick."

"Are you? Sick, I mean?" I ask.

"No. I just didn't want to listen to Holden talk about you all day. You're going to have to deal with him, Jayne. He's got it bad."

"We're just friends."

"Might want to tell Holden that."

She offers me a stack of papers from the coffee table. "But just because I didn't show my face at the paper today doesn't mean I haven't been working. Take a look."

Sales reports from the online retailers. This is surreal.

"The second book has almost a hundred and fifty reviews on it already. Can you even believe that?" She hands me a printout with a name and address. "We have an appointment next week—he's an accountant and financial advisor. He's seeing us on a personal recommendation from my father because he's booked months out, but these are big numbers happening and once these checks start rolling in, things could get weird fast."

The tone of her voice hints that maybe things are already getting weird.

"Are you able to sit down and talk about a few things, or do you have plans?" she says.

"I'm home now. I didn't mean to be gone all day."

"Well, I called and texted. I'm guessing you were with Luke. Bummer about the food truck."

"Yeah. He was upset, so I spent the day trying to cheer him up."

For a moment, the playfulness returns to Gretchen's eyes. "I'll bet you did." And then it's gone again. "So, we need to go over a few things ..."

And off she launches into what she talked about with two different publicists, an agent working very hard to woo Jaina Jacen, emails from another agent interested in talking, the early designs for Jaina Jacen's new website and logo mock-ups from the graphic designer, printouts of different swag packs we should consider ordering so we can give back to the readers through giveaways, a long list of book-signing events and conventions that "we should really be seen at."

So much information, so little ability to focus. Because I kissed a boy today.

"Are you even listening?" she says.

"Yeah. I'm—this is amazing. I can't believe you've done all this."

"It would be great if we could talk about the third book and when you think you'll have it done. Even a ballpark would help. Do you have a synopsis written yet?"

When our eyes meet, I notice that Gretchen looks tired. And the guilt wiggles like drowning earthworms after a hard rain. She's working really hard to make Jaina Jacen a success, and I'm sort of sucking in the effort department.

"I think I might have to hire an assistant or an intern to help me. I *do* have a life outside of this, and I want to hit a few fashion shows in the next month," she says.

"Right. Absolutely. We can do that." I don't want to overwhelm my friend. I feel like shit. "Hey! Luke saw the window at the bookstore on the way home. He wants a signed copy." That perks her up a little.

"Of course he does." She leans back in the chair and crosses her legs. Gretchen makes ratty sweats look glamorous. "Wait—what did you tell him about all this?"

"Nothing. I said I'd get him a signed book."

"So he doesn't know it's you?"

"No." More guilt. *I am lying to Luke.* "He was genuinely excited for you."

"Cool. As long as we have our stories straight."

"I told him that I came up with the pen name, but the window display has your headshot front and center."

"Is it the black and white one? I look cutest in that set."

Quack hisses at the corner. The empty corner. "Did you give the cat her medicine?"

"I'm one person, Jayne. I can't be everywhere at once."

And that's what this comes down to. The resentment begins here. Gretchen is pissed that I was out having a day while she was here slaving away. Fortunately, I know how to play this game.

"Mani-pedis this weekend?" I say. She leans over her laptop again, frown twitching. "Gretch, I know you're working hard, I appreciate everything you're doing, and I will get you an assistant and I will help out more, and I will treat you to a mani-pedi this weekend."

"You're not coming with me?" I hate pedicures. I have weird toes. I don't want anyone touching my feet. But I know if I don't agree to allow some underpaid esthetician to scoop out my cuticles, Gretchen will find something else to piss and moan about.

"Yes. I will come with you."

"And you'll pay for it?"

"Yes. I will pay for it."

"And you'll come right home and work on the third book so we don't fall flat on our faces?"

Drama queen. "Yes, I will come right home and work on the third book."

"And you'll tell me everything that happened today with Luke without leaving out any of the naughty bits?"

I pause. "Yes. Although the naughty bits weren't really naughty."

"I spied on you through the window, Jayne. I saw his shit-eating grin as he climbed into the cab. And you're wearing an article of his clothing. This is front-page news."

As long as I have Gretchen's face smiling and her mouth not nagging, I will agree to whatever conditions she sets forth.

Even though all I really want to do is hug my pillow and bury my face in Luke's sweatshirt that still smells like Luke and get lost in the delicious memory of the last twelve hours.

24

THE FUNNY THING ABOUT HAPPINESS—IT sometimes sneaks up, taps you on the shoulder, and then tiptoes away, leaving only shadowy footprints behind. And then you're not sure if it was really ever there at all, or if those footprints were left by your crazed cat or perhaps a pervert who snuck in to watch you sleep who then got spooked and left without so much as sniffing your underwear.

In the week and two days since Luke Piewalker's burned to the ground, I have seen him exactly zero times. I have received exactly six text messages lamenting his busy schedule, bemoaning the endless paperwork, teasing that we should get together for more rainstorm kissing and cooking lessons, confirmation that it was Tiana who melted the food truck to bolts and tears, inquiry about his favorite sweatshirt and how he hopes I'm still wearing it, and lastly, an announcement that the Walker twins are definitely going to their parents' in San Diego for Thanksgiving.

I knew chances were slim he'd be available to go with me to Circus Dandy tomorrow, but I sort of hoped that maybe a last-minute change of plans would happen and he'd text and say, *hey, flight*

canceled due to too many free-range turkeys on the runway I'll be right
over to kiss your face some more.

For anyone outside the United States, that fourth Thursday in
November is just another day. But here, it is the granddaddy of glut-
tony, the crown of consumption—and for some, the gateway to grief.

Sure, there's food. Lots of it. Even on the Wednesday just before,
the air thrums with excitement as people prepare to take four consecutive days off to spend with loved ones, watch football, and enjoy a
long-awaited reunion with fat pants. It's the "loved ones" part that's
got me worried.

Family.

If you cannot hear me across the distance, that sigh was a
heavy one.

The pissing match between my parents has only grown longer,
hairier tentacles. Which means tomorrow is going to be a blistering
good time. I'd start drinking now in preparation, but I have to pick up
the Tofurky for my suddenly vegetarian sister. She can't get it herself
because she's flying in late tonight from some zit conference in Phil-
adelphia; Frankie won't get it because he's a sexist and says his penis
precludes him from being in the kitchen on Thanksgiving; and my
mother can't get it because "I have to cook everything else plus clean
this house and your father is too busy with his demon-whore to
provide any help at all this year." What she means is my father
refused to have Thanksgiving catered for the first time since I was in
pigtails.

Breaking news: Sheila Dandy is cooking.

Maybe we should put the health department on alert.

Gretchen has offered to come along and run interference. My
friend, saving my ass yet again.

And without the food truck to occupy my afternoons, I have had
copious quantities of time to focus on writing. Which logically
suggests that I should have copious pages to show for it.

Instead, I have rewatched every version of *Pride and Prejudice*
ever produced (sorry, ladies, but Matthew Macfadyen, and not Colin

Firth, is my Mr. Darcy), followed by the Bridget Jones series, the BBC's *North and South*, and pretty much every romantic film released in the last decade ... all in the desperate search for inspiration. While Gretchen doesn't know the depth of my angst—when she pops into my room at random times, I make it look like I'm typing furiously—I will exhaust Netflix's supply of "research materials" soon, and Gretchen will demand to see pages.

Which I do not have.

I remind myself with daily affirmations that I am the writer who controls the story, and not the other way around.

"Ha ha ha, you're a funny one, Jayne Dandy," says the story.

Absolutely, I know I have to get this third book done to keep the growing fan base happy. But this has all happened so fast—it's ... overwhelming. What started out as a way for me to work through the intimacy problems festering in my head has exploded into a business. Never in a million years did I foresee this.

Plus when I'm not worrying about my horrifying lack of literary output, I've been trying to keep Sheila Dandy out of jail by tag teaming with Margaret to take Mommie Dearest out every few days for a meal. As a result of this busyness, I've canceled my last two appointments with Dr. McCoy, although I am very excited to tell her about the progress with Luke—or what progress there was. The little troll who lives in the cluttered room behind my ear whispers that Luke doesn't really like me, that if he did, he would've made time to see me. Which is silly because I haven't made time to see him, either. Be quiet, little voice. You're mean when you're drunk.

And about that third book. I've already given poor Miranda and Alec their fair share of problems—a near-death experience, a miscarriage, an unjust arrest, a kidnapping, sex in every possible position and dangerous locales. It's probably time to pull out the big guns and kill someone off, although Jaina's readers, I'm guessing, really just want the sexy vagina funtime. But how many different ways can two people collide physically? And don't their parts get tired?

Oh, imagination, don't fail me now. If you do, Gretchen will leave the *Kama Sutra* on the kitchen table again with a Post-It note that says, "READ ME."

"Uh-oh, that red face tells me someone is having impure thoughts." Gretchen sashays into the kitchen, dressed for work. "Or maybe there's whiskey in that coffee cup. Real writers drink whiskey for breakfast, you know."

Before she sits, she plunks down an envelope in front of me.

"Open it, Miz Jacen." Gretchen's eyes twinkle. "I do believe it's payday."

My—our—first royalty payment. I'm so nervous. "You do it." She takes the envelope from my outstretched hand and slowly slides a finger under the flap, lips puckered. Only Gretchen could seduce an envelope.

"Stop teasing," I say. She giggles. And then upon unfolding the pages within and staring at the check, her giggles turn a little maniacal.

"Look, look, *look!*" I hold her shaking hand steady. That check has my real name on it. And numbers. Six of them, broken in half by a comma, followed by two more little numbers after the decimal point.

"Oh ... whoa ..."

Gretchen snatches the papers and tosses them on to the table and jumps like someone's lit her ass on fire.

"You did it! You did it! You did it!" Gretchen shrieks. And then I'm jumping and shrieking and tears trickle and we're giggling and bouncing like we did that time when Mateo McDonald asked her to the junior prom.

I stop and hug her tight. "*We* did it. Not me—we. Without you ..."

She straightens her blouse and stuffs our bounty back into its envelope. "I will be back here no later than three. You be ready to see the world. We have banking to do." She squeezes my cheek. "Oh, before I go, I need a book. Holden has discovered Jaina Jacen," she says, winking. "Throw me a Sharpie." She signs a book and as an added bonus, she kisses the page, leaving a red, heart-shaped stain behind.

"Little jerk thought he was being clever yesterday when he asked about it," she says. "Oh, what he would do if he knew it was you writing all this. He'd come undone. Literally."

"Stop."

Gretchen laughs. "Oh, Jaynie Prudie, get your head back in the gutter. You have another book to write." She throws her trench on and starts toward the door.

"Tomorrow, you're going with me, right?" I say over my shoulder.

Gretchen freezes and pivots slowly on her impossibly high heel. "Don't be mad."

"What? No way! You cannot leave me alone with my family."

"It was last minute—Eric hired a jet ..."

"A jet? Where are you going? Are you leaving me forever? And you can't go! We have the *reading* on Saturday. At the s-e-x show?"

"I'm only gone Thursday and Friday. Quick overnighter to Aspen. Naked snowball fights. Sex in the hot tub. And maybe in the snow. Excessive champagne consumption."

"But I thought you said he has a small wiener."

"You did hear the part about the private jet, right?"

"Why do you even work at the paper—or anywhere, for that matter—if you have men shuttling you about on their private jets?"

"Because I'm an independent woman of the twenty-first century. And Daddy says I have to have a job. Plus, free shoes. Duh." She blows me a kiss and moves to make her escape once again.

"I can't believe you're leaving me alone with the Dandys."

"What about Luke Piewalker?"

"He's in San Diego with his folks."

"Oooh, sucks—okay, what about Food Critic? Do you still have his lame coupon that promised 'any favor, any time'?"

Light bulb. "I do."

"No time like the present. And don't forget, banking. Three

o'clock. Oh, remind me—I need to get new crotchless panties before the stores close."

Why would I remind her of that?

I do not understand crotchless panties. What's the point? Doesn't the crotch part of the panty serve a specific purpose? Is that some sort of turn-on to a guy that his woman has underwear with a big hole where the panty part should be? Because if that's the case, I have some in my drawer from college, and those are nearly crotchless secondary to time and wear. I knew a kid in elementary school who had a cotton allergy so he never wore underwear, but he was a little boy—and he had a medical reason for going commando. Pretty sure the only medical substantiation Gretchen could claim is atrophy of the G-spot.

Erogenous zones aside, I have to figure out how to survive my family for consecutive hours without the aid of Gretchen's sharp tongue or hip flask.

Holden's coupon is pinned to the bulletin board in my room, right next to the shelf where Valerie Vibrato and her pouty red smooch sit collecting dust.

But if I invite him, he's going to read more into it. And I am very much not into Holden. Then again, I'm also suffering significant Dandy Family fatigue, and even if Holden is there to run interference, it will definitely be better than going alone.

Perchance it's time to collect.

EIDER: CHAPTER ??

Jaina Jacen (November)

JAYNE DANDY IS BROKEN.

SHE LOST HER WORDS.

I AM SO SORRY, POLLUX AND ILLYRIA.

Anyone wanna get drunk?

25

IT TOOK some strong-arming but Holden sits in my passenger seat, en route to the miraculous Thanksgiving jubilee at the Dandy residence. Even though I had a valid favor coupon from Holden himself, he insisted that he would only go with me if I promised to stop at his parents' after dinner for pie. Fine. Whatever. I like pie.

Aw, pie. I hope Luke got to San Diego all right. He texted me last night from the airport. Said he missed me and that he is coming back into town Friday night because he promised his buddy he'd help out at the Copper Horse over the weekend. And Gretchen better make sure her darling, sexed-up ass is back in Portland by Saturday morning. No way in hell am I getting up on stage and reading *Resist Me Not* for a crowd of horny onlookers.

"Any ground rules I should know before we go in?" Holden says as I pull the emergency brake.

"Don't let anyone goad you into a conversation you're not comfortable having. Don't ask about my father. Don't mention politics. Don't make pool-boy jokes. And try to ignore it if my brother farts." I pause—what am I forgetting? "Most importantly, turn off your food critic. I make no guarantees if what we're about to encounter is edible. If not, I will take you elsewhere and feed you real food after."

Because I can. I have money in my bank account.

I stop him at the door. "Remember, less is more with these people."

Maggot, apron stained and wrinkled, accosts us before we've one foot inside. "I need to get this in the oven, thank you very much," she says, plucking the boxed Tofurky from my hands.

"You're welcome," I say to her dust as she hustles back toward the kitchen. I turn to Holden. "Buckle up, sweet cheeks."

As expected, my father isn't here, and the house is big and weird without caterers running around setting the table and shooing my mother out of the kitchen. It smells different too—usually the Dandy Thanksgiving kitchen smells like fresh-baked bread and steamed vegetables and basted, roasting turkey. Today it smells like someone forgot it's a major holiday. I peek a look inside the oven and see a sad little naked bird sitting in its roaster, a few carrots and wilted mushrooms to keep it company.

This is going to hurt going down.

I'm not sure what Sheila Dandy was complaining about in terms of cooking responsibility—prepackaged dinner rolls sit on the counter, their fluffy, carb-infused tops waiting to be unleashed on the world. Maggot reads the box of Stove Top stuffing like it's a medical journal. She's managed to get vegetables sliced and it looks like she's attempting homemade cranberry sauce. Lumpy mashed potatoes simmer uncomfortably in a Dutch oven, splattering starch all over the stovetop. Two cans of gravy sit unopened on the counter.

"Where's Mom?"

"Follow the wine bottles."

And then I hear her voice. "Jayne, this isn't the guy you brought to dinner last time. Aren't you just turning into a regular Girl About Town."

Oh God, she's going to molest Holden.

Sure enough, she has a hand in his curls, the other hand wrapped around a half-full glass of Merlot. "Introduce us to your loverboy," she says.

"This is Holden. You've met him before." *You'd remember that if you weren't drunk.* "And he's a friend, Mom. Don't embarrass him."

"A *friend* ... mmm, what *kind* of friend?" So gross.

"We met at the Grill that night and again at Piewalker's—I'm the food critic?"

"Ohhhhh, I remember now. You're much cuter than that food-truck boy," Sheila coos, sliding an arm around Holden's. "Wine?"

"Mom, stop hitting on Jayne's friends," Frankie says. "You a Seahawks fan?"

"Of course."

Frankie slaps Holden on the shoulder and rescues him from my mother. Frank seems happy that I brought testosterone to keep him company. I don't need to ask where Dad is—Sheila has made sure the text messages of the last week have covered every possible scenario of where he is and what he is doing and who he is doing it *to*.

Just as dinner is carted to the table, Frankie's latest squeeze pops in, and sadly, she's just as vacuous as all the others. Apparently she took the mailroom job I turned down. My mother has a good time making fun of her, and the poor dear doesn't even recognize what's going on. Sheila Dandy should offer clinics in how to peel someone's skin away without them even realizing it's happening.

As feared, the food is terrible, although Holden makes a valiant effort to taste a little of everything, Maggot's hopeful eyes on him as he chews. I feel bad for her—she's a great dermatologist and a savvy businesswoman, but she's a terrible cook. But she tried today, even giving up her skiing trip to help my mother, so I should choke down a few bites. At least with chewy and dry, the meat isn't undercooked. I can't die from salmonella if it's overcooked.

"So Jayne, tell us about Gretchen writing porn," Sheila slurs. And there you have it.

"It's not porn, Mom," I say, cheeks ablaze. *Please do not let her figure this out. Please please please.*

"That's not what I heard."

"Mother, I've read Gretchen's little books—her pen name is Jaina Jacen—and under all the sex, they're actually quite good. Strong love story, interesting characters—"

"You know Jaina Jacen?" Frankie's girlfriend shrieks.

"Yes. She's Jayne's roommate," Maggot answers. The girl squeals and claps her hands.

"OMG, I can't believe you KNOW her! No one is going to believe this. Can you get me a signed book? Can you arrange for me to meet her? Her sex scenes are incredible. OMG, OMG, I can't believe you *know* her."

"Have you read the books?" I ask.

"Oh yeah! Everyone in the mailroom has. We read them out loud in the break room during lunch and then we talk about who reenacts what scene in their own—"

"You can stop," I say.

"My little sister has ... issues ... with sex," Frankie says behind his hand.

"What kind of issues? Oh, you should totally read these books. They'll help you get over that. Dude, they are so hot."

"I do not have issues with sex. I just don't think it's appropriate Thanksgiving conversation."

"Sex is a completely natural part of life, Jayne," my mother says. "I don't know why you're so weird about it. You're not still blaming those shriveled-up church ladies, are you?"

"Honestly, are we going to talk about this now?"

"Well, anyway, I think Gretchen did a fine job on her books," Maggot says. "I'm looking forward to the third one in the series, actually. And I think it's great that Gretchen put herself out there. Brave, if you ask me."

"Well, aren't you just the little book critic," Sheila says.

"Mother, don't be rude." Only Maggot gets away with talking to Sheila that way. As annoying and pretentious as my big sister can be, I'm grateful that she's defending Gretchen—

because that means she's defending me. Only she doesn't know it.

"Whatever it is, she's writing about people screwing." Sheila tops off her wine glass. "It doesn't take a genius to write a scene about two people bumping uglies."

Frankie's girlfriend giggles.

"The stories are much more than that, Mother," Maggot says.

"Whatever they are, I'll bet Gretch is laughing all the way to the bank," Frankie says. As a matter of fact, Frankie, we did laugh on our way to the bank yesterday. It was fun. So was buying the $400 buttery leather boots beckoning my feet from my apartment bedroom.

"What about you, Jayne? You've always talked about writing the Great American Novel. You think you could write some smut and make a name for yourself? Have you even started looking for another job? You had your chance at Frankie's firm, but you blew that, didn't you." Sheila looks over at Frankie's tart. "Jayne used to write obituaries and classified ads. Straight to the top of the *New York Times* bestsellers' list with those." She laughs at herself. "But then she got fired—"

"Downsized, Mother. Not fired."

"Then she got *downsized,* so she worked at a food truck. You weren't the reason it burned down, were you, Jaynie?"

Holden's eyes are saucered. "I'm sorry," I whisper.

"Truth be told, Jayne didn't burn down Piewalker's. And she makes a mean éclair," Holden offers. I don't interrupt to tell him I actually don't make the éclairs. "Some crazy ex of the truck's owner had a vendetta, and she Molotov'd the truck. They were really lucky that no one was seriously injured or killed."

Sheila pauses for a beat. "Jayne cooked something other than oatmeal? Now I know you're lying."

I shake my head at Holden and mouth my thanks. He reaches under the tablecloth and squeezes my hand.

Without waiting to see if anyone's done eating, I stand and take our plates. I'm done here. Maggot follows me into the kitchen.

"Jayne, don't be mad."

"I'm not mad."

"You just broke that plate in half."

Tears sting my eyes, but I cannot let anyone see. I just need to clean up and leave.

My sister's hand rests on my shoulder. I jerk away from her and toss the broken plate into the trash. Margaret exhales heavily. "Mom's under a lot of stress. The split from Dad has been hard on her."

"Sheila Dandy is the devil. And she deserves whatever hell she brings on herself."

"Don't be like that—"

I spin and glare at Margaret. "You know what? I'm glad Dad left her. I hope whoever this new woman is, I hope she's nice and she doesn't say mean, hurtful things or make him feel like shit all the time. Because that's what the spiteful beast in there has done to him for thirty-four years. Dad deserves to be happy before he dies."

"Maybe. It's not our fight, so we just have to be there for Mom when she needs us."

"Knock yourself out. I only protect those who protect me."

My coat and bag in hand, I poke my head around the corner into the dining room. "Holden?"

"Thank you for dinner," he says to my family. "Happy Thanksgiving."

I ignore my mother's cackles from behind us as she shouts about how it's just like me to leave the scene of the crime.

"I'm really sorry," I say as we pull away from the house. "She was in rare form today."

"Are you okay?"

"I'm fine." I'm really not. My innards are in disarray. "Just embarrassed."

"Now I can see why you needed backup."

"It's usually not that bad—my father refused to pay for a caterer this year. And he has a new girlfriend. My mother is clearly not dealing with it well."

"That doesn't mean she has to take it out on you." Holden squeezes my shoulder as I drive.

I will not cry I will not cry I will not cry.

I maintain control over my tear ducts until the threat abates, just in time to meet Holden's family. His parents are down-to-earth and funny, and his mom's pumpkin pie is one for the record books. Grandma Mary is so in love with her curly-haired grandson, telling stories about how toddler Holden adored her budgies and begged her every weekend to go to the aviary at the zoo. She even gifts me with a hand-knitted scarf to apologize for him leaving me at the hospital when she had her budgie emergency.

His parents don't flinch when they ask what I do for a living—Gretchen and I have been using "freelance writer" now that I'm not gainfully employed in a company listed in any phone book or stock exchange. Holden tells them what he knows about my volunteer activities at the Tigard farm, and it's fun to tell them about my ducks and the wild versus domestic duck problems at so many of Portland's city parks.

When the conversation turns to their son's accomplishments, they seem genuinely proud of Holden, even if he didn't become an architect. His dad ribs him a little about minoring in folklore, but then notes that without his son's appreciation for literature, he wouldn't have found his way into the collection of books now consuming one wall in the dining room.

It's a delightful finish to an otherwise disastrous day.

When I pull into the lot of Holden's building, the nervous gut gurgles return, especially when he turns in his seat instead of saying *hey thanks Jayne see you next week* and bouncing out of the car to go upstairs and dig into his mom's leftovers.

"Thanks for coming with me today," I say. "Your favor has been redeemed in full."

"Thanks for hanging out with my family," he says. He's angling closer. "My mom really likes you."

"Your mom seems wonderful. Both your parents, actually. And Grandma Mary." I lean back against my door, fluffing my new red scarf.

"I feel bad that our date didn't work out, you know, last time. And I know things have been crazy lately, for both of us, but I'd really like to take you out on a proper date again. If you're interested."

I don't know how to say no without sounding like a dick. Holden's a nice friend, and I like him, but ... Luke.

Before I can answer, he's bridged the distance between us, his hands on my upper arms pulling me close for a kiss. He smells cinnamon-y. And then his lips make contact, and he's smooching away, but it's not soft and gentle like how Luke kisses. It's—weird. And slobbery. And he groans like he's eating the most delicious ice cream cone ever scooped.

This is the opposite of romance.

I don't want to be kissing him.

This isn't right. Too much spit. And his lips feel rough, chapped even.

I pull away.

"Did I offend you? Oh man, I should've asked first. Your brother mentioned—"

"No, it's fine. Just took me by surprise."

"Isn't that sort of the point, though?" he says, smirking. "What are you doing this weekend? We could grab some sushi, maybe go see a movie. And I promise to keep my hands to myself."

"I have a thing this weekend. With Gretchen."

"What sort of thing?"

I pause and take a deep breath. I can't lie my way out of this. "She—Jaina Jacen—is doing a reading at the Spicy & Sweet Sexhibition. Saturday afternoon at the Convention Center."

"Are you kidding? That's so cool! What time? I will so be there!"

Crap. "She's scheduled to go on at three."

"Sounds perfect. Then after, we can all get food."

"Yeah, let me talk to Gretchen. I'll text you."

Holden smiles and grabs the fabric grocery bag from his mom, planting a chaste kiss on my cheek. "Looking forward to it."

Gosh. Me too.

26

GRETCHEN DOES NOT SPARE any details of her Aspen debauchery, including the parts where she and Eric christened the private jet bathroom, the leather chairs in the main aircraft cabin, the hot tub and every room at the condo he rented. It's a miracle she's able to walk given the workout her reproductive organs have had over the prior forty-eight hours. And I only listen because I'm desperately seeking new material for the next book.

This morning, however, my intestines are in revolt. Why am I so nervous? The best part: I feel like I've lost five pounds. The worst: if this keeps up, I will be tethered to the Convention Center bathrooms instead of cowering backstage to listen to the crowd's reaction to Jaina Jacen's words.

I'm not the one who'll be on the stage. Although really, I am. Maybe not my body, but feathery pieces of my brain will be filtering out of Gretchen's mouth and into the ears of willing listeners.

And like the time before at the little bookstore over in St. Johns, I stuff the trunk of Gretchen's car with everything we might need while she primps and preens. The newest load of paperbacks—*Tempt*

Me Softly is now available as a real book!—fills the back seat, leaving just enough room for our new foldable dolly.

Gretchen vocalizes as she drives, like a deranged drama kid. "Me me me me me me, ma ma ma ma ma ma, mo mo mo mo mo mo, la la la la la la."

"What are you doing?"

"Warming up."

"You're reading, not playing Lady Macbeth."

"I am a serious artiste," she teases.

"Are you nervous?" I ask.

"Not as nervous as your pissed-off gut. Eat the banana in my bag. It'll keep you from pooping again."

At the venue, the promoter we met at the bookstore greets us at the front entrance and leads us to where we can set up, along the far wall next to the stage. We'll do the reading first, and then Jaina Jacen will be available to sign and sell books at the skirted table. The promoter invites us to stay set up for the rest of the day and mentions that she's had a great response to their advertising in support Jaina's/Gretchen's appearance.

Eyes forward, I concentrate solely on not taking out anyone's ankles with this wobbly, wheeled contraption. We pass table after table of explicit toys, lubes, clothing, mechanical devices, and weird body contraptions that make Hamlet's slings and arrows look like child's play.

I'm trying so hard not to look, but seriously—who designs all this stuff? *Who uses all this stuff?*

Oh, the Satan Squad would have a field day saving souls in this joint.

When we emerge from the end of the side aisle flanking the performance stage, Gretchen inhales sharply. I expect it's because someone is doing something naughty under the bright lights.

But then I look up from the patterned carpet and see an ocean of excited people already seated in the folding chairs, many, *many* Jaina Jacen postcards in hands throughout the space.

They're here for the reading.

My heart gallops across the room and abandons me, my chest left open and empty for the whole world to see.

Gretchen's face pales briefly, and then she shakes her head, runs a hand along her perfect ponytail, straightens her shoulders. She is so good at this.

The promoter suggests that Gretchen go backstage out of view for now while I set up. "Sure. No problem," I say to their backs as they walk through side doors and disappear. Now it's just me and a trunk full of stuff that has to come inside.

I should've corralled Holden into helping today instead. This would've been a much better way to cash in my favor coupon. The thought of making more solo trips along Bondage Boulevard or Down-n-Dirty Drive as I cart the supplies in ... I smell a long day.

My phone vibrates in my pocket. "Hey, are you guys here yet?" Holden. Like magic.

"Yeah. Gretchen just went backstage. Are you here?"

"At the front entrance."

"Perfect. Stay there. I'll meet up in a sec."

Holden packs gear in with me and then helps arrange the table for after the reading. The crowd has only grown, and people mill around picking up the paperbacks and asking if they can buy one now.

As I pull the last book from a box of twenty of *Tempt Me Softly* paperbacks, the promoter requests that everyone find seats so we can get started.

Gretchen texts: *"Where R U? Get back here ASAP."*

I leave Holden in charge of the table and head backstage. Gretchen, while still her controlled self, paces in long strides behind the curtain. "Oh, thank God. What took so long?"

"I—"

"Never mind. I need you to peek through the curtain and look at the front row, toward the left."

I do. My chest again does that bungee-jump thing that happens when I get letters from the IRS or a callback for a repeat Pap smear.

Luke is here. In the front row. He is no longer in San Diego.

"What the hell is Luke doing here?"

"What? No—who cares about Luke." Gretchen looks through the curtain herself. "Shit, she moved."

"Who moved?"

"Suzette. She's here. With the whole writers' group. They're here."

"Okay. That's okay. They've heard you read before. You read at the meetings. They're just excited for you."

"Right. Okay. You're right. I'm just worried that Suzette is going to be a dick again—"

"Again? When was she a dick the first time?"

"That night, when we had the sex toys and you left, she confronted me in the kitchen when Beth wasn't around and said she didn't believe that I actually wrote these books."

"Why didn't you tell me this?"

"I forgot. And it never came up. We've both been so busy, and I didn't think anything about it."

"Okay." This will be fine. "Okay, you'll do great. Just read and do your thing—"

The promoter talks into the mic, drowning out my voice.

Gretchen hugs me, harder than necessary. When I hand her the books with the preselected passages, her manicured hands are shaking. It's weird to see Gretchen rattled.

"We got this. Ignore Suzette. Make Jaina Jacen shine."

Fist bump.

Applause.

And she's through the curtain.

I'm offstage listening with my thumbnail between my teeth and my heart in my throat. Gretchen's delivery is much stronger this time —she must've practiced since our last event—and when she gets through the section from the second book, she's got the crowd eating out of her hand.

I'm spying from the wings, and when Luke sees me across the space, his eyes light up and he smiles. Commence thundering heart. Oh how I have missed that smile. Two weeks is too long.

Our goofy grin-slash-staring-contest is interrupted when the promoter opens the floor for questions. Gretchen handles herself with total grace, repeating the rehearsed answers to the *where do you get your ideas*, and *how many books are in this series* and *when is the next book coming out*.

"We'll take two more questions, and then Jaina Jacen will be available for autographs over at the table along the wall."

Second-to-last question from a tall woman in black angel wings and a very tall hairdo. Her wingspan blots out the sun. "Do you ever find yourself falling in love with your characters?"

We didn't rehearse this one, but Gretchen manages. We're almost done.

And then the questioner and her wings step aside, and left in the shadow stands Suzette.

Gulp.

"Hi, 'Jaina Jacen,'" she says sarcastically. "I happen to be a fan of waterfowl, and I was wondering how you learned so much about Australia's Blue Duck population."

Gretchen pauses and pulls her ponytail over her shoulder. "Oh, research. Lots and lots of research. I spend a great deal of time on the details for my stories."

"Wow. That's really interesting, considering the Blue Duck is endemic to New Zealand, and is also called the *whio*. But of course, if you did your research, you'd know that."

Gretchen titters nervously. "Oh! Well, thank you for letting me know. Did I get that wrong in the book?"

"Actually, you didn't write about the Blue Duck in either of these books."

The crowd buzzes a little. A few people holler at Suzette to shut up and move on.

"Do you have a point here?" Gretchen asks, her smile tight.

"I do. I've been in a writers' group with you for two years and never seen you write anything other than airheaded summaries of overpriced shoes and clothes that no real human being could ever wear. And now you're trying to tell everyone here that you wrote not just one but two romance novels where you have characters talking about endangered animals you've likely never even heard of? I call bullshit. I think this is fraud, and I think people deserve to know the truth."

The immediate silence is deadly, underscored by a backbeat of a pole dancer's boom box in the section over as she shimmies and glides her way around her apparatus.

"Are you a fake?" someone yells.

"Sit down, lady!"

"Who cares? Shut up!"

A few wadded postcards bean Suzette in the head, but she clamps down on the mic and presses her lips against the mesh, growling like a rock god. "Tell us the truth, **Gretchen**. It's more than a pen name, isn't it? Did you buy this material? *Did you steal it?* Tell everyone here the truth."

Gretchen looks at me. The girl who can handle anything can't handle this.

I ... I have to rescue her. I have to rescue Jaina Jacen.

One foot after another, I hold my breath, mumbling a prayer to a god who probably doesn't remember my name and certainly won't after I'm done here. I put a hand on Gretchen's shoulder.

"Hi ... hi, hey, if you could just settle down for a second." The crowd quiets. "First, Suzette, you're a jerk and I feel sorry for your triplets. Second, lots of people write under pen names. It's how we protect ourselves professionally and diversify—Stephen King wrote as Richard Bachman, J. K. Rowling writes as Robert Galbraith," I hear Dr. McCoy's voice in my head, "and Mary Ann Evans wrote

Middlemarch as one George Eliot back in the 1800s so she would be taken seriously."

"Did she write the words or not?" someone shouts.

"Jaina Jacen did write the words."

"But who is she? Is she even here?"

I lock eyes with Luke where he sits in the far left front row. "I'm Jaina Jacen."

"Her name is Jayne Dandy. She's lying to save her friend," Suzette chirps, looking smug.

"You're right. My name is Jayne Dandy, and I am the writer behind Jaina Jacen."

"Prove it!"

"Why do you care so much about this, Suzette?"

"Because people demand the truth—we deserve the truth!" she hollers. "And you're selling us a product that you say is original, but we have no proof that you didn't just buy it off the Internet, or that you didn't steal it from some other unknown writer. Is that what you did? Did you guys plot this out and steal the content from some poor writer who doesn't even know yet?"

The promoter steps in front of me. "This is ludicrous. You need to leave the venue right now or I will have you escorted out—"

"No, wait a second. If this lady wants to know she's getting her money's worth, I have her proof," I say. I step backstage and grab my bag. From it, I extract another new journal, again draped in the *Pride and Prejudice* book jacket. "I'll give you the first five pages of book three. And then you tell me who the fraud is."

Gretchen stands just behind me. I'm so glad. Without her nearby for support, I might crumple under the weight of the audience's stares.

Especially when Luke stands and walks down the side aisle, disappearing from view.

I thrust the journal into Gretchen's hands. "You finish. Thank you for coming!" I say to the audience, and then I fly down the stairs, chasing after Luke.

He's almost at the front door before I get to him.

"Wait! Luke, please," I holler. He stops but turns slowly. "You're leaving?" He doesn't answer. And his eyes are hard.

"You lied to me about that. I saw Gretchen's picture in the book-store window, and you could've told me right there that this business was all you."

"Is it really that big of a deal? I was embarrassed."

"About what?"

"Because—" I lower my voice, "Jaina Jacen writes erotica."

He laughs under his breath. "You know what? This isn't even any of my business. You can do whatever you want, Jayne."

"Don't be like that—please. I don't understand why you're so mad at me for being embarrassed."

"Because you weren't honest. You didn't trust me enough to tell me about this part of yourself, for whatever messed-up reason you've got going on in your head. You let me believe something other than the truth."

"But I'm telling you now, and I would've told you—I just had to get the guts. I didn't want you to think less of me because I'd written this stuff."

"Why would I think less of you?"

"Because ... it's naughty."

"But it's not. It's normal. You're the only one who thinks it's naughty."

Please don't call me Jaynie Prudie ...

"You know what's even weirder? I should've figured it out. I downloaded the books, and then I went in search of anything else written by Jaina Jacen. It's all sci-fi and fantasy. Gretchen hates that stuff. I'm the idiot for not figuring it out."

"You're not, though. I should've told you." I pause and stare at him. His face looks as hurt as my chest feels. "That day the truck burned down—when we kissed," I say quietly, "I've never allowed anyone to get that close to me. My feelings for you—they're signifi-cant. I thought maybe we were ..."

"We were what? A couple? Together?"

"I thought maybe it was the start of something. At least it was for me."

Luke moves closer. "It is—or it was—for me too. And the last couple of weeks have been weird and busy, but I came home early from Thanksgiving because I wanted to see you. Not because I had to work at the Horse but because I was hoping I could whisk you away for a surprise weekender at the beach." He pulls a piece of paper out of his back pocket and hands it to me. An email confirmation for two nights at The Inn at Cannon Beach. "But you didn't share this part of yourself, even though we've talked about how much I value honesty."

"I know. And I am so sorry for that. But if we could go somewhere and just talk about it, I promise I'll tell you everything." *Including the part about how my main character, Alec, is you.*

He steps back and looks down at his feet, his exhale shuddering his shoulders. "Jayne, this isn't about the books. You know what bothers me most? You're so afraid to be yourself that you let everyone around you dictate who you should be and how you should act. You don't own anything—accomplishments or otherwise—because you're trying so hard to fit in to some impossible ideal that your family has created for you."

"You don't know anything about my family," I growl.

Luke cups my face in his hands. "I know everything about your family, Jayne. And I know you will never be happy until you get honest with yourself. It sucks that you lied to me, but what's even worse is that you spend so much time lying to yourself."

And then he's gone, and I'm alone, standing in a crowd of leather-clad cowboys and whip-carrying sex bunnies, hating Luke because everything he said is the absolute truth.

27

SURPRISINGLY, a number of people stayed behind and wanted their books signed—by both Gretchen and me. That was weird. And fun. But mostly weird. Holden hung back to help us clean up once attendees scrambled away to catch the fashion show where models were sporting far more flesh than leather and mesh.

The plans to go out for post-reading food dissolved when Gretchen complained of a headache, and although I think Holden was disappointed, I was glad that we were going home to quiet. I don't think I can handle any more titillation—of any kind.

The drive home is strained. "You okay?" I ask.

"Fine."

Gretchen pulls in front of our building. En route, we've had no witty banter, no silly commentary on the free show of boobies and leather chaps, not even a snide remark about Suzette's choice of stained sweater.

"You're not okay," I say.

"It's not a big deal."

"What's not a big deal? Clearly something is a big deal if you're upset. Are you mad at me too?"

She sighs. "I'm not mad at you. I'm just not happy about how things went down today."

"I can't believe Suzette pulled that shit. Maybe we should go drown our sorrows in wine," I say, pulling a bottle out from the gift bag the promoter gave to me. "It's called *Pop My Cherry*."

Her smile takes effort.

"Gretchen, come on. What's going on?"

She turns in her seat. "You should've let me handle those people today."

Oh. Wait, what? "But you looked at me—I thought you were begging for help."

"No. I may have been for a sec, but I would've handled it. I just needed a few seconds to get my bearings."

"Okayyyyyy. So you're mad at me because I stepped in and tried to help?"

"No—it's not that I'm 'mad.' I'm just ... disappointed. I've done a lot of work on Jaina Jacen, on the marketing and her image and everything, and now ..."

"And now I screwed it up."

She doesn't respond.

"You think I messed everything up, then. Is that what you're saying?"

"Jayne, while you've been playing food truck and hiding in your room—"

"Because that's my job!"

"I know, but while you've been doing that, I've been doing *this*, and it's disappointing that now it's all going to change."

"How? How is it going to change? What, because you won't be the face of Jaina Jacen anymore?"

She looks right at me, but her eyes aren't friendly or playful.

"Seriously, this is about your ego?"

"Be careful, Jayne. I've taken very good care of this for you—"

"Because I'm paying you!"

"You're paying me twenty-five percent when I'm doing eighty

percent of the work!"

"Oh my God, so this is what it's all about. Money. I thought you of all people—Miss Silver Spoon, Miss Want-for-Nothing—would rise above the call of cash."

Gretchen gets out of the car and stomps up the stairs. I'm hot on her tail.

"You can't leave in the middle of an argument," I say. "It's not healthy."

"You're one to talk."

The *Sssshhhh Little Hipster Sleeping* sign is on the neighbors' door, so the fight is paused until we're in our apartment. Gretchen slams her keys down and hisses back when Quack's sleep is disturbed.

"This isn't about money, Jayne. It was never about the money. You said you'd hire an assistant—that hasn't happened. I've asked about a title for the next book so we can get a spot with this amazing cover designer, and you haven't given me anything. You show up today with a handful of new pages written, but where's the rest of it? How long have you even spent on writing the next book? I'm holding back the wolves who want more, and you're not helping me here."

"I know. And I'm sorry. Now that the food truck is out of the picture—"

"You didn't even need to keep that job once we started seeing the numbers come in from *Resist Me Not*."

"Luke helped me out when I got laid off—as things started to pick up with the first book, I didn't want to just dump him. What kind of friend would that make me?"

"What about me? What kind of friends are we? I'm supposed to be your best friend, and I'm burning out because I'm one person doing the work of five. Do you even have a synopsis for the third book?"

I don't answer.

"You don't, do you. Why?"

"Because. I ... I've got writer's block or performance anxiety or *something*, knowing that people are reading MY words. I'm terrified I'm going to let them down if I can't make this book as good as the other two."

"You will let them down if you don't get that next book out there."

"I know that! And now the whole world is going to know it's *me* writing this stuff, not you—they're going to know that I'm writing sex. Plus Luke is pissed because I lied to him—did I tell you he's downloaded the books? Yeah, it's only a matter of time before he figures out that HE IS ALEC. I'm sorry if I'm not coddling your ego right now, Gretchen, and I'm sorry I haven't hired an assistant—I will—but I am freaking out a little. Okay?"

"No. Not okay. You should've thought about this before you started playing author. Your neuroses are what got you into this mess —now they're going to have to help get you out of it."

She moves into her bedroom and starts packing a bag.

"Where are you going?"

"I need a few days away from all of—this." She swings an arm toward the section of the living room that has become Jaina Jacen headquarters.

"So you're leaving? Just like that?"

"Call it a mini-vacation."

Fine. Two can play this game. "Well, I completed that stack of blog interviews you emailed me the other day, and they're going to need handling, so make sure your mini-vacation involves your laptop."

She laughs, although it's not friendly. "Oh yes, Jaina Jacen, your wish is my command."

When she slams the door, Quack hisses again and then licks her favorite spot on the wall.

I, on the other hand, call Dr. McCoy and leave a message for a Monday morning emergency appointment. I throw *Star Wars: Episode I* in the DVD player and crack open the *Pop My Cherry* so I can slurp my way into a parallel, alcohol-soaked universe.

28

"IT'S BEEN a while since you've been in, so I was pleased to get your message." Dr. McCoy slides a cup of tea across the coffee table.

"I don't even know where to begin," I say, squishing back into the cushions. So I begin with tears. She lets me cry for a handful of minutes and then starts with the questions to unpack everything that has happened in the weeks since I last darkened her doorstep.

I tell her about Jaina Jacen, the success of the books, the situation at the Sexhibition this past weekend and how I haven't heard from Gretchen, the carnage with my parents' splitting and the Thanksgiving fiasco with Holden—and of course, I tell her about Luke. When I spill that we kissed, she claps. Quietly, but it makes me smile nonetheless. For most people, something as mundane as kissing a cute guy wouldn't be grounds for balloons or skywriting. I'm not most people.

"How are you feeling about everything?"

"Lost. Confused. Sad. Scared."

"Why do you think that is?"

"I think Luke said it best the other day. I'm not living for myself. I'm afraid of disappointing everyone, especially my family—"

"Which you know is irrational because your family has made it clear that no matter what you do, it will never be good enough."

"Yeah. I know. But that doesn't mean I don't feel that pull to want them to be proud of me."

"Of course. And you probably always will. But what you need to do is find a place where you're able to say, *hey, this works for me and it doesn't matter what you think,* and move on from there. You're not doing anything illegal or immoral here, Jayne. In fact, quite the opposite. Yes, you are writing material that some might find offensive, but those people don't have to read it. Instead, you've taken ideas from your own head and turned them into a very profitable enterprise, making more money than either of your siblings have likely made in the last three months. You're independent, strong, and smart. You're standing on your own two feet. You've shared your good fortune with Gretchen by giving her meaningful employment and what sounds like a generous share of the pie, which underscores your devotion to her. I think you're doing remarkably well, even if you don't."

When she puts it that way, I smile through tears.

"But I lied. To Luke. And he said that he can't tolerate it when people lie to him. That's how he and his ex-girlfriend parted ways."

"This wasn't a lie told to hurt him, though. This was about self-preservation on your part. I think if you give Luke some time, he'll come around. Sounds like he's sustained a little trauma of his own with the food-truck arson."

I nod. He has. I'm being selfish. Jayne Dandy isn't the only one with real-life problems here.

"And now there's the pressure of needing to write this third book in the series," I say.

"Think about the worst-case scenario. If you don't write it, what happens?"

"Well, I lose fans. And the book sales stop, and then I won't be making any money. Which is dangerous because I'm unemployed."

"Okay. And what's the best-case scenario if you *do* write the next book?"

"More fans. More sales. I avoid homelessness."

"And what about in here?" She taps her chest.

"I love writing. It makes me happy. And whole."

"Both excellent emotions."

"Yeah, but it's the content. I'm terrified to write this stuff and have people know it's me writing it."

"Because it's content of a sexual nature?"

I blush. "Yes."

"But that's why you're Jaina Jacen. You have a pen name so you can keep this separate, right?"

"Yeah. But people want a face to go with the name. And what if I fail? What if the readers hate the new book?"

"Have they hated the other two books?"

"No. Well, some people have left crappy reviews ..."

"You cannot please everyone. No one pleases everyone."

"I know."

"And pleasing yourself is important too."

"Maybe."

"Jayne, I think you're worrying about the wrong things right now. Baby steps. You've got this great momentum going—if you can step outside yourself for a brief moment and take a look at all you've accomplished in a very short time, the pressure of being a failure will abate and the ink will again flow."

When I'm sitting on this couch, with Dr. McCoy walking me through the shadows, everything feels manageable and quiet and calm. But as our last five minutes approaches, it's like I'm sprinting, that I have to say everything else I don't want to forget because I'm not sure when my next appointment will be and the world outside will confuse me all over again as soon as I step foot outside the door.

She leans forward and hands me a business card.

"Dr. Rae Ellis-Garrett," I read. "Who's this?"

"I want to introduce you to her."

"Why? Do I need a specialist? A different kind, I mean?"

She chuckles. "No. You're doing great. She's a colleague—I'm referring you."

"Why?"

"I'm retiring, Jayne."

"What? No!" I'm on my feet, hands fisted, before I reclaim my self-control. I sit. "You can't. Please. I need you—how will I survive?" *No no no no no.*

"My dear girl, thank you for your confidence, but this is all you. Over the last ten months, you have grown in incalculable ways. The young woman who sat on my couch almost a year ago couldn't even say the word 'penis' out loud—and now you've written two books where the male anatomy plays a lead role."

Burn, cheeks, burn. "The verdict is in: therapy has turned me into a pervert."

Dr. McCoy laughs. "Not a pervert at all. During our time together, you have faced some formidable demons. With patience and practice, using the tools I have given you as well as any others Dr. Ellis-Garrett can provide, you will finish knocking down these walls and find the life waiting for you on the other side."

"Wow. You should write this stuff down," I tease. "But there won't be anyone like you. Ever."

"You're almost there, Jayne."

"No. I don't want you to go." Ladies and gentlemen, put your hands together for more tears. "This Dr. Whoever won't be you. She's going to think I'm weird."

Dr. McCoy laughs. "Jayne, she will not think you're weird. She's going to think the same of you that I do—you're intelligent, brave, and resourceful."

"Ha."

"One more thing," she says, handing me a small wooden box. "Open it."

I do. Inside, atop a bed of raffia rests a smooth river rock the color of our dreary November sky. "What's this for?"

"It's a reminder." She points to the black-framed papyrus scroll on the wall. A quote from Khalil Gibran, it reads, "*March on. Do not tarry. To go forward is to move toward perfection. March on, and fear not the thorns, or the sharp stones on life's path.*"

"The rock will serve as a reminder that the sharp stones can be sanded, their jagged edges lessened and tamed. And that every step forward is exactly that: a step forward."

"My very own magic pebble," I say, sniffing.

"Now: you need to go home and write that book. Standing on your own two feet and pleasing yourself will take you farther than any therapy sessions ever could."

After we hug our goodbyes, I keep the umbrella sheathed. The sky gives my tears company, and right now, I need all the friends I can get.

29

AS I PULL alongside the curb, I spy a human sitting on my steps. A human shaped like a food critic. In his lap, he holds a box.

"Holden?"

"Hiya." He stands and places the box on the stair.

"What are you doing here?" It's only twelve thirty. He should be at work.

"Brant Cole closed the paper."

"What?"

"He just shut the whole thing down today. Everyone got pink slips." He digs into his corduroys and pulls out a folded memo—sure enough, on pink paper. "'The *Rose City Register* is to cease operations as of 5 p.m. ... Retrieve any personal effects from the office environment by close of business today.'"

"Holden. Wow. I'm so sorry."

"Easy come, easy go. I left early. What's the point in staying? Everyone's depressed and crying. And I can't get hold of Gretchen, so I brought her stuff. Just in case."

"Thanks. Gretchen will appreciate it."

"Do you know where she is?"

"No. She's ... mad at me."

"Oh, I grabbed something for you," Holden says, smiling as he digs rope-lid pens from Gretchen's box. "For all the books you'll have to sign."

"Thanks." I chuckle and pull one over my head. "So ... what are you gonna do?"

"Take a couple days off, and then I'll start looking for another job. Maybe you need a personal assistant?" I do, actually, but ... not Holden. "Suppose I'll have possibilities lined up out the door—minor in folklore and all that."

"You'll land on your feet."

"Feels like I just went through this. But I will miss all those free meals ..." Probably as much as I miss the éclairs and turnovers. I feel his pain.

"Hey ... what have you got planned for the rest of today?" I say, feeling impulsive.

"My options are open."

"You like ducks?"

WEEKDAYS ARE quiet on the farm. The animals aren't as skittish when fewer city folk are shuffling and raking and scooping. The weather is typical for the first of December—darkened skies thick with clouds awaiting their chance to explode, the occasional breeze short but fierce, reminding us which season is in charge. When I was a kid, I always felt sorry for the autumn trees stripped of their leaves. I asked my dad once if we could bring the trees in our yard inside so they wouldn't be so alone or cold during the long rainy months. Oregonians—we like trees.

I introduce Holden to the farm's owners and then lead him into the barn, although his Top-Siders aren't great for the muddy pathways. Inside is a little better—hay has been thrown down—but his reticence to get too close to the goats or Mildred the horse makes me laugh.

"They won't hurt you," I say, handing him a green apple from the bucket near the door. "Like this. Flat palm. Granny Smith's are Mildred's favorite."

The old brown mare chomps down, leaving a slobber trail on Holden's palm. He looks at me like he's been painted with acid.

"Seriously, city boy? You're making me look bad." I throw him a shop towel. "Come. Meet the ducks."

The last stall in the barn has been refitted for the waterfowl—it has a pond and benches and plenty of hay and alfalfa for the birds to cuddle in. Spoiled critters.

"This one's Beru." I point over the stall's half door at my little mottled duck curled in her hay. "And that one over there with the brilliant green neck is Owen, her partner."

"Did you name all of them?"

"No. Just these two. I helped rescue them from Westmoreland Park in the spring. We sort of adopted each other."

"Why do you do this? The farm and everything?" he asks.

"Because I love animals. And I want to do something to help," I say. "Don't you have a 'thing'? Something that's just yours?"

Holden is quiet for a moment. "You know, I don't. That makes me sound so lame."

"Well, no time like the present. You're unemployed—"

He slaps a hand over his heart, as if injured. "Thanks for reminding me."

"You'll find another job soon. Hell, you could write a food blog."

"I've been thinking about going back for my master's."

"In folklore?" I tease.

"Very funny. No, I need a teaching certificate. I could teach high school English."

"You're afraid of a horse and a few goats, but you would willingly walk into a room full of teenagers?"

"Yeah. Wow. What's wrong with me?"

Just as my hand is on the stall latch into the ducks' enclosure,

Holden lets out a blood-curdling scream. Attached to the end of his finger is a goat.

"Fang! No! Release!"

"Dear Jesus, you named the goat Fang? GET HER OFF!" he screams. I know it hurts, but he sounds like a little girl. Dale the farmhand comes running and shoves his finger into Fang's jaw, releasing her grip on Holden's hand.

What is pulled free is a bitey, bloody mess. Shit. That's going to need stitches.

Holden sinks to his knees and looks up at me. He's very pale, very quickly.

"You'll be okay. You're okay. Right? You okay, Holden?" It's not funny. *STOP LAUGHING, JAYNE.*

"Why are you laughing at me? Omigod, this fucking hurts! Ohhhh ... I'm going to throw up."

And he does. He leans over right there in the barn and upchucks his breakfast into the hay.

I apologize to Dale on the way out—he's laughing too—and escort Holden to my car. I don't know where the hospitals are in Tigard. I opt for Emmanuel.

It is a quiet ride back into Portland, interrupted only by Holden sucking in pained air through his teeth.

I drop him off at the emergency exit and then retreat into the lot to park.

And then I see it—the Piewalker truck parked at the lot's end. Shit, does that mean Luke is here? Is he hurt? Is Leia okay?

Holden's fingers are meaty and bloody enough that they don't make him wait long for a bed. My, how the tables have turned. Now if only I could get someone to call me about a budgie emergency ...

It's unfortunate that my friend had his fingers gnawed on by a curious goat but I can't stop worrying about why Luke's truck is here.

I text him.

A few minutes later, his response: *I'm fine. Leia fell off her bike. Broken wrist. Why R U here? U okay?*

I don't want to have a text conversation about the fact that I'm here with Holden. Instead: *Can we meet up? By the front entrance?*

Be down in five, he says.

My hands don't know what to do with themselves and I am glad I'm in a hospital because my chest is thunderous and my heart might stop working knowing that Luke is here and I am going to see him imminently and my hair is a mess and it doesn't help that I smell like the barn because after all I'm wearing my barn clothes so duh—

"Jayne," Luke says behind me. I jump a foot.

"Hey! How are you? How's Leia?"

"She's all right. They're talking about whether she'll need surgery. Something about a free-floating bone chip at the head of the radius."

"In English?"

He laughs under his breath. "I don't know. I'm just waiting."

"But she's okay otherwise?"

"A few scrapes and bruises. Some asshole knocked her down in a crosswalk. Could've been much worse."

"I'm glad she's okay. Tell her I said hi."

"I will."

Awkward pause.

"So, why are you here? You don't look swollen," he asks.

"No, not me this time. I, uh, I took Holden out to the Tigard farm today and Fang bit him."

"Fang?"

"A goat."

"Named Fang."

"Yeah ... she's bitey. I should've warned him."

"So ... you're hanging out with Holden?"

Shit. I was worried he would think this is something other than it is. "No. Not really. He showed up at my apartment today—Brant Cole closed down the newspaper, so Holden brought Gretchen's stuff by. Anyway, he seemed depressed so I thought maybe some time at the farm would cheer him up."

Luke's face warms a few degrees. "I'll bet he didn't expect to be a meal for a goat."

"I should've known. He was really uncomfortable around the animals, and Fang capitalizes on scaring the city slickers every chance she gets."

"Good to know," he says, smiling. And then the smile fades. "You know, in case I ever go."

"Any time. I'd love to take you out there."

His phone goes off. "Shit. I gotta run. They're going to take Leia in for surgery after all."

"Right. Yeah. Okay." *Do it, Jayne. Apologize. Right now. Before he leaves.* "Luke ... about everything ..."

"Not today, Jayne. I gotta go."

And with that, he's off, the elevator doors swallowing him into the belly of the beast while I stand here and try to think of the best way to untangle the knots clotting my heart.

30

AFTER AN IMPRESSIVE NUMBER of stitches have been looped through the chewed flesh on the pinky and ring fingers of Holden's left hand, he's loaded with antibiotics and released to my care, doped up on OxyContin. He slurs the instructions to his parents' house. Perfect—even though it's technically my fault that he was Fang's chew toy today, I don't feel like playing nursemaid. Not tonight.

My apartment is dark and cold without Gretchen buzzing around and the stereo on and her laptop glowing. I chirp involuntarily when I step around the room divider and see a body sitting on the couch.

"Mom? What are you doing here?" Quack is sprawled across Sheila Dandy's lap, purring. Of course she is. "And how did you get in?"

"Those hippies who live downstairs gave me your key. They didn't even ask for ID. You really shouldn't trust hippies."

I move to turn a lamp on.

"Don't. I like it dark. I think your psycho cat likes it dark too," she says. "Nice outfit."

Ignoring her commentary, I sit across from her. "Why are you here?"

"I want to know the truth." She waves a hand at the Jaina Jacen stuff on the wall. "Is this you and not Gretchen?"

This could go one of two ways: she's either going to be proud that I've created this little empire, or she's going to be disgusted that her youngest daughter is writing what she calls "porn."

"Margaret already told me. You don't have to think so long before answering or else I'll know you're lying." How did Margaret find out? Oh God—was she at the Sexhibition?

"Yes, Mother, Jaina Jacen is my pen name. I write the stories."

"Why is Gretchen involved?"

"I was embarrassed. Plus she's prettier than I am—pretty faces sell books. A lot of reasons. Why does it matter?"

"Because if the people at the club find out that my daughter is writing pornographic material, I will never be able to show my face there again."

My mother's truth revealed. Silly me hoping against hope.

"Well, I'm sorry if you don't approve, Mother, but this is me, and this is what I did—what I still do—and I've made some serious money in the last three months, which is great because as you know, I don't have a 'real' job anymore, so I'm going to keep doing it because people like my words, and really, they're the ones who matter—"

"How am I supposed to tell anyone about this?"

"I don't know, Mother. Don't tell anyone. And don't worry, the pseudonym will prevent sullying of the Dandy family name."

"You have talent, Jayne. Which is why I'm shocked that you'd stoop to write pornography. And I'm glad you're not at that paper anymore."

"Wait—what?" Did she just admit that I have *talent*?

"Languishing under that weasel Cole was a terrible waste of your time. And it's not like there were any husband prospects."

"In the twenty-first century, women work for reasons other than to find husbands." She snorts at me, startling the cat. "And how do you know Brant Cole?"

"His parents belong to the country club. The whole family is corrupt."

"Oh."

Her phone buzzes. Again. She silences it and flops her hand against the couch cushions. She's quiet, but only because she can't speak through tears. And I am totally at a loss as to what I should do because I've only seen my mother cry twice before, and both incidents involved stains on expensive clothing.

"Your father is leaving. For good. He's selling the house. I have to move into a—" she pauses and whispers, "a condominium."

"Wow. I'm sorry, Mom."

"There goes next summer in Europe. Plus he says we have to give up the timeshare in Maui, and so much for Christmas this year. My phone won't stop ringing with creditors from accounts he didn't know I opened, and the allowance he's put me on isn't enough for a pauper's funeral. And I'm sure whatever annual bonus he's due, I'll never see a penny of it."

"Mom, you guys were together a long time. He'll have to pay you alimony."

"If he'd left when you guys were still at home, I could've nailed him for child support too."

Wow. This is a gross conversation.

"I think this is a good opportunity for you to start over, Mom. Dad will make sure you get into a nice place, and you'll never need for anything."

"Easy for you to say. You don't have any overhead to speak of, living in this dump. Oh, I know—maybe I can start writing trashy stories and make some money that way."

God, why does she do this?

"That demon-whore he's with—did you know she's thirty-eight? I thought she was some hot young secretary. Turns out she's a lawyer. Works in the brokerage's legal department. And yes, she's pretty, but she has bigger hips than I do. I know what's going to happen—she's going to get pregnant on purpose and then he'll be trapped with new babies." She laughs to herself. "Let's see how well he does in his sixties with a newborn. Then again, she'll just hire a nanny to take care of everything. Hell, she'll probably hire a surrogate so she doesn't have to interrupt her busy lawyer schedule to incubate. Not like me—not like how I raised all of you. Not how I let my body be destroyed by pregnancy after pregnancy, just to keep my man happy. I gave him, and his children, the best years of my life. And this is how he repays me?"

"Did you ever stop to think that maybe he got tired of you being so mean?"

She stares at me, eyes hardening. It's like watching an iceberg refreeze under the influence of an arctic wind. "You hold your tongue, young lady."

"Why are you here, Mom? Were you thinking that I was going to agree with you and tell you the things you wanted to hear? Because I don't even begin to know what that would be."

"You always were a daddy's girl. Just like you to take his side." She knocks Quack off her lap.

"I'm nobody's girl. Dad was always working, and you've always treated me like I was the kid you didn't want—"

"I was fine with two children."

Ouch. When I was little, Frankie used to call me the mistake, but I thought he was just being Frankie. "Well, sorry, Mom, but you've got three."

"Yes, I do. A dermatologist, a lawyer ... and a writer of pornography. I will likely win Mother of the Year."

I hear Dr. McCoy's voice in my head: *"You need to find a place where you're able to say, hey, this works for me and it doesn't matter what you think, and move on from there."*

"I think you should go." I stand. Sheila Dandy looks at me, wide-eyed. For a brief second, I see fear flash in her face and I feel bad. She's been handed a big shock, and I should be there for her.

And then I laugh quietly.

"I wasn't planning on staying anyway. I only stopped here to let you know what's going on with your father. I suppose I should've just saved us both the trouble and sent you a text message."

"You can send future messages via text. Save yourself the embarrassment of standing in my den of iniquity."

Quack swipes at my mother's leg as she stands. "There is something seriously wrong with that animal."

"Who, Quack? She has perfect instincts. Don't you, Quack?" On cue, she hisses and spits, ushering Sheila Dandy toward the door. Mother straightens her pantsuit and tucks her hair around her ears.

"I have no idea what this means for Christmas," she says, hand on the doorknob.

"You can text me."

When Sheila is finally gone, Quack yowls, springs into the kitchen sink, and curls up for a nap.

"Me too, kitty cat. Me too."

31

FORTY-EIGHT HOURS. That's all I get until someone taps my forehead and waves a maple-smelling delight under my nostrils.

Eyes squinted. The room is too bright. Head is hurting. I vaguely remember wine, definitely some Bailey's, marathon television on Netflix ...

"Get up, lazy bones. You stink."

Gretchen's home!

"Hey! Hi," I say, sitting up. An open box of donuts sits on the table. I did smell maple. A whole box of maple bars. They're not Piewalker turnovers but beggars need sugar. "How are you? Are you okay? Did you hear about the paper?"

"Yeah. I'm fine. I just needed a few days away. Brant Cole's a douche. I'm surprised it didn't happen sooner."

I bite into a pillowy fluff of baked dough. "Are you still mad at me?"

She plops into the chair across and drops her purse to the floor. "No."

"Holden brought your stuff home. From the office." Ah, poor Holden.

"Thanks."

The cat smells the maple. She jumps on to my lap and takes a healthy bite out of the opposite end of the pastry in my mouth.

"That's not good for her," Gretchen says.

"Are you going to tell her no?"

"I value my life too much." She chuckles and shakes her head. "What'd I miss in my brief absence?"

"Dr. McCoy is retiring. And Holden got attacked by a goat at the Tigard farm."

"What the hell?" A smile crinkles her cheeks.

I share what happened with Holden, and how I ran into Luke at the hospital. And how weird it was.

"You could always call and check on Leia. If you needed an excuse."

"He didn't seem too interested in talking to me."

"He was probably stressed about his sister."

"Maybe."

"I'm sorry to hear about Dr. McCoy. What are you going to do?" she asks.

I look around the apartment, at the box with Dr. McCoy's river rock on the coffee table. The kitchen table holds stacks of paperback books that need signing and mailing; boxes of swag and postcards Gretchen designed and ordered sit under the fold-up table that serve as Gretchen's office, notebooks and file folders thick with spreadsheets and notes in organized piles. So much evidence of her industry and devotion to Jaina Jacen.

"She's referring me to her colleague. But until then, I'm going to write another book. And then maybe after that, I'll write another one."

"Sounds like a good plan."

"First, though, I need to make sure my best friend is still interested in acting as my manager."

A small smile pulls at Gretchen's cheek. "How about if your best friend helps you find an assistant so you can keep writing?

Because it might be hard to manage Jaina Jacen's career ... from Milan."

I yelp when Quack bites too far into the donut and sinks into flesh. "What did you say?"

Gretchen's teeth shine in the dim light. "I've been offered a job. It's just a temporary thing for now—Eric's sister works as a designer at a fashion house over there, and she's asked me to come and be her assistant, to document what she's working on for the next two seasons."

"Eric? As in, little-wiener Eric?"

"Duh. Why do you think I was dating him?"

"God, you're so shallow and devious. And brilliant."

"I sort of am." She grins.

And then we're again on our feet, jumping like freaks, hugging, wiping tears from faces.

"Gretch, this is huge. When do you leave?"

"A couple of weeks? It sort of depends on if you want me to move out of here—if you do, I have to get everything into storage first. Otherwise I could go as soon as next week. If my visa comes through without any problems."

What am I going to do without her here?

"You leave everything where it is. We can deal with that after you figure out what's happening in Italy. What if you get there and Eric's sister is a dragon lady and you have to come home? You need a place to come home to."

"Wherever you are will always be my home," Gretchen says, wrapping her arms around me. "But you really need a shower."

"Wait, though. What about the band? I have a new name for it."

"Hit me."

"I think we should call ourselves 'Penis Fiction.'"

Gretchen cackles. "Omigod, you said *penis* and didn't hyperventilate. I think my job here is done," she says. "Don't worry, little rock goddess. We'll always have the band."

32

AND JUST LIKE THAT, Jaina Jacen is on her own.

It's a whirlwind ten days of Gretchen getting me up to speed with where the business is at, showing me the social media ropes, introducing me to the new webmaster handling Jaina's online forums and all the other folks who make these books saleable. We interview and hire a college intern—Liesl, an English major from Portland State —to help out so I can focus on writing.

Which means I spend a lot of time in my room staring out the window at the brick building next to us because every sentence I start sounds ridiculous. You know, if you stare at something long enough, faces and shapes start to form, likely conspiring against you. A rather interesting hole between two bricks could fit a tiny camera—is that where the government is spying on me? Maybe I should go hide under my covers again. I was able to write when I didn't think anyone was watching.

Words, Jayne.

His velvety touch sent shivers down her spine.

No. Erase.

His velvety lips scorched her breathless abdomen.

Seriously? Delete.

"Lips are made for kissing, and you should be kissing mine."

Whose idea was this?

A knock on the apartment door—I let Liesl get it, but when I hear a male voice, my heart flutters. It almost sounds like ...

"Jayne! You have company," Liesl says through my door. A quick check in the mirror. I'm so glad I remembered to tuck the girls into a bra.

Breath mint on board. Tidy the stringy hair. This Stormtrooper shirt is cool enough, right?

Bedroom door open. Deep breath. I've really missed him and I can't believe he's here to—

"He says he has a singing telegram for you?" Liesl says. That voice didn't belong to Luke. It belongs to a skinny guy dressed as a Christmas elf.

"Are you Jayne Dandy?"

"If I say no, will you not sing?"

The elf looks at Liesl. She nods and smiles.

"This is from Holden:

POINSETTIAS ARE RED,

> *Snow is soft and white,*
> *I'm sorry our first date ended in anaphylaxis,*
> *With lips swollen and throat tight.*
> *Your goat friend, with teeth so sharp,*
> *Nine stitches were my prize; on that, I shall not harp.*
> *If only we could try again,*
> *At this festive time of year,*
> *We could skate and shop and laugh,*
> *I'll even spring for beer.*
> *And I promise this time,*
> *To you I shall be true,*
> *Budgies and goats will have to wait,*

Until our time is through."

AND THEN THE elf stops singing. "Best wishes for a happy Christmas, from your friend Holden."

Liesl claps excitedly—I sort of stare at the guy, unsure of what just happened. When he doesn't leave, I realize he's waiting for a tip. All I have is a fiver and a Starbucks card with enough left on it for maybe one and a half coffees.

As soon as he's out of my doorway, Holden takes his place, bouquet in bandaged hand.

"What did you think?"

"You didn't have to hire a Christmas elf. You're unemployed, remember?"

"He's my neighbor. Just starting out so he needs practice. You were actually doing him a solid."

"I want a pair of those striped tights," I say. "Come on in." Holden steps through the door and hands me the flowers. "Liesl, Holden. Holden, this is Liesl, my new assistant." It still sounds weird calling her that. I'm like a grown-up—I have an *assistant*.

"Is she working you too hard yet, Liesl? A real slave driver, this one," Holden teases, a gentle nudge in my ribs.

"How are the ..." I nod toward his left hand. He lifts it, the last two fingers buddy-taped together.

"Sore. Stitches are out. I think my guitar will be plucked again."

"Again, I'm so sorry."

"It was an adventure," he says. "I wanted to come check on you and see how you're doing, you know, with Gretchen off to chase Italian shoes."

"I'm expecting the first FedEx shipment of stilettos and straps any day now."

Liesl hands me a stack of notes and grabs her bag. "I gave Quack her medicine in a hot dog. She seemed to like that much better."

Hunh. Hot dog. I hadn't tried that one.

Once Liesl is gone, I am overrun by anxious quivers—and not the altogether good kind. Holden is here, and we're alone, and he's brought flowers and he's asking me out *again*. And he's standing very close as I fill the vase in the kitchen sink.

When his hands migrate to my shoulders and commence massaging, I realize I'm in trouble.

"You're tight. Our little writer has been spending too much time hunched over her computer, me thinks," he says. "Come sit. I'll rub this out for you."

Oh God. I can't do this. Not with Holden.

I feel lightheaded. Flirting with nausea. "You go sit. I'll put on some coffee. Oh, beware of the cat."

I have to get him out of here. I cannot be alone in this apartment with Holden when he's just done two nice things for me because maybe he's expecting some sort of repayment and of course he is because he had his hands on my body and now he's going to want to kiss and maybe touch me and the last time he kissed me it was like noshing on a banana slug and ...

Oh, Gretchen, I miss you so much. If you were here, you could shoo him out and tell him to go find food to critique or perms to buy.

Food. We could get food. That will get him out of the apartment and maybe curtail any thoughts about touching my roundy parts.

"Hey, I was just about to grab an early dinner. You up for it? I'm buying," I say.

Holden's made himself comfortable on the couch—loafers are off, revealing mismatched argyle socks. "Uh, sure. Yeah. That sounds good."

I've commandeered the BMW while Gretchen is out of the country, although she was careful to install seat covers before she handed over the keys. "I've been friends with you for too long to trust white leather interior to Jayne Dandy." Of course, she had to choose leopard-print seat covers, but the stereo system overrules the humiliation. I can afford a new car of my own, maybe even a shiny little number like Gretchen's, but why buy the cow when I'm getting the milk for free?

I choose a pub—loud, busy with holiday revelers, no booths. Conversation is friendly enough, if not a little strained. Holden is an affable guy, but I can't stop worrying about what's going to happen when the bill is paid and it's time for us to leave. And then I feel worse because I thought I was making such great progress, and even Dr. McCoy said she was proud of me for working through some of my man-related anxieties. It feels like one step forward, forty-two steps back.

And then I realize what's missing here: I was able to work through those anxieties because I was with Luke—not Holden. The common denominator isn't me being frigid; it's me being here with the wrong guy.

"Hey, you want to head over to the Copper Horse tonight? I heard that Leia Walker's band is playing. Apparently they're pretty good," Holden says.

Oh God. No way. What if Luke's there? He supports his sister. And his buddy owns the Copper Horse, so what if Luke's helping out again, which is very likely because the food truck is bye-bye, and then if he *is* there and he sees me with Holden ...

"You know, I'm actually really tired tonight."

"Come ooooon, Madame Scribe. You can't hide behind your screen forever. One night is all I'm after."

"Holden ..."

"I'm not taking no for an answer, so you can sit there and wiggle all you want," he says, finishing his beer. "Thus far, I see no signs of anaphylaxis, so I'm taking it as a sign that you are meant to hang out with me. Tonight." And before I beat him to it, he swipes the car keys off the table and dangles them in his face. "Checkmate."

Shit.

33

THE COPPER HORSE IS PACKED.

I scan faces, trying not to be too obvious as I look for Luke. I don't see him behind the bar, but that doesn't mean he's not here. Leia is, though, rocking her heart out on the cramped stage—even with a neon pink cast on her right wrist and hand, she's jumping and slamming a tambourine into her scantily clad butt. I laugh to myself. Can't keep a good twin down.

Holden takes my hand and leads me to a table in the corner where some of his friends are already halfway to drunk. Thank heavens. We're not going to be alone.

He introduces me the best he can given the lack of space left for conversation over the blaring amps. A quick finger up and over his shoulder, and he's swallowed by the crowd to retrieve drinks. It's damn loud, but I'm grateful—no awkward chats with Holden's friends about the status of our relationship or how I know him or how long we've been dating. Because we're not dating. Holden knows that, right?

Tell me he knows that. It takes more than a singing Christmas elf to inspect the thread count of my bed sheets.

Holden returns with two sweating microbrews and slides on to a chair shoved a little too close to mine. And then his arm is around the back of my chair and he's leaning into my ear. "What do you think? Pretty good, yeah?"

I nod and swallow a protracted sip.

"Hey, I didn't know Luke worked here," he says. "He told me to tell you hi."

"He's here? Tonight?" I look over at the bar. A huge, bearded guy moves enough to his right that I get a clear view of the counter—and Luke's face as he grins and hands over a beer to a patron.

My breath catches.

I can't believe how much I've missed seeing that smile.

I have to talk to him. But is that rude? If I leave Holden sitting here to go talk to another guy? No. It's not, right? Luke's my friend. My former Piewalker's coworker-slash-boss. A fellow fancier of Jedis and the Rebel Alliance. Baker of divine treats and the only boy who hasn't induced a panic attack when he put his mouth parts against my mouth parts.

"I'm gonna pop over and say hello," I yell into Holden's ear. Thumbs up.

Commence gastric clenching.

I muscle through flirty conversations and booze-addled debates to slide in between bodies at the end of the bar. Luke's busy, so I wait. And wait. And wait.

Until finally he sees me. While his smile is there, it's not the melter he usually throws my way. "Ms. Dandy. Can I get you something?"

"I just wanted to come say hi. I've ... I've missed you. How are things?"

"Things are fine. A lot of paperwork, like you said," he says, wiping the bar down in front of me with a bleach rag. The smell reminds me of the food truck. Fun times. And they weren't so long ago. What a difference a month makes.

"So, have you decided? If you're going to open up another food truck, or ...?"

"We're still considering our options. Tiana's father is pretty embarrassed about what happened, so he's settling out of court for the damages. Plus the insurance money. We're looking at properties for a real café."

"Wow! Are you serious?" I'm so excited for him, my hand lands on his before I realize what I've done. We pause, and then he looks down at the floor and slides his hand free. "Luke ... please. I want to talk. I feel terrible about—everything. I really miss you."

"And that's why you're here with him?" He nods in Holden's direction.

"God, no. Holden—he's just ... Holden. He doesn't know what he wants."

Luke chuckles. "Yes ... he does."

"We're just friends. And I've been lonely. Gretchen left for a new job in Italy, and I've been trying to write a new book but I'm really struggling ... I'm trying to get my bearings without the two most important people in my life."

He pauses, his face softening a little. And then it's gone again. "Well, thanks for coming to support Leia and her band," he says.

"Why are you still mad at me? I didn't mean to keep anything from you."

"That's the problem, Jayne. You *did* keep something from me."

"But I had a good reason! Didn't I?"

Another quiet pause. Then he flips up the hinged section at the end of the bar and indicates for me to follow him. A quick peek back at Holden, engrossed in his chums, and I'm clinging to Luke's fingertips as he pulls me toward the front door.

The outside air, while chilly, refreshes instantly. He pulls me along the walkway, out of the way of the front door.

I speak first. Before I lose my nerve. "I can't stop thinking about you, and I check my phone about a thousand times a day to see if you've returned any of my texts." *Keep going, Jayne.* "I didn't think that what I did was bad enough to drive you away."

"You didn't drive me away. I've just been busy."

"But you haven't texted me back."

"Stuff's been crazy. My dad had a health scare while we were down for Thanksgiving—"

"Is he okay?"

"Yeah, he's fine. But then the crap with the food truck and hiring a lawyer and dealing with the police and Leia's bike accident. It's been a lot of stuff."

"But ... I would've helped you through it. That's what friends do."

He nods and looks down at his feet briefly. "Jayne, based on what I know about you—what you've shared with me—it must've been really, really hard for you to write those stories. And I think what you did at the reading, saving Gretchen like that—you were very brave right then."

"You think so?" My voice is barely audible.

"I just wish you would've told me about it before. Because not telling me about it indicates that you have problems with honesty. That scares me."

"But Luke, given what you know about me, telling you, *hey, guess what, I wrote about people having sex because my therapist thought it would be a good exercise and oh by the way now I'm selling it to the public*—"

"That's all it would've taken. What you just did right there, rather than me finding out when I came to a sex-toy convention and learned the secret alongside all those weird strangers."

"But it's not that big of a secret! It's so dumb and insignificant—I don't understand why you're so bothered."

"If it's not such a big deal, why were you so embarrassed?"

"Because. You know why. I have ... issues."

"But beyond that, Jayne, you weren't honest. It's the principle. And I wanted to be that guy—the one you could come to with your secrets."

"I've told you things about me no one else knows. Except maybe Gretchen."

He steps closer and tugs on a few strands of my hair. "I know."

I grab his hand. "Please, trust me. There are no more secrets. It was just a bizarre thing to tell you and I didn't want you to be ashamed or embarrassed by me."

"I'm not your mother, Jayne."

I nod and look down. My eyes sting. I hate that Sheila Dandy has this ridiculous power over me. His finger lifts my chin.

"I would never be ashamed or embarrassed by anything you've done. And especially not by anything you've written."

I laugh against the threat of tears. "You don't know that. You haven't seen—" He grins like a canary. Oh man. "Omigod, you've read the books?"

"I told you I downloaded them."

"Yeah, but I didn't think you'd *read* them."

"You're a terrific writer, Jayne. I've never seen anyone turn a heaving bosom into something so ... real."

"Oh God ... Luke—my main character, Alec ... I am so sorry."

"Don't be sorry. I'm flattered. And Alec sounds like a total stud."

My neck and cheeks and ears are so on fire, they throb. Even my eyeballs ache.

"That's one of the reasons I didn't want you to read it. I'm so embarrassed ..." I cup my cheeks in my hands. They're near feverish from fluster.

"Stop being so embarrassed. You should be damn proud of yourself." And then Luke is closer again, and I inhale his scent, cologne and bleach and sweat, and I want to throw him against the building and do ungodly things to him in front of Jesus and everyone because we're both licking our lips and I think he might be remembering that night we made dinner because I know I am—

But my buzzing phone has another plan.

"Holden?" he says, taking a step back.

"I swear, we're only friends. He's not the one for me." I grab just above Luke's elbow before he can step farther away. "Honest. I have everything to lose by you not believing me."

A fingertip brushes my cheek. "Go back in. Before he comes looking for you."

"When can I see you again? I'm having serious Piewalker withdrawals."

"You only want me for my cream filling."

Uproarious laughter. "Oh my God, I can't believe you said that."

"You—or rather Jaina—can use it. No charge."

I reenter the pub ahead of Luke, though when I weave through the pulsating crowd of sweat and tequila, it's not the sight of Holden that makes my heart pitter-pat but the promise that I might have found my way back into the good graces of the one person whose company I desire most, above all else.

34

SOMEONE HAS LINED UP SHOTS. And already the tabletop is littered with empty shot glasses, so Holden and his friends have been very busy in my brief absence.

"Everything okay?" Holden says as I retake my seat. His breath is flammable and his eyes appear to be floating in their sockets.

I nod. "Brilliant." I smile. "You guys having fun here?"

"Every time the band uses foul language in one of their songs, you do a shot."

Which means every twelve seconds. I've been reseated for less than a minute and the girl to Holden's left has already downed two, one behind the guy sitting to her left. These people are going to be corpses before night's end.

This is why I'm always the designated driver. Getting plastered in public and then puking my way across the city is so uninteresting.

Two hours later, the crowd has thinned and the band finally finishes the longest set in the history of garage bands. And Holden is plastered. Fantastic.

One of his buddies, a nondrinker, helps me get him into Gretchen's car. No sign of Luke as I'm leaving, which is disappointing. Their truck is still in the lot, but that doesn't mean anything—could've been Leia using it for the band.

I roll the car window all the way down and threaten Holden. "Do not barf in this car. Gretchen will kill you and they will never find your body." He probably thinks I'm kidding.

He snores all the way back to my apartment. There's no way he can drive in this condition, and if I lock him in his crappy car overnight, he'll become Holden the Popsicle. And I don't know where he lives. I sort of remember where his parents live, but showing up after midnight with their soused son might not go over so well.

"Holden, we're at my place. Can you get up the stairs?"

"Yeah ... sure. I can do that." His head flops in my direction. "God, Jayne, you are so beautiful."

Great.

"Okay, thanks, Holden. Let's get you upstairs."

Our noise wakes the hippies and the husband, Rand, upon opening their door, sees I'm struggling to drag Holden's drunken ass up the stairs, so he jumps in to help. I unfold the sleeper sofa and we plunk Holden down.

Quack loves Rand, so she's at his leg, purring and rubbing. I think it's because he always smells like weed, and through an unfortunate but memorable "we accidentally smoked weed instead of finishing our taxes" incident one night a few years back, we learned that Quack has a strange fascination and taste for sandwich baggies filled with dried green plant.

"Jayne, tell me you're going to cozy up in here with me," Holden says.

Rand kisses Quack's head and passes her to me. "Good luck. If I hear the rockin', I won't bother knockin'," he teases.

When the front door clicks closed, I am alone with a very drunk food critic.

I give him a tall glass of water, two ibuprofen, and a banana. He's still going to be hungover but this will mitigate the worst of it.

"You're a keeper, Jayne Dandy," he says, flopping against the flimsy sofa mattress. And when his snorty breathing turns to a bona fide drunk-induced growl, I'm so relieved.

Doesn't mean I don't wedge my office chair against my bedroom door, though. I want an early warning system should drunk Holden become undrunk Holden with a boner at 3 a.m.

THE KNOCK on the front door beats my alarm clock. Although at first I'm not sure it is knocking because maybe it was just in my dream —you know how that happens when noises in your environment work their way into a sound sleep.

And then I hear footsteps and the cat hisses and the chain-lock is sliding and the deadbolt disengages and I know someone's answering the door.

Holden—answering the door!

I'm up and out just in time to see a pink box placed in Holden's hands. Holden, who is wearing nothing but plaid boxers and his hipster glasses and his hair is a mess of wild curls.

He's holding a pastry box. With pastries.

I fly to Holden's side and watch Luke's backside as he skips down the stairs.

Shit. No.

"Luke! Wait!" He doesn't. Oh God, and I have morning breath and terrible hair and raccoon eyes and no bra and I'm in my sleeping shorts. But I have to stop him. He's out the front door before I find a second shoe to throw on to go after him.

His hand is on the truck's door handle. "Luke!"

He turns. "Just friends, huh?"

"Oh, no—I know what this looks like. Nothing happened. I swear."

"Then why when I handed over the box did he say you were still curled up but he'd tell you I came by?"

"Jesus, Luke, you of all people should know that I wouldn't do—

that—with him." It's freezing out here. "Can we go back upstairs and talk? Come up and have some coffee."

"I think one man in your bed is enough."

"He is not in my bed! Will you just listen to me? He was too drunk last night to drive himself home, and I couldn't very well leave him to freeze to death in his car. Ask Rand—ask my neighbor—he helped me carry him upstairs."

"It's okay, Jayne. I should've called before stopping by."

"Please ... Luke. This isn't what you think."

"Jayne, everything okay?" Holden shouts from the main door. *Go away, Holden.*

"I'll call you," Luke says, and he's in the truck sliding away from the curb before I can make him believe that I'm not a scheming, slutty freak show.

35

I DON'T GIVE Holden time to inspect what's in the pastry box. I pile his clothes into his arms and shoo him toward the door, despite his protests that he thought we could have breakfast and go Christmas shopping and something about meeting his parents later for a movie.

"Holden, no. Please. You're a nice guy. But no—"

"You're friend-zoning me. Aren't you. That's what this is, right?" He pulls on his corduroys. He has very skinny legs for a food critic.

"You are a great guy. And a lovely friend. And I think we should totally hang out—as *friends*. But I'm not ever going to be that girl for you."

"Because of him?"

I look at Holden's blue-gray eyes. "Maybe. I don't know."

"And I screwed this up for you, didn't I?" I don't answer. When his shirt is over his head, Holden sighs and pulls me in for a hug. "You're awesome, Jayne. If I can only be your friend, that's what I'll take." He kisses my temple. "But I might try again. In case you change your mind."

I won't. I keep that to myself.

I need Gretchen but she's nine hours ahead and she might be sleeping or out partying with her new fancy Italian friends. Next best crutch: Dr. McCoy. I know she's not seeing patients anymore, but I call her and leave a voicemail anyway. Maybe she's at her office packing up her *Star Trek* memorabilia and she'll invite me to come help. I have pastries!

Liesl shows up. Of course she does. Because that's what I hired her to do. But because technically, I'm her boss, I can't tell her my life problems. That would be too weird. Plus she's all of nineteen or twenty and she probably thinks I'm an old woman with old-woman problems. I remember being nineteen and thinking twenty-six-year-olds were ancient—practically *thirty*. O.M.G.

The only alternative until I find someone reasonable to talk to is to force a pen into my hand and scratch words on to paper. As in, write. Something. Anything.

Which is impossible because I cannot concentrate with that creepy brick pattern staring at me. I draw the curtains but then it makes me sleepy. I need the rare, almost-winter sunlight to remind my cells to vibrate.

Speaking of vibrating, I should reorganize and dust my rubber duck collection. Valerie Vibrato wears a filmy coat that could warm her wings in a minus-twenty ice storm.

That takes all of twenty-three minutes.

And then the blank page resumes its death stare. No returned messages on my phone.

I again pull the curtains and try hiding under my blankets with the flashlight to see if that will bring back some of the inspiration I found when writing *Resist Me Not* and *Tempt Me Softly*. This vexing third book has its title—*Hearts Collide*—groan—but that plus ten or so handwritten pages does not a book make.

And Liesl has already pulled on Gretchen's designer hip-waders and tiptoed into the Nag Pond about when I might have crap available to start planning a launch campaign.

Please just stop being so mean, brain. I need to make this happen.

People are relying on Jaina Jacen. An impressive number of house-wives have written to me about their improved sex lives. Embarrassing, but it also validates this occupation in a small way. "Hey, Sheila Dandy, there are women writing to tell me I've saved their marriages. That's almost as good as building orphanages for orphans and shelters for homeless dogs. Hand me my cape. Because HEROES WEAR CAPES."

But my brain is instigating a strike. The kind with picket signs and angry shouts and arms crossed against stubborn chests.

Luke thinks I showed Holden my girly bits—shudder—and now he's not gonna talk to me and that makes my heart hurt a little. Or maybe a lot. Or maybe it's just gas. I shouldn't have eaten that second turnover. But they were bloody good. I hope Luke gets his café. He deserves good things.

"Jayne?" Liesl is outside my blankets. "It's after three. I'm just heading out."

I flop the blankets away. "Three in the afternoon?" Dammit, I fell asleep.

"If you could sign the stack of books on the table—I've written the recipients' names on Post-Its—then I can go to the post office Monday morning."

"Right. Okay."

"And a florist delivered something for you. I put it in the fridge because Quack sort of attacked it."

"Okay, thanks."

"Have a good weekend. Get lots written!" She clicks the bedroom door closed quietly. I wait until I hear the downstairs door slam before getting up.

The flowers in the fridge—sure enough. "Thanks for taking care of me last night. I'm glad we're FRIENDS. xoxo H."

Guilt, guilt, guilt.

A quick check of my phone reveals I've missed a call in my lazy slumbering. This self-employed business is tough. Nowhere to be at a specified time every day, no Gretchen here to make sure I eat and bathe and floss and trim those weird hairs that have recently sprouted from the first knuckle of my big toe.

The voicemail—it's from Dr. McCoy. "Hi, Jayne. Audra McCoy calling. I got your message. Unfortunately, as you know, I'm not seeing clients anymore. But I would love to get together. As two friends having coffee. How does tomorrow morning work? We could meet at Lloyd Center, by the ice rink in front of Macy's. If 10 a.m. works for you, text me back to confirm."

We can meet. As friends. Music to my ears.

WHEN SHE WALKS TOWARD ME, Audra McCoy lacks the usual *trust me I'm a doctor* stride. She's wearing yoga pants and an oversized Irish-knit wool sweater with some great boots. Her hair, usually in a tight bun, is longer and grayer than I remember. She looks ... normal. And relaxed.

"Hi," I say. "It's black but I brought cream and sugar."

"Thanks." She sits next to me on the bench and takes her mermaid-printed cup.

"How's retirement treating you so far?" I ask.

She chuckles. "I'm still working, just not with patients. Loose ends, closing up the office. But it feels weird, to be honest. I'm trying to find that work-life balance when there's less work to be done."

Dr. McCoy—Audra—pats my hand. "Let's not talk about me. Let's talk about you. One friend to another. First, though—have you called Dr. Ellis-Garrett yet?"

I shake my head no.

"Why not?"

"She's not you?"

Audra laughs again. "Well, you'll call her when you're ready. And you'll love her. She's terrific."

"Maybe. We'll see. I've been hanging on to my rock and working through stuff with your toolkit of advice."

"Solid plan. Baby steps, remember?" I nod. "Sooooo ... how's

Luke?" I tell her how Holden just can't seem to pick up what I'm dropping down, and how Luke likely thinks I've lied to him again and even worse, he probably thinks Holden and I are sleeping together, which is insane. But mostly I talk about the writing, how fear has broken my brain and I can't write anything decent and I'm sort of terrified because nothing is working and I feel like a fraud.

"What about if you went back to writing something for yourself? Something completely unrelated to Jaina Jacen's erotica books? What about if you wrote another science fiction or fantasy story? Just to get things rolling."

Illyria and Mooney. It's been a while.

And as she talks, the little wheels grind into gear to the point where she quiets and hands me her pen. "Write it down—before you forget."

If I finish their story, I can send it to Luke. It's something he would appreciate—set on another planet, strange beasts, ships, laser guns, the works—it's an allegory for us, whatever "us" is at this very second. Somehow I must convince him that I am true and real. And falling in love with him.

Because I am.

Oh man, that's what this is.

I go to return her pen but she digs into her bag ... and pulls out two copies of Jaina Jacen's books. "I'd like your autograph, Ms. Jacen," she says, grinning.

"Why did you buy these? I could've given you some."

"Hey, I'm all about supporting my artist friends." I laugh. Me? An artist? Hardly. "I'm very proud of you."

"Thanks," I say. Hearing nice things makes me self-conscious.

"Whatever you do, keep going."

"But how am I going to do that without you?"

She pats my cheek. "You don't need me anymore. Everything you need to make this work is in your head, and in your heart."

"That sounds like a Hallmark card."

"Maybe I can get a job writing cheesy jingles. I'm only going to be able to reorganize the linen closets so many times." She laughs. "Seriously, though, you keep out the Sheila Dandys and the crazy writers' group women and anyone else who doesn't recognize what a force you are. You deserve all the greatness life has."

"Sheila Dandy ..." I say, sighing. "Yay, Christmas. Thanksgiving was awful. I don't know how I am going to deal with another holiday."

"Jayne, I can tell you this now because we're talking as friends, right?" I nod. "My mother and I were not close. She didn't like that I had a female partner, and she stopped talking to me. For years. People—my own therapist—told me that I would be sorry if I didn't make up with my mother before she died. So I did. And she tore me down again. She's still alive, and we don't talk. But it was an important lesson that I've tried to pass on to my patients: just because society dictates certain norms and delivers them on a packhorse of guilt, it doesn't mean we have to climb on. You deserve to be treated with respect by everyone you choose to have in your life. You deserve to be accepted for who you are. You have the right to be yourself because there is only one you. I think Dr. Seuss said it, didn't he? Something about there is no one you-er than you?" She smiles.

"My young friend, if someone does not grant you the respect you are due as a human being, no matter what their relationship to you, friend or blood, you have no obligation to suffer their presence in your life."

Listening to her is like watching the strings sever on the lead balloons wrapped around my chest.

"You're a good kid," she says, patting my hand again. "You're going places. Take those with you who will appreciate the ride. And Jayne—give Luke a little time. He'll come around. You're good people, and he knows it."

She tucks the signed Jaina Jacen books into her bag and stands.

"When can we hang out again? You know, as friends?" I ask.

"Let's get together after the New Year. My partner and I are heading to the Oregon Coast for Christmas. Watch the California grays migrate south to Baja."

"Thank you. For everything."

She hugs me tight. "Thank you, Jayne. You've taught me just as much as I hope I've taught you."

UPON ARRIVING HOME, I'm met with an unexpected, and rather sad, gift. Outside my door sits a banker's box—full of the remaining numbered paper bags. From Luke. An envelope taped to the box lid holds two things: a photograph of Loki and a certain delicious Spartan against a white background, and a ticket for the January Portland Comic Con at the Convention Center.

I guess this means the game is over. I can open the bags. Not that their contents matter anymore.

This photo. We were happy and things were new and this can't be over because it hasn't really started yet. What would Loki do in this situation?

And this box means he thought about me, that he was here in my building—which tells me there's still hope.

I sit down at the keyboard and remain there for four solid days, minus breaks for food and potty and some slobbery snoring and of course Quack's Prozac. It's not the Jaina Jacen story that tumbles out of my head, much to Liesl's chagrin.

It's about those crazy kids, Illyria and her Mooney, the heartbreak of their lives separated by class distinctions, and the impossible love story that explodes out of the planet's core like the last moments of the Death Star.

EIDER: CHAPTER 12

by Jaina Jacen (DECEMBER!!!)

I don't dare hire transport to get me to the turbines. And forget a trihorse. They're huge and ungainly and so noisy.

It is astounding how I am able to traverse undetected along the busy road leading out of the inner compound's grounds. Even the heat sensors are immune to this longcoat's technology. I smirk when I consider how long it will be before the guard commander realizes one of his prized coats is missing.

It's a fair trek by foot. The moons have long since risen by the time I arrive, though fear that Mooney will have given up and departed moves my feet with stealth and speed.

I'm careful on approach—this could be a trap. It wouldn't be the first time a highborn was lured away on the promise of love or adventure. I don't desire to serve as tomorrow's headline in the meeting hall.

I watch from behind a massive tree, its girth easily the width of ten tall men. Eider is renowned for its remarkable forests that stretch as high as the sky is deep. As children, Pollux and Lyrie would challenge one another to see who could climb the highest.

How funny that Mooney and Illyria now choose to meet each other in the shadow of their childhood haunt.

And then I see him.

He's looking about, checking his timepiece, muttering under his breath. He looks nervous. He paces, speaking to himself. He bows to one knee. He stands. A winged creature shoots out from the unseen side of the turbine, and Mooney jumps.

I giggle.

He starts and turns in my direction.

"Who's there? Lyrie, is that you?"

I am found.

I pull my mask away and my face appears as if out of ether. His smile widens like the sunrise as he jogs toward me.

Breathless, he stops a few paces outside the tree line, careful to keep the required respectful distance. His face shows evidence of the trouble I caused him in the square. My stomach clenches with remorse.

"I never would have seen you had you not laughed. I was beginning to worry you wouldn't show."

"And miss watching you catch a fright from a night bat?"

"The night bats here are huge."

"Good eating, I hear," I say, smiling.

"You've eaten night bat before?"

"Of course not. At least, not that I know of. But you never can be sure. Perhaps the kitchen staff has been industrious and creative with their culinary offerings when other foods are scarce."

Mooney laughs out loud, an unrestricted sound that the forest behind me drinks like fresh water. "It is so good to see you, Lyrie. Always the joker. I'm so pleased that hasn't left you."

"So, Mooney," I emphasize his adult name, "why are we here? Word about the compound is you are to be married."

His smile dissolves. "I do not love her. You know how these things are, Lyrie."

"But you are not free to choose. Neither of us is."

"Perhaps we could be."

274

"What you suggest is treason."

"Treason is conspiring to overthrow the government. The only thing overthrown here are my senses." He reaches out and offers a hand.

I'm shivering not from cold—on the contrary, the longcoat is too warm—but from fear. Happiness. Excitement. All of the emotions my father has tried to whitewash from my personality are on grand display right now, like a pyrotechnic display on Eider's Twelvemonth.

I take his hand.

He leads me to the dark side of the turbine, through which a door has been carved and covered with a well-loved cloak.

"Is it safe?"

"I've been here all afternoon and sustained no traumas."

"Except for the night bat," I tease.

He holds the cloak to the side and gestures for me to enter.

Inside the hollowed chamber, the light of a hundred candles consumes whatever darkness was here before. Flowers abound—in every shape, color, and fragrance. Upon a makeshift, cloth-covered table, wine rests in a tall decanter. Sweetcakes are arranged on a plate, surrounded by yet more flowers.

"Happy Twelvemonth," he says.

"How ...?"

"I, like you, am resourceful." He escorts me to a seat, a huge rock covered in a lush blanket. "It's dry here. I made sure of it."

I unbutton the longcoat before I overheat.

"Hey, there you are," he says, nodding at me. "I thought perhaps you were simply a floating head sent in Illyria's place."

"These longcoats—I'm never giving this one back to the guard commander."

Mooney offers me a checked cloth; into it, he places a small cake. "If I remember correctly, Lyrie preferred cacao over fruit cakes."

"Always." I take a bite. Fresh and moist, the sweetcake melts against my tongue. "Pollux ... this is amazing. Unrivaled by any of my Twelvemonths before or to come."

"I have a lot of years to make up for."

"You have nothing to make up for," I say.

The conversation continues through too many cakes and at least two—three?—glasses of the bubbled wine I've only ever been allowed to taste at special gatherings. Sure, Taisa and I have been known to steal a decanter and hide in my chamber until our giggles threaten to wake our neighbors, but this—this is wholly different. My head is lightened and my heart swells in my chest.

When talk turns to our futures, Mooney stands and raises his glass to the sky. "I knew then, as I know now, that the only way my feet can continue to step one in front of the other is if your matching set marches with me."

Time stops for that moment. Even the candles freeze in their flickering. Such a proclamation, though heard by only our ears—it is too bold.

"I understand the drink makes you playful, Pollux Mooney, but you cannot tease such things."

He plunks the chalice haphazardly on the tabletop and drops on his knees before me, clasping my hands in his. "This is no tease. We can go—right now. Tonight. Before the moons drop back behind the rocky heights and the sun returns to warm the dew. We could be on our way to Merganser. I have a Scaup—an old starcraft—it could get us there. We could start anew, just you and me. They'll never find us."

"Your words are dangerous, Mooney. Remember your station." The wine no longer warms my stomach but churns against it.

"These are not dangerous words—they are words of possibility. And don't throw your station at me. We were once friends. In the uppermost branches of an old tree, you promised you would marry me one day. Do you remember that? I tied a whiteflower around your thumb and you said that you would keep it forever."

I did keep it. The whiteflower.

From my sack, I pull the tiny book from my tutor. The flower, though long dead, lies pressed between the pages.

Mooney's face lights up when he sees it.

I slap the book closed and stand abruptly. "We cannot make such foolish choices, Pollux. We are adults now. I am of age. There are expectations—"

"You do not WANT those expectations, or else you would not have insisted I meet you in the square. You would not be here right now. You would not have risked so much—the wrath of your father, the scorn of your agemates. I would not have risked so much—the very real promise of physical punishment if, and when, we were caught, the possible loss of my position with the government."

"Please stop."

"I will not." He seizes me and before I can tug free, his lips land on mine. I taste the wine, the sweetcakes, our past together ... and our future.

"Come with me. Please, Lyrie. I love you. I've always loved you."

An alarm sounds across the space, severing the moment as if slicing a grandsheep's throat. "What is that?"

Disquiet consumes Mooney's features. "You have to make a choice: either go with me, now, tonight, or you hide in those woods in your longcoat and watch me fly away."

"What? What are you talking about?"

"I've set a watch on the compound corridor and at the edge of the wood. If it was discovered by guardsmen that you had stolen away, my watchmen were to notify me. You have been discovered, Illyria. You must decide what you want."

I move aside the cloak hanging over the door. "How do I know this isn't trickery? That you're not coercing me into leaving with you under false pretenses?"

Mooney throws a heavy bag over his shoulder. "Because it's me. And you trust me."

"I ... I cannot. What about Taisa? What about—"

"My Sovereign, my friend and only love, I wish you all the best." He kisses me desperately and then bolts through the fabric and into the meadow, footsteps light and agile.

Behind me, I hear the roar of approaching armed carriers as their wheels devour the pristine vegetation. Red flares of compound-wide alarm explode against the backdrop of the massive double moons, alerting everyone within a dozen leagues that someone important has gone missing.

They will all know it's me.

I have to decide. Stay behind and endure a life I have no passion for with people who want to hear nothing of dreams or wants or desires, who live by archaic rules mutated and warped from their origins, carry forth the next generation given to me by a man my father has chosen, who knows nothing of whiteflowers or climbing trees or shared childhood secrets.

Illyria, decide.

The carriers growl closer.

"Pollux Mooney! Please! Wait!"

He stops and turns to me, waving me forward. I sprint as hard as I can to catch up. When our hands clasp, he pushes a kiss against my head and pulls me on toward our future.

Elsewhere, together.

36

I ALMOST PEE the bed when my eyes creak open to find a shadowed figure standing over me.

"Wake up, sleepyhead," she says.

"GRETCHEN!" I'm out of the covers and wrapping myself around her and we're dancing and she's shushing me or else the hippies are gonna knock on the ceiling because it's 6:30 in the morning. "I'm so glad you're here! Wait—why are you here?"

"Because. It's January tenth. Which means it's your birthday weekend, and there was no way I was going to let my best friend start her new year off without a righteous celebration." She plops down on my bed and pulls me with.

"Really? You came all the way from Milan for my birthday?"

"Of course not. I came all the way from Milan because those people are insane and I was desperately homesick and no matter what they say about Italian men, they all just want to touch my boobs."

"So, you're *home* home? Like, forever?"

"Like, forever."

"And just in time for my birfday!" I hug her again. Quack yowls in the light spill from the hallway.

"How was your Christmas?" she asks, rubbing my hand wrapped around her middle.

"Terrible. Well, not entirely terrible. I met my dad's new girlfriend. They're engaged. She's actually amazing."

"And how's Sheila Dandy taking it?"

"Her usual fire-breathing way. Drinking like a fish, making fun of her pornography-writing daughter. Although she's started picking on Maggot and Frankie, so at least I wasn't the only one licking wounds around the Christmas tree."

"Why'd you go, then?"

"To be sure I was making the right decision."

"About ..."

"About being Jaina Jacen and not caring what my mother thinks."

Gretchen hugs me tighter and kisses the side of my head. "Proud'a you, Jaynie Prudie."

"I'm proud of me too."

Now that she's home, and I'm awake, we have to catch up. But because it's my birthday, we throw on clothes and hiking boots and drive east out of Portland for hazelnut-crusted French toast and Mimosas at the Multnomah Falls Lodge.

It's beautiful here. One of my favorite spots on the whole planet. Not that I've seen a lot of the planet, but I doubt there are many places as gorgeous as this. Multnomah's water tumbles from over five hundred feet up on the first level and another seventy-ish feet from the second. Not as ostentatious as some waterfalls, these are breathtaking in their simplicity. And the Native Americans said that the falls were created to win the heart of a young princess who desired her own private bathing pool. How is that not the most romantic thing ever?

A slow but quick hike along the path takes us to Benson Bridge, which today is sparse with tourists secondary to the bitter January cold. Even in winter, the greenery abounds—Oregon's calling card—

although today the green wears white from the waterfall's freezing, billowy spray. Though we're shivering around cups of cocoa, there's no other place I'd rather be.

I fill Gretchen in about Holden, happy to share that he's met someone—hallelujah!—a sweet little sous chef from the Pearl District. He emails me every other day to tell me all the sweet things they do for each other. It's nauseatingly cute.

Gretchen tells me about Nico, a delectable morsel she picked up in Milan, and how much of a bummer it was when not only Eric unexpectedly flew in and found them together but when Nico's wife and little boy showed up to add more color.

"I'm so glad you're home," I say, hugging her.

"Me too." Hugging keeps us both warmer, so we stay wrapped around each other for a little while, watching the water trickle down massive icicles along the spill line, savoring the quiet of a wintry scene. Until some Japanese tourists slide on the icy bridge deck and then ask to have their picture taken with tall, blond Gretchen.

"So ... how's Luke?" she asks, once the bowing tourists have skated away.

My chest feels heavier whenever I think of Luke. I haven't seen him since the morning he found Holden at the apartment. How long has it been—three weeks? He's texted a few times but he's been swamped with whatever is going on with their efforts toward a new café, and he and Leia are taking turns in San Diego as their dad did in fact have a stroke.

"Do you think there's a chance for the two of you to ...?"

"I don't know. I sort of wrote a story for him."

Gretchen laughs. "Like, a sexy story?"

"Noooo. But if I tell you about it, you have to promise not to laugh." She crosses her heart. "I mean it, Gretchen. Don't laugh."

"Jayne!"

"It's something along the lines of this: it's set on a distant planet called Eider—"

"What the hell is an eider?"

I smile. "Um, it's a duck."

"Of COURSE it is. Okay, continue."

"It's about a young, highborn woman named Illyria who has to marry someone her father chooses for her, but then when the annual collection of her blood specimen for the planet's archives happens, she crosses paths with a young man named Mooney ..." Gretchen's eyes glaze over. "Anyway, there are spaceships and weird animals and stuff."

She breaks her promise. "Omigod, you're such a major nerd."

"I am, aren't I?" I shiver against a rogue wind.

"What did he think about it?"

"I haven't sent it to him."

"Jayne Dandy, queen of dorks, we're leaving." She weaves an arm through mine and pulls me toward the path.

"But I want to stay here and freeze some more."

She stops and puts her mittened hands on my shoulders. "We're going home right now so you can send this little love story to Luke Piewalker post haste. He needs to know that you lurve him and he cannot waste another moment fondling pastry bags when he could be fondling these." She gropes me. A day is not complete until Gretchen feels me up.

I clap my hands. "And let's give it up for Gretchen! Here for an encore performance!"

"He needs to see Australia, Jayne." She nods at my chest.

"Yes, let me call him and say, 'Gosh, Luke, I know you're mad at me but I have this weird birthmark on my boob that looks like Australia I'd love to show it to you it's imperative we get together immediately be sure to bring cake.'"

"Perfect! Just like that."

I sigh at her.

"You need to deal with this, Jayne. Do you think he could be—THE ONE?"

"You mean like 'The One' in the context that we would pick out china patterns and walk down aisles and buy townhouses and plant kale in our section of the community garden?"

"No—simpler. 'The One,' as in you will introduce him to your vagina."

Thank God the people walking by just as that word somersaulted out of Gretchen's face don't seem to speak English. "You're incorrigible."

"Duh, but I'm also worried about your health. Did you know that cardiologists recommend at least three orgasms a week for optimum cardiac health? And for men it's even more because they need to keep their wiener pipes clean or else their prostates get all funky and then it's like they're walking around with a third nut."

"You are so gross."

"I am an ambassador for science."

"Sleeping with doctors does not make you an ambassador for science."

"I slept with *one* doctor—no sleeping involved, for the record—and I was infused with the love of all things sciencey."

"You were infused with wine."

"Don't knock it till you try it," she says. "And Jaynie, I think once you discover the Big O, you'll be thanking me."

"Why? Are you going to give it to me?"

"You're cute, but not that cute. Although I think Luke would disagree with me. I think he should do the honors. Let him be the first to blow your mind."

"I'd like to talk about something else now," I say, laughing. "Or wait—there are some people over on the other side of the path who didn't hear you say *orgasm*. Try again, only with more spirit this time."

We grab steaming coffee for the trip back to the city. En route, Holden texts: *Live music at the Copper Horse tonight. Come by. Drinks on me & Tess.*

Copper Horse. That means Luke might be there.

I can't go.

I should go.

Maybe he's out of town dealing with his dad. Or maybe he's here. But what if he is here and he's working, or what if he comes by to listen to the band and he has a girl with him?

I don't think I'm ready to handle that.

"Everything okay?" Gretchen asks.

"You feel like going to the Copper Horse tonight?"

"You're the birthday girl."

Indeed I am. And I only have eight more hours to talk myself out of this.

37

AGAIN THE LOT is at capacity—and when Gretchen sees the dumpy Piewalker pickup against the fence, her grin widens. "Ahhaaa. The plot is revealed. You know, I called from Italy to get those reservations at Papa Haydn."

"I wanted to do something casual."

"Casual as in Luke falling into your underwear."

Laughter. Because that's all you can do with Gretchen since justifiable homicide is still considered rude in most jurisdictions.

Holden and Tess have a high-top table saved for us, and Leia's band is mounting an attack on the health and safety of eardrums everywhere. When Holden greets me with a beer, he says close to my head, "He's not here, Jayne. Sorry."

Which is double-edged: I can relax because I know he's not here, but then I'm sad because I won't see his cheeky grin while he flirts with cosmopolitan-slurping vixens vying for his attention.

"But this might cheer you up," he says, handing over yet another duck. This one's holding a feather quill. "It's a writer duck. Like you."

"Thanks, Holden."

The band's new material—good stuff, actually—has the crowd on its feet most of the night, including Gretchen who dances with a guy whose tattooed arms are works of art. And Tess with her pixie cut and infectious laugh is adorable. She and Holden really are perfect for one another.

When the band takes a momentary break before launching into a bar-wide rendition of "Happy Birthday to Jayne," I swear again that I might find a creative way to end Gretchen's wretched existence.

Instruments down, Leia plops on a stool and shares her performance sweat via a tight hug around my neck. She shows off her new camo cast, followed by the newest tattoo—a Tie Fighter behind her left ear. "I got it for my dad," she says. My eyes widen. "Oh, no, he's not dead. He and I both got one while I was down there last." She smiles.

Phew.

She tells me he's doing better but they're having to reteach him most of the basic life stuff. Apparently Luke is there installing mobility aids in the townhouse, and their whole sci-fi community has rallied around to make sure the Walkers are taken care of.

"Hey, your birthday—" Leia digs in her bag. "I didn't know so I didn't get you a gift, but I have the perfect thing." She hands me an envelope.

"What is it?"

She waggles her eyebrows.

Inside is a ticket—for a speed-dating event at the Portland Comic Con. "Are you serious?" I say. Hilarious. "For me?"

"It was for me, but ... I met someone." She giggles. I've never seen Leia giggle in public.

"You did?"

"He's in real estate," she whispers. "*Please* do not tell anyone that. If my parents find out I'm dating someone respectable, I'm afraid my dad will have another stroke. And my mother will start in about the whole grandchild thing again."

A blip of sadness pings my chest. Mrs. Walker teased Luke about grandchildren when he and I were at Whitaker Ponds.

And while the ticket is a darling gift, the idea of going to a speed-dating event stomps on my giant red *no* button.

"I know Luke gave you a costume and a ticket, so you have to go. The food truck obviously won't be there, but I'm definitely going. If Luke's still in California, I'm using his ticket for Mr. Real Estate. He's a closet geek."

Luke didn't give me a costume. And I returned the Loki costume ages ago.

"Think about it," she says, pasting a smooch on my cheek. "Break's over. Time to rock."

Gretchen drags me out on to the tiny dance floor and for a few minutes, I forget that I'm now twenty-seven and that I have writer's block and that the boy I love is in another state and doesn't know it's my birthday.

I end up chauffeur because, lo and behold, Gretchen partook of Sambuca shots with the tattooed guy and now she's got her head out the BMW window crooning bar songs she learned during her brief sojourn abroad.

Once she's tucked in and Quack has coiled up at the end of my bed with the chewed remnants of her favorite stuffed animal, I brew a cup of tea and stare at my computer screen, specifically at the story I wrote for Luke.

It's too cheesy. I cannot send this.

Cheesy is good. Cheesy is what we want here. Allegories are melodramatic and sloppy and ripe with maudlin proclamations of swelling hearts.

A burst of bravery detonates in that part of the gray matter we all have, the one that encourages us to text the guy despite the bottle of wine we just offed, the one that tells us tattooing unicorns or our favorite song lyrics is a good idea, the one that tells us that releasing ten thousand crickets into the high school commons is a good senior prank.

I click send.

And then I spend the next two hours trying to find out if there is a way you can unsend an email. Apparently there is not unless you're on the same server.

Around 4 a.m., tea cold and fridge emptied of anything resembling a pastry, I flop on to my bed. The envelope from Leia stabs me through the front pocket of my jeans. I pull it out and reread it, wondering which costume she meant when she said Luke had given me one.

And then I remember the numbered bags.

I tear into one after another until I'm laughing out loud: Princess Leia's Boushh the Bounty Hunter costume is now assembled on my bedroom floor. Oh, I have to try it on. This is too much.

Despite the many ill-advised dietary choices of late, I am thrilled to find the costume fits. A twist here, a pose there, and the bedroom mirror doesn't lie: I look cool. This is a badass get-up.

It would be a shame for it to go to waste.

Right?

38

I CHANGE my mind about a hundred and twelve times in the thir-teen-day span between my birthday and the Comic Con. I've heard from Leia via text that she's definitely going, but she never mentions her brother. I'm too chicken to ask.

And then a follow-up text settles it: *Luke's still in SD. He says hello.*

Heavy sigh.

Now that Gretchen is back, she's reassumed the Jaina Jacen reins from Liesl who is more than happy to watch and learn. Gretchen is in her element—sure, she knows a thing or two about fashion, but watching her market and promote is like watching a ballet. A caffeine-soaked, fast-talking, hip-popping ballet. She's organized and ruthless with a side of unpredictable, but that's what makes her so good at everything she does.

Especially nagging.

She puts me on a schedule: two thousand words a day minimum so we can have a working draft for book three within a month. When the first five days go by and I fall dismally short of her word count projections, she does two things: locks me in my room with the first two books so I can get reacquainted with the characters and their stories to help bulldoze through this infuriating block; and she buys me a tent for my bedroom. The kind you use to keep off the sun at the beach. She sets up my laptop and notebook on a TV tray and rolls my office chair inside and takes my phone away and then zips the tent behind me.

"Think of it like being under the covers, Jaynie. Just you and the words. No one else. No distractions."

The most bizarre part? It totally works.

I reread the first two books in the series, blushing through the steamy scenes (I can't believe I wrote this!) but smiling at the good parts and even tearing up at the sad bits. Love is hard, man. I did a good job making it as hard as possible for these crazy, mixed-up characters. I almost feel like I should apologize for sullying their cute pants with so many plot turds.

By January twenty-second, I have fifteen thousand usable words. Progress at last.

When Gretchen gives me my phone back at day's end, there's a single message from Leia: *Be there or SUCK. See you tmrw!*

Today's the first day of Comic Con. I can't go tonight because Holden and Tess are making us dinner—it's her birthday this time, so we're apparently celebrating as a group. I suppose it's fine. Saves me from having to drive one or all of their drunken butts home at night's end.

"Hey." Gretchen knocks and enters. "You got tampies?"

"Do you ever buy your own feminine hygiene?"

"Babe, I'm just happy that I need it this month. I was a little worried I'd be introducing Nico's DNA into the American population."

"You serious?" She hadn't mentioned being nervous about that.

"Nah. I just wanted to see your reaction." I smack her arm. "But still, I need tampons. Gimme."

I throw a thumb over my shoulder toward my tiny bathroom. Gretchen stops at my nightstand.

"Speed dating? At Comic Con? Holy shit, Batman—this is for tomorrow. Where'd you get this?"

"Leia. She gave it to me on my birthday."

"You're so going."

"I don't think so ..."

"Jayne, why not? What have you got to lose?" I look at her and I wish my eyes didn't look as sad as they feel. Gretchen moves across the room and grips my shoulders. "You cannot sit here and pine for a guy who doesn't know how great you are. You have to get out there. Look at how well you're doing with everything else. You need to strike while the iron's hot."

"Maybe now isn't the right time, though. There's a lot going on—and I don't have time to date or worry about all the bullshit and anxiety that happens when I get too close to a human male. I have to finish this next book, and I really should be doing more marketing stuff so you can have your life back."

Gretchen squishes my cheeks in her fingers. "Do you have a costume?"

I nod.

"Do you like nerds and Jedis and strange things I will never understand?"

Another nod.

"Then you are going tomorrow, if for no other reason than to prove to yourself that you can do this. That you can move past Luke and look into other galaxies for love."

I giggle. "You said galaxy."

"If you tell anyone I uttered geek-speak, I will disown you."

"Be careful, Gretchen. It's like a disease—you start out saying things like *galaxy* and *rebel alliance*, and before long, you're hanging out in comic book stores and standing on street corners asking people where the mothership is."

"Speaking of motherships, Chewbacca," she nods at my hairy legs, "definitely shave before you let some nerd peek under your helmet." Her eyebrows wiggle suggestively.

"No one will be peeking under my helmet."

"Still, that's a lot of hair for one body," she says.

"It's January. We don't have to shave in the winter. Or didn't you get the memo?"

She helps herself to my supply of feminine hygiene. "The only memo I'm concerned with is the one where Operation Get Jayne Laid is a go for launch."

"It's speed *dating*, not speed *copulating*."

"What do you think speed dating leads to?"

"Dinner. A movie. Two years of holding hands before going our separate ways."

"You are a terrible Jedi."

"I'm still in training."

She steels her hands on my shoulders. "Tomorrow, you will find yourself an Obiwan Kenbobby or whatever the hell he's called and just get it over with. You are a GO FOR LAUNCH, Jayne Dandy."

T-minus twenty hours and counting.

39

I'M SO NERVOUS.

Once all the pieces are on, I'm afraid I'll overheat. The costume is so detailed—helmet, tunic, vest, cape thingie, waist wrap, bandolier, canister backpack, arm gauntlets, shoulder pieces, boot covers, puffy pants, staff—it's a lot of stuff. I hope I don't pit it out before I get through the event.

I throw deodorant and body spray in my bag just in case. Smelling like an exploded garden is better than smelling like terror-induced sweat.

Driving to the venue, a minivan filled with kids pulls alongside. Two little boys stare and just before the light turns green, their faces erupt in recognition. My window's down to prevent my face from melting off, so I hear the older boy yell, "Dad! Look! A bounty hunter!" I smile because it's adorable—and then when they park next to me in the Convention Center lot, I pull on the helmet and pose for a photo.

I'm so glad these parents are keeping the geek alive for the next generation. Hope abounds!

One last check of my face before going inside—I pull down the mirrored visor and the photo of Luke and I dressed up at his buddy's costume shop falls into my lap. I have to let this go. I have to let him go. I hurt him, and now he's afraid of me, and I have this speed-dating ticket in my bag and I need to be brave and go find my nerd. Maybe he's in this building right now and he will have the magic in his wand that will melt my neurotic defenses and I can move on to the next dimension.

Magic in his wand.

Gretchen would be so proud of me. Jaynie Prudie becomes Jaynie Pervert?

Inside is a madhouse. Comic books, action figures, and movies have come to life in broad-spectrum color. Fans of every size, shape, and species roam the massive building, the intricacy of the costumes competing for supremacy in every aisle I walk down. You think you've seen the most incredible costume ever, and sure enough, something even more outlandish or phenomenal comes around the corner.

I had no idea nerd culture was so vast. Or awesome.

I really have been missing out all these years.

And in a brief but powerful moment, I feel the bite of tears in the back of my throat—these are my people. We are all crazy and fun and silly together. I've never felt more un-alone in my entire life. Which is ridiculous because I'm talking about grown adults dressed like Spiderman and Gandalf and the princesses from Mario Bros. and a fully masked Bane and the Little Mermaid and a lot of half-naked Superwomen and Link from Zelda and some badass Lara Croft wannabes ... This is like nothing I have ever seen before. Luke was right. This is unreal.

An hour in, I've posed for photos with half a dozen people—I had no idea Boushh (Princess Leia) the Bounty Hunter was so popular. Then again, this costume is really something else. Those Walker twins know their stuff.

I text Leia to see where she is in the building. I'm dying to see what she's wearing and if she's brought Mr. Real Estate along. She buzzes back: *Meet at 6 in Hall C near Tauntaun exhibit.*

My eyes hungrily inhale all the pretty things, soon followed by my wallet that helps itself to a few select *Star Wars* T-shirts I cannot live without. And the Ewok bobbleheads. And the C-3PO purse I saw online last year and haven't been able to find in real life. Until now.

Gretchen will tease relentlessly. So worth it.

The PA announces an event starting in the Portland Ballrooms 254 and 255. It's time.

I can't do it.

I have to do it.

I pull the ticket from under the bandolier. My scheduled time is four thirty. I should go line up and check in or whatever they make you do. I feel lightheaded. I'd blame it on the costume but I know better. I shouldn't be doing this. Why am I here? Why didn't I tell Leia *no way speed dating is for crazy people and I am no crazy person.*

Rumble gurgle growl squeeze.

My stomach is pissed off. I can't swallow.

I should run. I should run out to my car and drive to my apartment and hug my deranged, monocular cat and hide in my tent with my new toys.

But if I do, Gretchen will never let me forget that I chickened out and she will find some other way to trick me into the Big Bad World of Wieners, and with Gretchen handling my dating life, it could go much, much worse.

Two tables greet the participants. Once we're signed in, the ladies are led inside to choose a seat. A husky redhead in a barely there Superwoman outfit shoves ahead of another girl dressed as *X-Men's* Storm (the white contacts are freaky as hell) to get the front table. They can duke it out—I'm totally content to find a table near the back corner, preferably near an exit.

The rules dictate that participants with masks can leave that part of the costume on until the seven-minute dinger, at which time masks should come off so participants can properly introduce themselves. I guess no one wants to be scared into a date without inspecting the goods first.

Fine by me. My bounty-hunter headgear is too stuffy and hard to talk through. I'll just keep it off so any potentials can see what I look like from the starting line.

Four thirty on the nose, the first round begins.

My first suitor: Captain America. Works at a multimedia start-up in Beaverton. Talks about himself for seven minutes until the warning bell sounds and then he asks me what I do. I tell him I'm a writer; he asks if he's ever seen my books. I tell him I write travel guides. Because why not? DING. Time's up.

Suitor number two: the Hulk. It's hard to figure out what he looks like because his face is totally green and he's wearing some sort of headpiece to make his head larger than it is—or at least I hope that's a headpiece. He has lovely straight teeth and asks me about myself right away, a change from Captain America. Asks me what my three favorite things are; I tell him I love ducks, rainy days, and pastries. Because that's all I can think of on short notice and it's true, right? His smile fades a little and he mentions that he's a vegan from Los Angeles and he's having a hard time adjusting to the climate here and he can't wait to get back to LA once he's done with his training year at a major insurance company headquartered in Portland.

I talk to Wolverine (stockbroker), Ironman (works at a comic book store—had the best costume in the room), a Teenage Mutant Ninja Turtle (I think he said he was Raphael—works in lumber sales), a guy who sort of looked like Indiana Jones (currently unemployed, which would explain the half-assed outfit), and Doctor Who (lovely British accent, hoping to find an American wife so he can immigrate to Yankee Land).

One round remains before my session is up. I'm exhausted. And I need to skip out if I'm to meet Leia and her new squeeze on time.

I grab my helmet and bag of purchases and scoot my chair out just as a Stormtrooper in full costume sits down across from me. The bell rings and he offers a hand. I shake it and sit down. One more can't hurt.

"Finally! A *Star Wars* fan," I say.

He laughs, voice muffled. "You've not met one yet today?"

"No. Just about everything else, though. I was starting to feel so underrepresented."

He doesn't say anything else. I can't tell if he's smiling or even looking at me or if he's staring at the very buxom girl in the *Fifth Element* Band-Aid costume next to us. Even I was staring earlier. How does a person get a body like that, and why is she in need of speed dating?

"Soooo, are we going to talk, or ...?"

He reaches down and digs into a messenger bag.

Atop the table, he places a Darth Vader rubber duck.

I can't help it. My eyes sting and then I'm sniffling and I just ... smile. "I love ducks."

"I've heard that about you."

"What else have you heard about me?" I say.

"That you write books. That you know how to stuff a mean éclair. That you love real ducks and cats with possible brain damage. That you might be allergic to shrimp. That you have good friends who care about you. That you are," Luke says, pulling off his mask, "by far the best kisser a man could ever hope to meet."

My heart. It stutters.

"But you're a Stormtrooper."

"Yes. I am."

"I'm a bounty hunter. And a princess. And my father, Lord Vader," I gesture with the duck, "he will have you, his lowly minion, killed if he knows you're talking to me."

"I'm prepared to take my chances."

He removes his gloves and plucks the duck from my hand. "I searched all of San Diego for him."

I wipe my wet cheeks with the back of my sleeve. "He's perfect."

Luke grabs my hands and leans forward, pressing my fingers

against his lips. "I'm sorry I doubted you. I was an ass, and I hope you can find it in your Rebel heart to forgive me."

The seven-minute bell rings. "I suppose I can give you my contact information once we're done here," I tease.

He chuckles. "I'd like that. Very much."

"But isn't this a little predictable? You showing up at the last minute to sweep me off my feet?" I lean closer, closer, until there is nothing but an inch and a breath separating us.

"You're the writer. You can make this ending whatever you want it to be."

I smile and wrap my hands around his head, pulling his face against mine. The tables next to us erupt in applause. I'm pretty sure we've broken the event rules, but everyone here is in the mood for love.

Luke smiles against my mouth, our foreheads touching.

"I can go with predictable," I say.

40

"YOU PROMISE YOU CAN'T SEE?"

"I cannot see a thing. Please tell me you're not going to drop me off a cliff." I smell ... fresh paint. Newly cut plywood. And flowers. A lot of flowers.

"Ready?"

"Will you hurry up!"

Luke fiddles with the bandana he's had around my eyes for the last fifteen minutes of rather disorienting travel. Good thing I trust him. Because I do. Trust him. And I'm pretty sure we're alone after we left Leia and Mr. Real Estate (named Adam, a sweet guy from what I could tell, which worries me because Leia might eat him alive). They're still back at the Con, dressed as Ahsoka and Hans Solo, but we're here. Alone. Luke and me. Together. And we could be in the middle of a medieval torture chamber and I would be none the wiser. Although where would he find a medieval torture chamber in Portland? And why would it smell like flowers? Maybe he's building one and that's why I also smell plywood and paint. I'm not sure if medieval torture is my thing—*Star Wars*, sure, but medieval—

"Jayne, you're shaking. Are you okay?" I can hear the smile outlining his words.

"Yeah. Yes. I'm fine. I'm just—this is weird. I'm blindfolded and you're taking forever and my mind is going a thousand miles an hour."

"When is it not going a thousand miles an hour?"

The blindfold releases my face. And I am certainly in the midst of a construction zone, albeit one that has been overwhelmed with flowers of a hundred colors and types. Booths in red and black line the walls. Tabletops in stainless steel are still covered in their protective plastic sheeting. Space-inspired light fixtures dangle from thin wires and give the place a warm, welcoming glow, despite the plastic tarps and unfinished flooring and the kitchen appliances that await installation.

Along the far wall, a brilliant mural in neon reads "Welcome to Piewalker's."

"You did it."

"I did it," Luke says, a quiet grin stretching across his face.

My heart swells with excitement and pride and all those happy feelings you float in when someone you love has something fantastic happen to him.

"I can't cook dinner for you here yet, but ..." He clasps my hand and pulls me toward the back, into an office that is much more put together than the front half of the building. From inside a small fridge, he pulls out a plate of chocolate éclairs dazzling in their whipped cream hats.

"I could be persuaded to eat those for dinner."

"I was hoping you'd say that."

I take the plate from him and set it on the desktop. "A futon. Very enterprising of you, Luke Piewalker."

"I have no ulterior motives, your highness."

I pull him toward me, the plastic of his Stormtrooper costume clicking against the accoutrements of my still-intact bounty-hunter outfit.

"How does this happen?" he whispers.

"One layer at a time, I'm guessing." I reach over and give the door a mighty push. It clicks closed. The steps I took to dress a few hours ago, I do in reverse.

My bandolier.

His chest plate.

My backpack and arm gauntlets.

His leg pieces.

My waist wrap.

His arm guards.

Until only a few pieces providing essential coverage remain. I shiver when his fingers trail down my bare arms; he smiles when my hands land on his bare chest. He kisses one cheek, then the other. Then my lips. I'm shivering so hard, he reaches behind and pulls a quilt from the futon and wraps the two of us in it.

"Better?"

"Mm-hmm. Thanks."

"So, Miss Best-selling Author, help a guy out here—at the end of *Eider* ... do Illyria and Mooney get their happily ever after?"

I smirk. "Well, Mr. Amazing Café Boss, that's what the sequel is for."

"I like sequels." He kisses me again, longer this time. When he pulls away, he looks down.

And sees Australia.

"Birthmark?" he says, lightly tracing it with his fingertip. More goosebumps. I nod. "I can see your chest moving with the speed of your heart. Are you okay?"

I nod again.

"You want to narrate me through this, Miss Jacen?"

"For this, it's all me—just Jayne Dandy."

"I'm thrilled to hear that." He brushes my lips with his; a finger dances along the edge of my jaw, to my ear, down my neck. "Alec and Miranda and Illyria and Mooney are great, but I was hoping you could write our story."

"How does it start?" I ask.

"With this." Another kiss. Hands around my waist. Very little other than skin between us. "Question is," he says, "what happens in Act II?"

I bite his bottom lip as my bra coupling sproings free. "I'm sure if we put our imaginations together, we can come up with something."

ACKNOWLEDGMENTS

Thanks go to these special ducks who generously provided their assistance during the creation of this work:

David Purse and Debbie Purse at Inked Entertainment for the new energy brought to the Eliza Gordon library. Without their savvy, professional help, we wouldn't have the books on audio or representation at United Talent Agency (UTA) for film/TV development.

Victoria Doherty-Munro, who is always quick with a friendly word and razor-sharp editorial feedback. Thanks, Julie Trelstad of Julie Ink (https://julieink.com/), for help in the early days of Eliza Gordon.

To the bloggers and readers who become fans, *thank you for reading and loving and sharing* our books. Authors couldn't be authors without you.

To Yolander Prinzel, for your astute reading and consistent cheerleading (oh, and Princess Stella is indeed a Class I kitty); and to Jane Klassen Omelaniec, for unconditional love and friendship all these years, the use of the cabin when I'm on a deadline, and for introducing me to Jamie Fraser.

Thanks, Candace Robinson with Candace's Book Blog and

Promotions, for your most excellent skills with the megaphone; to Shana Benedict with A Book Vacation, for your wholehearted endorsement of my work.

Special thanks to Mariyam Khan with Oh Panda Eyes for the fantastic support of both *Luke Piewalker* (formerly titled *Neurotica*) and *Must Love Otters*—the wonderful book-inspired jewelry, the quotes and graphics to showcase the books, the playlist you built for Jayne, Luke, Gretchen, and Holden (Woodkid, where have you been all my life?), and for your enthusiasm about all things Eliza Gordon.

Thanks to Emily Wulff, you diva, whose vast knowledge of the Portland fashion scene gave Gretchen her name and her sea legs.

A special shout-out to London Sarah (McDonald) Dessent for being my First and Best Fan. I cannot wait until my not-so-wee bum finds itself on your side of the pond so we can be groundlings at The Globe and then Sir Toby can drive us around Scotland. Tell Lucien I love him.

And of course, mad props to the folks who occupy the rooms in my heart—Yaunna, Brennan, Kendon, and Gary. Thank you for your generosity with hugs and chocolate and for not hating me even though I'm always spouting off about how I can't possibly leave the house or put on real clothes because I have to work. (Someone check on Nuit—I think she's playing Spider-Man on the deck again.)

ABOUT THE AUTHOR

A native of Portland, Oregon, Eliza Gordon (a.k.a. Jennifer Sommersby) has lived up and down the West Coast of the United States. Since 2002, home has been a suburb of Vancouver, British Columbia.

When not lost in a writing project, Eliza is a copy editor, mom, wife, bibliophile, Superman freak, and the proud parent of two very spoiled tuxedo cats. Eliza writes stories to help you believe in the Happily Ever After; Jennifer Sommersby writes young adult fiction. Her debut, *Sleight*, was published in 2018 by HarperCollins Canada, Sky Pony (US), and Prószyński i S-ka (Poland). The sequel, *The Undoing* (*Scheme* in the US), published in April 2020.

The name Eliza Gordon was chosen to honor two amazing people, Martha Elizabeth (Porter) Young and Kenneth Gordon Young. Not a day goes by that we don't love and miss you. Your devotion to one another continues to inspire.

Follow Eliza on social media or visit her website at www.elizagordon.com, and sign up for her newsletter.

DEAR DWAYNE, WITH LOVE

FROM LAKE UNION PUBLISHING

DREAM BIG. MOVIE-STAR BIG.

Wannabe actress Dani Steele's résumé resembles a cautionary tale on how *not* to be famous. She's pushing thirty and stuck in a dead-end insurance job, and her relationship status is holding at uncommitted. With unbearably perfect sisters and a mother who won't let her forget it, Dani has two go-tos for consolation: maple scones and a blog in which she pours her heart out to her celebrity idol. He's the man her father never was, no boyfriend will ever be—and not so impossible a dream as one might think.

When Dani learns that he's planning a fund-raising event where the winning amateur athlete gets a walk-on in his new film, she decides to trade pastries and self-doubt for running shoes and a sexy British trainer with adorable knees.

But when Dani's plot takes an unexpected twist, she realizes that her happy ending might have to be improvised—and that proving herself to her idol isn't half as important as proving something to herself.

Available for Kindle and in paperback, as well as via Kindle Unlimited, Audible, and audio CD.

This is a work of fiction. While Dwayne Johnson p/k/a The Rock is a real person, events relating to him in the book are a product of the author's imagination. Mr. Johnson is not affiliated with this book, and has not endorsed it or participated in any manner in connection with this book.

MUST LOVE OTTERS

BOOK 1 IN THE REVELATION COVE SERIES

Hollie Porter is the chairwoman of Generation Disillusioned. At 25, she's saddled with a job she hates, a boyfriend who's all wrong for her, and a vexing inability to say no. She's already near her breaking point, so when one caller too many kicks the bucket during Hollie's 911 shift, she cashes in the Sweethearts' Spa & Stay gift certificate from her dad and heads to Revelation Cove, British Columbia.

One caveat: she's going solo. Any sweethearts will have to be found on site.

Hollie hopes to find her beloved otters in the wilds of the Great White North, but instead she's providing comic relief for staff and guests alike. Even Concierge Ryan, a former NHL star with bad knees and broken dreams, can't stop her from stumbling from one (mis)adventure to another.

Just when Hollie starts to think that a change of venue doesn't mean a change in circumstances, the island works its charm and she starts to think she might have found the rejuvenation she so desperately desires.

But then an uninvited guest crashes the party, forcing her to step out of the discomfort zone where she dwells and save the day ... and maybe even herself in the process.

Available now!

HOLLIE PORTER BUILDS A RAFT

BOOK 2 IN THE REVELATION COVE SERIES

SEQUEL TO **MUST LOVE OTTERS**

ELIZA GORDON

raft (*noun*): when two or more otters rest together, holding hands, so they don't drift apart

Hollie Porter has put her old gig as a 911 operator and sad single girl in an attic-bound box, right where it belongs. She's rebounded nicely from her run-in with Chloe the Cougar in the wilds of British Columbia, and this new life alongside concierge-in-shining-armor Ryan Fielding? Way more fun. After relocating to Ryan's posh resort at Revelation Cove, Hollie embarks on an all-new adventure as the Cove's wildlife experience educator, teaching guests and their kids about otters and orca and cougars, oh my.

When darling Ryan gets down on one NHL-damaged knee and pops the question of a lifetime, Hollie realizes this is where the real adventure begins. It's all cake tasting, flower choosing, and dress fittings until a long-lost family member shows up at the Cove and threatens to hijack her shiny new life, forcing Hollie to redefine what family means to her. What is she willing to sacrifice to have one of her very own?

As Ryan's words echo in her head—"Our raft, our rules"—Hollie has to face facts: a raft isn't always tied together with blood and genetics. Sometimes it's secured by love and loyalty ... and occasional help from the clever creatures that call Revelation Cove home.

Available now!

LOVE JUST CLICKS

BOOK 3 IN THE REVELATION COVE SERIES

Francesca "Frankie" Hawes has felt one click short of a full roll her entire life. Her dad and brother—both world-class photographers—can't be expected to file paperwork, manage clients, or book their own dental cleanings. So Frankie does it for them. But when they ask her to step in and shoot the Meyer-Nelson wedding in secluded Revelation Cove, BC, they go one bridezilla too far.

It's one thing to take Instagram pics of her brother's dog, but unless an Alaskan malamute wanders into the bridal portraits, Frankie fears the worst. Enter wedding guest, childhood friend, and hot ginger snap Sam McKenzie, who brings with him the tricks he learned hanging around the Hawes family, possibly saving Frankie from full-frame disaster.

Her colorful reunion with Sam makes Frankie's Portland routine of work, sushi, and aqua-fit feel pathetically underexposed. When a family emergency calls her home, Frankie must deal with a jarring reality that'll require her to confront if life in her family's shadow is as cozy as it seems, or if she's strong enough to call her own shots in the harsh light of the world outside the studio.

Love Just Clicks is a standalone story set in the Revelation Cove universe.

Available now!

WHERE TO BUY ELIZA GORDON BOOKS!

Find the Eliza Gordon library of feel-good romantic comedies at the following retailers:

Amazon globally
Apple Books
Kobo
Barnes & Noble Nook
Chapters/Indigo
Google Play
Overdrive
Biblioteca
Scribd
and more!

Visit www.elizagordon.com for retailer links and to sign up for my newsletter. Join the Raft!